Phantom Fathers

The Maggie Barnes Trilogy

Mary VanderGoot

RESOURCE *Publications* • Eugene, Oregon

PHANTOM FATHERS
The Maggie Barnes Trilogy

Copyright © 2022 Mary Vandergoot. All rights reserved. Except for brief quotations in critical publications or reviews, no part of this book may be reproduced in any manner without prior written permission from the publisher. Write: Permissions, Wipf and Stock Publishers, 199 W. 8th Ave., Suite 3, Eugene, OR 97401.

Resource Publications
An Imprint of Wipf and Stock Publishers
199 W. 8th Ave., Suite 3
Eugene, OR 97401

www.wipfandstock.com

PAPERBACK ISBN: 978-1-6667-3703-5
HARDCOVER ISBN: 978-1-6667-9608-7
EBOOK ISBN: 978-1-6667-9609-4

JANUARY 10, 2022 4:38 PM

Phantom Fathers and *The Maggie Barnes Trilogy* are works of fiction. Names, places, characters, events, and institutions as they appear in these stories are products of the author's imagination. Used as they are in a fictional narrative, they are not to be taken as either real or referring to real persons, places, or events. Any resemblances are coincidental.

Quoted works in the order that they appear:

Excerpt(s) from LETTER TO MY DAUGHTER by Maya Angelou, copyright © 2008 by Maya Angelou. Used by permission of Random House, an imprint and division of Penguin Random House LLC. All rights reserved.

Phantom Fathers

For Henry

to honor your phantom fathers

I believe that one can never leave home. I believe that one carries the shadows, the dreams, the fears and dragons of home under one's skin, at the extreme corners of one's eyes and possibly in the gristle of the earlobe.

-*Maya Angelou*

Contents

Preface	ix
Acknowledgments	xi
Part One: Rowland Meets His Alter Ego	1
Part Two: Lillian's Story	57
Part Three: Ross's Story	105
Part Four: Guillaume Barone and Jeanne de Roose	143
Part Five: Stepping Into the River Twice	209
Part Six: Home	241

MAASTRICHT | BEAUVAIS | STRASBOURG

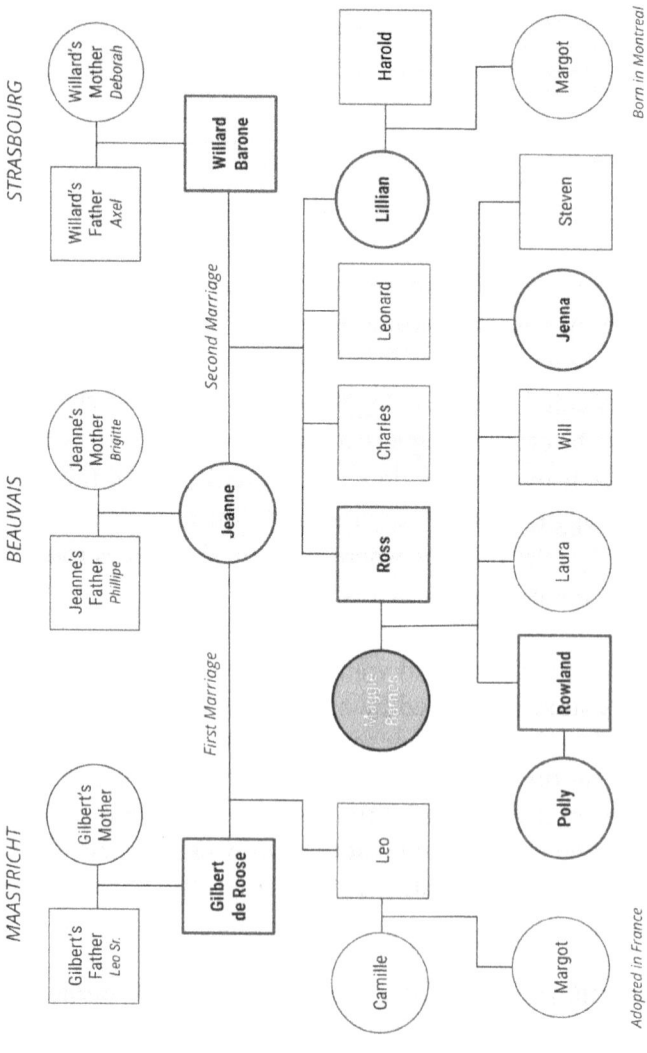

- Gilbert's Father *Leo Sr.* — Gilbert's Mother
- Jeanne's Father *Phillipe* — Jeanne's Mother *Brigitte*
- Willard's Father *Axel* — Willard's Mother *Deborah*

Gilbert de Roose — Jeanne (First Marriage)
Jeanne — **Willard Barone** (Second Marriage)

Children of Gilbert and Jeanne: Leo, Ross
Children of Jeanne and Willard: Ross, Charles, Leonard, Lillian

Leo — Camille → Margot
Ross — Maggie Barnes → Rowland
Lillian — Harold → Margot (*Born in Montreal*)

Rowland — Polly
Children: Laura, Will, Jenna, Steven

Adopted in France: Maggie Barnes

Acknowledgments

WRITING ACKNOWLEDGMENTS FOR the third novel in a trilogy is a special occasion for remembering again those who have stood by me during this venture. My special thanks to the two dear friends, both of them professors of literature, who did not grimace when I first blurted out that I would like to write a novel. You know who you are. You got me started and have kept me going. I'm so grateful.

Twice before I've thanked my writing groups. There's no way to describe how much it means to me to be in a circle of novelists who understand the challenges of long-haul writing. When I put my writing away and turn my attention elsewhere, they never let me forget that somewhere in the files on my computer a novel is waiting for my imagination. My other writing group has given me a place to experiment with poetry and short pieces. Although we've been sharing our writing for a long time and always encourage each other to keep writing, we've also figured out together that writing becomes a habit that no longer can be broken. Thanks to all of my writing friends for your choice company. I'm so lucky.

My stories are about people who have accumulated years; they are stories about the curious process of growing up and growing old. Since I began to share my fiction, I have been rewarded by a wealth of personal stories offered to me by others, many of them my readers. They've confirmed for me that stories about older characters deserve to be told, and that being old is as worthwhile as being young. I'm so grateful for the deep, rich, remarkable stories shared with me by people who've already lived long full lives. The courage of their Confessional Realism touches me; it inspires mine.

Part One

Rowland Meets His Alter Ego

Chapter 1

THE PHONE RANG, and Rowland answered. It was the familiar voice of his brother Will, who barked "Row?" The way Will started phone calls irritated Rowland. Although he pretended not to take it personally, he understood that Will was giving the order to "shut up and listen." Once when complaining about Will's phone manners to their sister, Jenna, Rowland admitted that hearing Will's voice coming through the phone made him feel like "a butterfly impaled on a pin and put on a tack board."

"Tell him how you feel," Jenna said. "Will won't know how he comes across on the phone unless we give him feedback." Rowland did give him feedback, to which Will replied, "Cut the poetry and answer your phone like other people do? Just say, 'Hey, Will, what's up?' That'll solve your problem."

Will and Rowland were twins, but they weren't identical twins, a fact obvious to anyone who knew them both. Long ago they'd spent nine months tumbling around together in a murky bag of water, and Rowland found the exit first. Will got backed up in traffic and arrived ten minutes later. Those ten minutes were a source of tension between the two of them, because Will had a firstborn's personality, and from the beginning he'd been trying to claim his rightful place.

Something else played out in the relationship of these two grown men. They wrestled with their names: Rowland and Willard. When they were kids, they had nicknames, simple monosyllabic ones: Row and Will. Rowland got teased plenty about paddling upstream or having the wrong end of his oar in the water, but he rolled with the punches. As a middle-aged man, however, he preferred to be called "Rowland," and almost everyone switched to calling him by what his mother referred to as his "baptismal" name. "It's odd to refer to grown men as Jimmy, Billy, and Georgie?" she said. "Better to call grown men by grown-up names." Strangely, she never shifted to referring to Will as "Willard," and no one else did either.

Will didn't like his name. When the boys were in junior high, Will confided to Row "I wish Dad had given me your name instead of mine. It's not fair that you got the good one." Although it was one of the only unattractive things about him, it was this handsome and successful man's bad luck to have what he thought was a nerdy "baptismal" name.

There was another backstory to Will's dislike of his name. It had to do with their grandfather, Willard Barone. Their mother disliked the man and his name from the first time she met him. She was courteous to Willard, but their relationship remained chilly, something surprising to anyone who knew her, because Maggie Barnes was seldom chilly toward anyone.

When Ross Barone and Maggie Barnes were married, she decided not to relinquish her surname in order to take her husband's. That was an affront to Willard Barone, who thought that the Barone family name came with a lot of cachet. Maggie thought otherwise; she thought it came with a lot of baggage. The matter surfaced again when Maggie and Ross picked names for their twin boys: Ross picked one, and Maggie picked the other. Rowland was named after Maggie's father, Rowland Barnes Barone. Will got the honor of being named after the family patriarch, Willard Barone. Before she'd changed Will's first diaper, Maggie began devising ways to free her son from the burden of this namesake. She called him "Will," and after the day on which the twins were christened, Maggie never used his "baptismal" name again.

Willard Barone was bossy, arrogant, and rich. He raised his sons to believe their family was special, and he expected them to act like "real men." He was equally determined that the females in his clan be lady-like and compliant. This he called "being refined," but it didn't sit well with Maggie, who got grafted onto the family tree by marrying Ross. Within earshot of her father-in-law, Maggie was known to say, "I prefer being natural to being refined." Maggie wasn't uncouth. She was mannerly and gracious, but she had a thing about over-bearing men and the way they expected women to act dainty to please them. More specifically, she had a thing about the presumptions of her father-in-law.

Willard Barone wasn't a he-man. On the contrary, he had a streak of that "refinement" he expected of women, a certain delicacy in the way he spoke. It was something like a lisp, or at least a strange slippage in the way he said certain words, and it was especially noticeable when he was uptight or angry. If his grandchildren got too boisterous, he'd say, "Maggie! Take sharsh of zeez boys!" It was the mothers he ordered to quiet children down and make them behave. He was a firm believer that children should be seen, if they were clean and well-dressed, but not heard. By association he assumed that also of their mothers.

Although Willard Barone's oddity of speech was the kind of thing kids could have had great fun imitating, in his family no one mentioned the way Grandpa Willard spoke. His grandchildren were scared of him. They suspected their grandfather had eyes in the back of his head and ears hidden in the walls, and they'd witnessed how he could shame a member of the family who didn't show him the respect he thought was his due. If you triggered Grandpa Willard's disdain, by the time he was done with you, your dignity was in shreds. In short, Willard Barone was a complicated character, and Will didn't carry his name proudly.

It reminded Rowland of Grandpa Willard when he answered the phone and heard Will's voice coming at him. "Row! Have you talked to Laura?"

"No, but obviously you have," Rowland replied. "What's up?"

"It's the family tree. The ancestry and genealogy stuff. She's unearthed some skeletons. Once you start excavating, you're bound to dig up something that's going to cause problems." Will couldn't see the smile that crossed Rowland's face as he silently judged how owning a construction company had shaped his brother's imagination. From Rowland's silence, however, Will did note his lack of interest, but he continued anyway. "It's information about names and dates. Thought ya oughta know."

After Ross Barone died and Maggie Barnes was still living, their daughter Laura started researching the family tree. She was a first-rate organizer and perfect with details. It was an ideal hobby for her, although Laura claimed she was doing it for the Barone family grandkids. Maggie never warmed to the idea, and when Rowland asked her why, his mother's response was: "Projects like this can be a Pandora's box. When you break the seal, you never know what's going to come out."

When Maggie died, she left her diaries with Rowland. Why Rowland in particular? Of all her children she must have speculated that he would be the one most likely to read the diaries because he had a curious streak. While that curiosity got him started, soon enough Rowland realized that going through family history is not light entertainment. He had doubts about the value of going over everything again. Maybe it was better to let the past be done. *Let it be water under the bridge,* he thought to himself.

"What did Laura find this time?" Rowland asked Will on the phone.

"It's Dad," Will replied. "You're not gonna believe this. He wasn't born in the good old US of A. He was born in France. Call Laura! Get the full story straight from her! Gotta go. I'm at a work site and have to keep an eye on it, but I wanted you to know."

Chapter 2

Rowland got off the phone with Will and called Laura. "It's not a good idea to make up stories about Dad" he told her. "He's not here anymore to defend himself or check whether what we're saying about his parents is true. I don't recommend defaming the dead."

"Hold your horses, Rowland! I'm not the member of the family who digs around in other people's business, and I'm not defaming them. I'm gathering information. I've found old records, and they're official, not just some gossip written in a diary." Like a big sister, Laura always knew how to put Rowland in his place. She was reminding him of the surprises on his mother's side of the family that Rowland uncovered in her diaries after she passed away.

Without pausing to let Rowland defend himself, Laura went on with the details. "Dad was born in France, not Maine. His family immigrated to the United States and changed their names when they became citizens. It sounds like his family got in trouble and ended up with a new identity. I'm wondering if they were in a witness protection program or something."

"Wait a minute! We're talking about *our* dad, the one and only Ross Barone?" Rowland wasn't done with his questions. "Are you sure there's no mix-up with names? Maybe there are two people named 'Ross Barone.' Did that ever occur to you? No way our one hundred percent, all-American, red-white-and-blue Grandpa Willard had a son born in a foreign country, even by accident, or even while he and Gramma Jeanne were on vacation. Something in this picture doesn't fit. For heaven's sake, Grandpa Willard had a family crest hanging on the wall in his den, and sooner or later every one of us grandkids got trotted over to it to hear him brag about his family name in the records of colonial Virginia. There's a problem with your story," Rowland said. "It doesn't fit Grandpa Willard's story at all. France? No way."

"It's complicated," said Laura. "I'll grant you that. I found his birth records in an online database. At birth Dad was named Philippe Guillaume de Roose. At age four he entered the United States at the Port of New York with his mother, Jeanne de Roose, and when they became citizens, his name was changed legally to Ross Philip Barone. I doubt there's another Ross Barone with that exact story."

"Before she got married Gramma Jeanne's name might have been de Roose. Still, what if there's a mix-up? What if you're going down a rabbit hole?"

"Now I'm the one going down the rabbit hole?" Laura shot back. Rowland heard the familiar ping of a seat-belt being released, and a car door opening. "I have to go," said Laura. "I'm in the parking lot. Got a meeting. Catch up with you later." Laura never wasted time. She was on the phone, multi-tasking while driving, and she needed to wrap it up so she could get back to work. It wasn't for no reason that her siblings called her "the schedule queen."

Rowland was left staring out the window with the phone still against his ear. There was a squirrel sitting on a branch in the tree outside. He wondered if it had been there all along, watching him grimace his way through a conversation with Laura. "Get lost, you snoop," he said to the squirrel. Without leaving the branch, the squirrel flicked its tail. *I wonder what that means*, thought Rowland. *When I have time, I'll look that up on the internet.*

Rowland called Will back. Two rings and then instead of "hello," the familiar voice announcing "Barone."

"This is your brother Row . . . land." He drew it out as long as he could for emphasis.

"Get over it, Row! You called Laura? How'd that go?"

"Quicksand," said Rowland. "The usual."

Will wasn't going to let Rowland set him up to cross Laura. The brother-sister relationship between Will and Laura worked with a very precise balance of control on each side. They both did what was necessary to keep it perfectly calibrated. He didn't question her, and she didn't question him, at least not very often and certainly not about anything as unimportant as some old-fashioned names of dead people.

Rowland filled Will in about Gramma Jeanne's name and admitted that it sounded familiar. "Laura may have that right, because I think Gramma Jeanne's name before she married Grandpa Willard did have something to do with roses."

"What would you know about Gramma's name before she married Grandpa? What did you say it was . . . Rose . . . something?" Will asked. "You're not making this up, are you, to keep Laura busy and get her off your case?"

"I'm absolutely not making this up. Don't you remember when we were in high school and had to take parts in a class reading of that scene from *Romeo and Juliet*?"

"Yeah, who was Romeo?"

"I'm sure you think you were, but that's beside the point," Rowland cut Will off. "Back to the point, if you can stir your cloudy memory for a moment. Mom was helping us practice, and for some reason Gramma Jeanne was around that day too, so Mom recruited her to be our audience. She told us that before she married Grandpa Willard her name was 'Rose,' but not pronounced exactly that way. It came from some dialect or something, but 'de Roose' is pretty close."

"Which rose was she, red or white? Gramma Jeanne was probably kidding. She was a half bubble off center, you know. I think you missed her joke. She was pulling your leg."

"No, she was serious." Rowland was becoming more convinced himself.

"How do you remember stuff like that?" Will asked.

"I have a good memory. That's why I win at Trivial Pursuit," Rowland said.

"And my ability to sort out trivia from what's important is why my income dwarfs yours," replied Will, not letting the challenge pass. He was addicted to winning, and though Rowland often lost, he still enjoyed setting Will up.

"Maybe Gramma was single when Dad was born," Rowland said. "Maybe that's why Dad had her name instead of Grandpa Willard's."

"Sure thing. Maybe our Gramma Jeanne was one of those mail-order brides who came with a tiny suitcase and a kid in tow," said Will, and they both laughed because their Gramma Jeanne was the last woman you'd ever think of as a mail-order bride or traveling with one small suitcase. "What else did Laura tell you?"

"Not much. This is already a lot to digest. It sounds like a Pandora's box to me."

"One more thing," said Will. "Laura considered not mentioning this to you before she's had a chance to check it out, but, what the heck, why shouldn't you know? She's checking if Grandpa Willard was a Nazi. After the war a lot of those guys, the low-level ones, tried to disappear in places where they could cover their tracks. But, Row, don't make more of this than it is! I doubt it will amount to anything. It won't hurt, meanwhile, to be nice to your sister. She's putting a serious amount of work into this. Give her some credit. Catch up with ya later. Gotta go." The phone went still, and Will was gone.

Sometimes it was hard for Rowland to believe that Will was his brother. Was there a gene pool that could randomly scramble the possibilities and come out with the two of them? What's more, it was hard for Rowland to believe that his Grandpa Willard was the branch on which they were the twigs. Rowland didn't like the thought of being genetically connected to his irascible grandfather.

And his dad? Ross Barone was a good guy like the principal of Rowland's high school was a good guy, but Rowland couldn't say he knew him very well. The public and obvious stuff, yes, but what went on inside his dad's head was a mystery about which Rowland didn't have a clue. Unlike his mother, who liked to chat and was a good story-teller, his dad seldom chatted and never told stories. He was a worker, not a talker.

Rowland had learned practical things from his dad, like how to pull the cord that started the lawnmower, how to cut in trim when painting a room, how to change the oil in his car and check the anti-freeze, and how to organize his receipts for the tax accountant. When it came to knowing anything personal or intimate about this mysteriously normal man, you could forget it. For Ross Barone, feelings were a distraction, an annoying distraction, when you were trying to get something more important done.

The connection Rowland once had to his father was rapidly fading. Sometimes weeks passed and not a glimmer of his dad crossed Rowland's mind. He definitely hadn't learned from his dad that digging up his past was important. As far as Ross Barone was concerned, the past was water under the bridge, and Rowland was inclined to think that way too about his dad's past. Why couldn't Laura let bygones be bygones? Why was she making a big deal of these family matters now? Rowland was tempted to call her and tell her to let it go.

"No, I'm in the laundry room, and they're watching TV," she said.

"You think of everything, don't you?" He put a little tease in his voice. "Polly, you're good for me. You're better than I deserve."

"We can talk about that later." She was teasing him back, because just when he was tempted to take her for granted, she had the good sense to drop a hint that she had expectations too. That's why she was good for him, and that's why Willard Barone wouldn't have known how to deal with her.

"Aren't you going to ask me what's so urgent at the library?" Rowland prompted her. He didn't want to seem secretive.

"I'm sure you'll tell me when you get home, when I'm not in the laundry room and the kids aren't waiting for supper," she said. "Right now, I've got to get going. And Row, stay as long as you need to, and get it done. If you're still hungry when you get home the leftovers will be in the fridge, and you can reheat them in the microwave."

"Thanks, Pol," said Rowland. "I really do."

"Ditto," said the voice coming back through the phone.

When they first met, they used to say, "I love you, I really do love you," at the end of their phone calls. When either of them was at work and didn't want to sound mushy, they'd use the short form and say "I do, I really do." It was code-talk. Rowland didn't know why he was using it now while alone in his office, and she was in the laundry room where even the kids couldn't hear her. Just a habit, he supposed. A habit of understating how much he appreciated her.

Chapter 4

As Rowland was leaving his office and heading to the library, he noticed dark clouds coming up. In the library, deep in the World War II archives, he momentarily forgot about the weather, but when he emerged again through the large main doors at the front of the library, it was pouring rain. He didn't feel like going straight home. The kids would still be up, and with the rain coming down, he wouldn't be able to turn them loose in the backyard to play. They'd want to play with him. As he drove away from the campus, instead of merging onto the highway, he crossed the bridge to the other side of the river, pulled into the parking lot of the Breakpoint Bar, switched out his wet dress shirt for the dry t-shirt in his gym bag, and headed into the bar.

Rowland wasn't the sort of guy who frequented bars to escape his family. During a first marriage to a woman with whom he'd been miserable, his home was a war-zone, and he looked for excuses to be absent from it, but when he met Polly all that changed. Ordinarily he liked going home to Polly and the kids, but this was not a usual night; Rowland was in a different frame of mind. He wanted to escape to a place where no one would talk to him, unless *he* started the conversation.

At the bar, Rowland picked a stool directly across from a TV, found the right distance for resting his elbows on the bumper, and ordered a beer. He would have preferred scotch, but in the company of the rednecks and jocks at the Breakpoint Bar, a drink preference could be an announcement of the kind of man he was. This particular evening Rowland didn't want to draw attention to himself with a drink order; he wanted to blend in and disappear for a while.

Rowland ordered a burger and asked the bartender to switch the channel to basketball. He took a deep breath and settled into the quiet, but it didn't last long. A guy came in, stood for a long minute behind the bar stool next to Rowland, and then sat down. He leaned just a little toward Rowland and said out of the corner of his mouth, without looking directly at him, "Sorry, don't mean to crowd you, but I like a spot across from the screen. It saves my neck."

"Sure thing," said Rowland, keeping his eye on the screen and giving the guy no reason to think he was inviting a conversation.

"The guy across from the other TV over there is a smoker," the stranger said as he glanced down toward the other end of the bar. "He was having a smoke outside when I came in. I check out the company and the sight lines before I sit down. Halitosis and BO are the last thing I want to have sitting next to me." He turned toward Rowland. "You're not a smoker, are you? You don't look like the type." It was a judgment, not a question, but Rowland thought it would be awkward to ignore it.

"No, I'm not." Rowland said. He felt a small churn in his stomach. Mentally Rowland ran through his avenues of escape. If the guy started up the conversation again, Rowland could take out his phone and check it. Thumb in a little message to his other number, and say loud enough for the guy in the chair next to him to hear, " . . . another emergency. Why can't a guy get a few minutes of peace and quiet to himself."

If that didn't work, Rowland figured he'd guzzle his beer, chow his burger, and look one more time at his phone while saying to the bartender, "I need my check. Gotta get back to work." Then Rowland would leave, and go to the Greenwood Pub where he could have a single malt scotch, and nobody would notice his drink order because the place was more upscale than the Breakpoint Bar. Normally strangers didn't barge into conversations with patrons at the Greenwood, but if they did, George the bartender was good at rescuing his regulars from guests who were too friendly. The Greenwood was closer to home, however, and there was the chance

Rowland would meet somebody there he already knew. It was the bar he used to go to when he was single and hoping to strike up a conversation with a woman. In tandem with this last thought was a second thought that flashed through his mind. He might not feel at home at the Greenwood wearing the t-shirt he'd retrieved from his gym bag.

As luck would have it, the guy who took the seat next to Rowland wasn't chatty after all. He ordered the corned beef hash plate and settled in to watch the game. It was a dull game, and all was quiet for at least a half hour. As the two men watched the screen, sandwiched in between an ad for shavers and another for deodorant there was a public service announcement that asked, "Do you know where your children are?" The man on the stool next to Rowland chuckled at the ad and said, "I'm escaping my family. They're home; that's where they are. Maybe the network should run an ad asking kids if they know where their fathers are."

Rowland didn't say anything, but he chuckled back, and the guy continued, "My kid just did his first run around the heart-break track. Fell for a cutie in his class and thinks he's in love. Apparently, she isn't quite as much in love with him as he is with her, because she told him she wants to be 'just friends.' In other words, it's over."

"Too bad," Rowland said. "The school of hard knocks can be brutal."

"Hey, most kids go through it and survive it. My boy will too."

"Yeah," said Rowland with a little nod.

"Meanwhile I can't stand his whining," said Rowland's neighbor. "What I really can't stand is that my wife is making chicken soup for him for supper. I don't want to be there to see him hanging over the bowl, and slurping up noodles as if he's a victim. I wouldn't be surprised if my wife slips him something to help him sleep so he's not up all night, pining for his lost love. Rachel thinks she's helping him mend his broken heart, but her method is driving me nuts."

"Moms want to help. It lets them feel needed." Rowland said it with a slight ironic twist so he wouldn't leave the impression he was some neurotic who'd barely escaped his own mother in adolescence.

"If my wife would back off, he'd do better. Let him do his wah-wah-wah by himself, and in a few weeks, he'll find another girl. He's a cute kid and other girls will like him. My wife is treating him like he has PTSD. That's what I'm trying to escape. How about you?"

What was it with this guy? Why was he dumping his stuff about a family crisis on Rowland, a perfect stranger? Did Rowland have "family crisis" printed across the back of his t-shirt? Rowland knew he had to say something if he didn't want to come across as one of those silent and sinister types, so he said the first thing that came to mind. "I'm supposed to be home helping my kindergartener get a project ready for show and tell. He gets homework; can you believe it?" Rowland laughed his snorty, cynical laugh. "Whatever happened to the 3R's? School used to be simpler when teachers took care of show and tell themselves." The moment he said it, Rowland felt shabby complaining about his kids and their school. He was doing it to make conversation with a stranger, but he knew Polly would feel betrayed if she heard him talking about his family this way.

Rowland tried to do repair. "Actually, my kid goes to a good school and his teacher is a creative type. They have a building project going on for a new library wing, and she has the kids all fired up about the construction. My boy is putting together a model with repurposed toilet paper rolls, into which they are stuffing paper-mache, reinforced with pipe cleaners. The teacher is introducing construction terms. I have to admit that a five-year-old wearing his hardhat and explaining to me about construction forms and rebar is pretty darn cute."

His neighbor grinned. "Sounds down to earth for kindergarten. His teacher must be under thirty. Better to teach kids about hardhats and rebar than about unicorns."

"I was supposed to help with the project tonight," Rowland said. "I called my wife to tell her I have an emergency at the office, and I'll be late. She asked if I wanted her to keep a plate of dinner warm. That's how she gets an ETA for how late I'll be. She's clever."

The guy listened, but he didn't take the bait on women and kids. That spoke well of him. "What do you do at your office?" he asked.

"I'm a consultant," Rowland said.

"What kind of consulting?"

"Mostly organizational, that sort of thing." Rowland stayed vague. No way he was going to tell a stranger that he was a Professor of English and that his wife was a specialist in Greek and Roman Literature.

"Money? That kind of consulting?" the guy asked.

Rowland didn't appreciate the interrogation. "Yeah, pretty much. Money's part of everything, isn't it?"

"I suppose it is." His neighbor let it drop.

"What do you do?" Rowland asked him after a long pause.

"Medicine."

"Well, that's money." Rowland said it with a little chuckle so the guy wouldn't think he was sizing up his wallet.

"My Dad chose medicine for me," he said. "Bad choice. I hate blood, don't like to deal with the stuff that comes from kidneys or intestines, and many infections are smelly. Families get quirky when people are dying. It's a bad field overall." He was serious. This guy clearly wasn't infatuated with his work.

"Which revolting part of medicine did you pick?" Rowland asked.

"Genetics," he said. "You only have to deal with a little blood, spit, hair, or scraps of tissue now and then. And, of course, you have to deal with the sins of the fathers upon the children."

The arcane language he used was odd for a doctor, but Rowland didn't know him well enough to ask what he meant. It did occur to Rowland that he might have been better off at the Greenwood Pub.

They watched the game in silence. Then Rowland asked the question that had been flipping around in his mind like a fish that had been landed in the boat, but still needed to be taken off the hook. "Genetics, huh. How far back do you have to go in order to know about your family tree? What does it take to get a clear picture?"

"Back to Adam and Eve if you want to be thorough, but the numbers get pretty large after a few generations." His neighbor laughed, and Rowland was relieved.

"Unless you're talking to my first wife," Rowland said. "In her case she'd take you back to George Washington and Daughters of the American Revolution to establish her pedigree." It was okay if the guy didn't want to talk shop at the bar. Rowland wasn't eager to discuss English literature either.

The stranger seemed to have missed Rowland's comment about his ex. "Your question's serious, isn't it?" He turned toward Rowland.

"It is," said Rowland. "I'm dealing with family stuff, but you didn't come to the bar tonight to work. Sorry to put the question to you."

"No problem," his neighbor said. "There's no sure answer, but three or four generations is a good start for getting clues about whether there is anything to be concerned about in a family line. It's harder than you think to trace a family's history."

"Does the bad stuff ever burn out and disappear? Do our kids have any chance of dodging the bullet?" Rowland asked.

"That's another one of those hard questions. It depends on whether people keep reproducing the problems. You start talking to people about family history, and they think they know a lot. They come into the office with little bits of paper on which they've written names and birth dates and strange medical diagnoses that don't exist. Sometimes they know plenty about their own generation. Sometimes they know a few things about their parents' generation, although you might be surprised how little most people know about their parents' youth. Get to grandparents and the available data falls off significantly."

"Do you think we should gather a bank of DNA samples from our relatives? That way we'd have it when we need it. We could hand it along to our kids, and if they end up visiting a professional like you, at least they'd have more than some scraps of paper with confusing details."

Rowland could tell the doc on the bar stool next to him wasn't convinced. "Just because you have the DNA doesn't mean you have the story. Unfortunately, there are things we'd rather not have everyone else know about us, and there might be things we'd rather not know about ourselves. For example, what if the person you've called 'Dad' your whole life isn't the man who conceived you? Do you want to know that? Might you be better off if you never asked the question?"

Rowland decided to end the conversation and go back to watching the game on TV. "You're probably right," he said. "Curious stuff, though, isn't it?"

"It is curious," the stranger replied, and then began telling Rowland about his own family. He admitted that his mother's penchant for creating drama about unimportant things might be playing into his impatience with his wife and his annoyance with his son. His father's story was grim. He was the only member of his family to survive World War II, after which he ended up in the US, where he married and became a cardiologist. His kids did well. It pleased him that his son became a doctor and his daughter married one. "The most striking thing about my dad is that he tried not to look back. His rule for life was 'Don't get distracted by what's in the rear-view mirror. Keep your eye on the road ahead.' That pretty well sums up his philosophy of life."

"That was your dad's advice? He said that in so many words?" Rowland asked.

"Not in so many words. It's how he lived. By the way, I'm Sam." The stranger reached out his hand toward Rowland.

"Rowland."

"Pleasure to meet you," said Sam.

Rowland figured, what the heck, this guy just told him about his family, why shouldn't Rowland say something about his? "It's an odd coincidence that we're talking about families because this afternoon I got a call from my brother telling me he had just figured out that my dad was born in France and had a name completely different than the one by which we knew him. I could have figured that my grandpa had secrets; he was an odd duck. A very odd duck. But I wouldn't have thought it of my dad."

"Whoa," said Sam. "That's what I mean. You go back a little way, and you start finding missing pieces. Something jumps up and grabs you. You've uncovered something that's going to stir things up, but you can't reverse course and undiscover it."

"We can't change the past. What difference does it make if we do or don't know about it?" Rowland took a swig of beer and waited for a response.

"What you discover has a way of working on you, like it or not. My life is making up for what my dad lost," said Sam. "Dad's passed away now, and I'm still doing it. He never asked it of me, but I feel the obligation. When he was living, he was at the sidelines mostly, caught up in his own work. Once in a while he'd say that if his children did well, it would all be worth it. I think he meant the hours he worked, the years he worried. I don't think he was going back any farther than that. Who would? What good could come from what happened to his family during WW II? What could ever make that worth it?" This guy was straightforward. It wasn't a pity-party. It wasn't a bid for attention. Here was a man on a bar stool, relaxing after a day's work, being friendly to a stranger on his left, daring to speak the truth about himself.

"I don't know much about my grandparents," said Rowland, "but I do know there's something weird in my family because there's been a lot of effort to cover it up. We don't even know what 'it' is."

"You want my opinion?" asked Sam.

"I do," said Rowland.

"The worse your family story, the more likely you are to know the worst of it. My grandparents, for example. I know where they died. I know the year. I know little more about them than that, though. I don't know if they liked music, or if my grandmother was a good cook, or if my grandfather was religious, or if he knew how to play chess. The worst stuff is what we remember after a disaster. The personal stuff, the things that would add color and warmth and make them real, that's what gets lost. I can't say I know who they were, and that gap in my knowledge makes it hard to honor them. To hold on to them."

"Never thought about it that way," Rowland said.

"It takes a while before the pattern shifts and you get into the zone in which the worse something is in your family's history, the less likely you are to know particulars. Take the plague years, for example. It's a genetic riddle. Twenty-five million people died. Half the population. I'm guessing that both you and I have ancestors who survived the plague. If they hadn't, we wouldn't be here. Working off statistics, we can assume survivors went through an ordeal to be among the living. No doubt some of it was ugly and shameful, but maybe some of it was heroic. Their particular story is lost; only a general story has survived. The accounts written up in history books give us big numbers, the loss of life and the percentage surviving, but the story is so leveled, it tells us almost nothing specific about our own family line."

"This isn't the first time you've thought about history, is it?" Rowland said. "You've got it worked through. Working on DNA, does that make it more real or less real?"

"Both," said Sam. "We know there have been dangerous times, but someone survived and handed on the legacy of life that got handed on to us. If there'd been a break in the line we come from, we wouldn't be here talking about it. To be or not to be. It comes down to that, but it's abstract. Personally, I'd rather not uncover one bad thing about someone I've already forgotten. At the same time, I'd like to be grateful for the good stuff, but to whom?" Sam took a deep breath. He looked down at the palm of his hand as if something were written there, and he was deciphering it. "You still want my opinion?"

"Yeah. We're into it this far. Lay it on me," said Rowland.

"If you half know something, and it keeps tugging at you, go after it. If you can lay it to rest, and it doesn't keep coming after you, maybe now is the time to let it go. For some families that's no longer an option. Once you start it's hard to stop. It sounds to me as if you're standing in front of that choice. But here's the thing: if you want to be serious about the future, you'll have to find a way to honor the past. That's honestly what I think."

"Hm-mm," said Rowland. He'd headed to the Breakpoint Bar so he could drink a beer in the silent company of hard-working guys, the kind who don't talk much. It was the last place in the world he expected to meet someone so serious. But here they were, two barstool philosophers putting questions to each other, and admitting there are no clear answers. They were oblivious to the other guests at the bar. They were two escapees who happened to meet up because they were hiding out in the same bushes.

Rowland signaled the bartender for his tab. The bartender brought Sam's too. As he was paying, Rowland noticed the name on Sam's credit card. Sam noticed that Rowland noticed, and he reached out his hand again and said, "Sam Cohen."

"Rowland Barone."

"Row . . . land?" Sam asked. "Like the knight?"

"More or less," Rowland said. "My brothers and sisters call me 'Row.' Either way works. I didn't get to pick my own name."

"I wouldn't have chosen to call myself Samuel either."

They both laughed, but later when he thought back to that moment, Rowland realized that he didn't choose to call the stranger he met at the bar that night "Samuel" or even "Sam." He called him "Cohen." And Cohen never decided between "Rowland" and "Row." From the very beginning he called him "Barone."

Cohen looked at his watch. "What time is it?" Rowland asked.

"It's 1:00. Do you drink scotch?"

"I do enjoy a good scotch now and then."

Cohen caught the bartender's eye and tapped two spots on the bar, one in front of himself and one in front of Rowland. "Balvenie," he said.

They raised their glasses. The bar grew quiet. The bartender turned off the TV. The comforting stillness was interrupted only a few times by the bartender's last chores of the night. Rowland watched him clean glasses in a sink with a device that worked like an electric shoe brush. He saw him wipe glasses with a towel and hold them up to the light to check for smudges. His mother used to clean silverware that way, drying it and then checking it for spots. Maggie Barnes had a way of showing up in Rowland's thoughts at odd times.

As the digital clock at the bartender's work station crept toward 2:00 am, the bartender came with the tab for the scotch. "It's on me," said Cohen. "You can get it next time."

"Thanks," Rowland said. "It's been a good conversation."

"A lot cheaper than therapy," said Cohen. They both laughed.

Chapter 5

A FEW WEEKS after he met Cohen at the bar, Rowland was at a neighborhood picnic. Polly was inside preparing salads with the wives, and he was outside with the guys, gathered around the grill. Next to him was Matt, the neighborhood lawyer. "Anything new with lady justice?" Rowland asked. "Is she still using her blindfold, and are the lawyers still checking if the weight pans are rigged?"

"I ran into a good one this week." Matt leaned in as he spoke, and the other guys gave him full attention. "It's probably not going to be a great legal precedent, but it was a memorable moment in court. It was a civil case. Property damage. My client is a lovelorn high school kid who went to the home of the girl who dumped him, and along the sweep of her parents' long driveway in tall letters he spray-painted the words, 'I'll love you forever.' Nobody got hurt, but it's an expensive driveway with fancy brickwork and underground lighting. The girl's parents weren't flattered by the kid's ardor for their daughter, and they wanted my client's parents to pay for sand-blasting the message off the bricks and replacing the damaged lights."

"The kid should pay," said Rowland. "What's the contest?"

"Of course, he should," said Matt, "but he doesn't have any money of his own."

"What did the judge think about that?" Rowland asked.

"The kid is a minor. The judge ordered the homeowner to arrange the cleaning of the driveway and directed that the bill be forwarded, via my office, to the parents of the lovesick boy." Matt smirked. "There wasn't much to defend. The kid messed up. Of course, he didn't think so. The little shit sat there pouting, sure that no one understood the depth of his love and the anguish of his broken heart. Sometimes with a kid like that I'd like to deliver one swift kick to the ass as part of the settlement."

"Okay then," said Rowland. "I guess we know what'll happen in cases like this when you become a judge. Is a kick to the backside allowed in court?"

"Unfortunately not, but I could tell the judge didn't have much sympathy for my client's broken heart."

After the judge decided the case, he asked Matt's client if he had anything to say. The boy shook his head "no," in response to which Matt leaned over and whispered to him that he had to answer the judge properly. The kid looked startled as if someone had just used a cattle prod to jolt him out of a trance. "No, Sir," he mumbled.

The boy's father was sitting behind him, and he stood up. "Your Honor, with due respect to the court, and in view of the fact that I'm picking up the tab for my son's foolishness, am I allowed to say something?"

"It won't change the court's decision," said the judge. "Let's be clear about that."

"I understand, but I'd like to be heard," the dad said.

Matt was amazed that a judge would let someone in his court make a personal statement that wasn't part of the proceedings. After making sure that the law has been followed, some judges do make moral declarations from the bench or deliver reprimands to parties who show lack of regret, but they seldom let anyone else offer personal opinions in their court. Judges want to get on to the next case; they have tight schedules. In this instance the judge allowed the father's request.

Before he spoke, the father squared his shoulders and clasped his hands behind his back. "I would like to say, here in this court and to my son, that I understand how the sins of the fathers are borne by the children, and sometimes for many generations. I have witnessed that firsthand. No argument. That does happen. There is something contrary to nature happening here, however, because in this case the sins of my son are being borne by me. I am required to pay the cost because he lacks money. It troubles me that the weaker is lording it over the stronger; the son is lording it over his father. It's not right. I believe I have a legitimate grievance. Thank you for allowing me to voice my complaint, Your Honor."

"Is that all, Mr. Cohen?" the judge asked.

"One more thing," said the defendant's father. The judge was surprised that the father intended to continue with his statement, but again he didn't stop him.

"I'm wondering, Your Honor, if in addition to ordering me to pay for my son's transgression, you also would order my son to apologize to me."

Matt described the scene. The judge was listening. The kid was slumped way down in his chair, looking at his feet, probably wishing he could disappear under the table. "Stand up and face your father," said the judge, "and take your hands out of your pockets!" The kid turned slowly, removing his hands from his pockets awkwardly, as if he were worried that hidden contraband might fall out. He was still pouting. Still convinced he was the victim.

"No doubt, another moment for which you would gladly deliver a swift kick to the ass on behalf of the court," Rowland enjoyed reminding Matt.

"Absolutely," said Matt. "The judge was considering the circumstances far more graciously than I would have."

"Mr. Cohen," the judge said, "what you are citing is another kind of law. Not the one we adjudicate in this court. You deserve an apology from your son. Whether you receive it will depend on how well his conscience serves him."

"Thank you, Your Honor," said the father.

The judge turned his attention to Matt's sulky client. "Young man, approach the bench!" The kid shuffled up to the bench. He had his hands back in his pockets and was looking at the floor. There was an awkward silence, and the kid looked up. "Your hands," said the judge. The kid dropped them to his side again. "And stand up straight," the judge ordered. "You've heard what your father has said. I will not order an apology because a coerced apology is seldom genuine. Whether or not you voluntarily offer that apology, without being ordered to make it, is a test of your character. Do you understand me?"

"Yeah," said the kid. Obviously, he didn't want to contradict the judge.

But the judge wasn't finished. "I recommend further to you that in addition to offering your father that apology, you think of some way to make restitution. Your current demeanor doesn't speak well for you. Forfeiting your allowance, given to you by your father in the first place, would be too easy. Do some yard work. Pull weeds. Pay your father back with sweat. Consider what this has cost your father, then make sure the sweat with which you make amends is in just proportion. You have an important decision to make. Even after damaging property and shaming your parents, you still have the chance to do something right. That choice is yours. Do you understand me?"

"Uh-huh," the kid said. Matt gave him the stink eye and whispered to his client to answer the judge properly. "Oh, I mean, Yes, Your Honor, Sir," said the kid.

"Young man, you may go back to your place," said the judge. While the kid's back was toward the bench, the judge nodded and smiled at the father.

This Cohen can't be the Cohen I met at the bar, can it? Rowland mused. *There must be other families with that name.* His mind was racing through the possibilities. *Cohen could have a son like the one Matt saw in court, but there are thousands of kids who do stupid stuff when they think they're in love. Could this be my Cohen's lovelorn son?*

Rowland didn't want it to be his Cohen's son. It was impossible anyway that in the two weeks since he'd met Cohen at the bar his son had spray-painted the driveway, the girl's parents had filed the complaint, and the court had scheduled the case. Courts don't move that quickly. Then it dawned on Rowland. Cohen was at the bar the evening Rowland met him because he was ticked off about his day in court. He preferred dinner alone to sitting across the table from his self-pitying son.

The other dads sitting on the patio listened to Matt's account of his appearance in court, and one after the other they measured out what they judged to be a fair punishment. No cell phone. No use of the car. No spring break trip. All of the dads, who thought they'd never have to stand before the judge's bench to give an accounting of the damage their own kids have done, were issuing tough sentences. Quickly the comments shifted over into recollections of the penalties their own dads had exacted back in the days when life was still hard and kids weren't spoiled.

Listening in, you might have thought these men spent their boyhood summers locked in stocks, and when their juvenile blunders cost their parents, the wages from their first jobs were garnished until every penny was paid. All the neighbors were Gen-Xers, however, children of Baby Boomer parents who had done everything they could to fortify the egos of their children. Whenever there was trouble, either in the neighborhood or at school, these parents were especially careful not to damage the fragile confidence of their precious offspring. They'd never known harsh discipline, and you can be sure if their kids were in trouble, they'd hire Matt to defend them. If there were costs for damages, they'd write the check.

What was this display of tough fatherhood all around him, wondered Rowland? Embarrassment possibly. The same parents, quick to judge others, weren't able to hold the line in their own families, especially if standards made anyone uncomfortable. Their children were raised on moral ambiguity, convinced they should never be blamed for anything or made to feel uncomfortable by anyone passing judgment on them?

Rowland was usually Matt's most appreciative audience for stories about events in the alternate universe of the halls of justice. He wasn't commenting this time, however. Matt noticed that Rowland had drifted off into his own thoughts. "You tired, Rowland?" Matt leaned over and spoke to him in a quiet voice while the other guys talked on. "Working too hard these days? When was it . . . a few weeks ago now . . . I heard your garage door at 2:30 in the morning? I was up taking a leak. From the bathroom window I saw you roll in real slow like you were trying not to side-swipe the garage or rip the trim off Polly's SUV. If you were at your office working, I'd say, you're getting too old to burn the midnight oil. And if you were out playing, I'd say that keeping late hours isn't the best thing for a family man." Matt knew that Polly was Rowland's second time around, and like a typical lawyer, he didn't beat around the bush when passing judgment or giving advice about risks.

"I've got it under control," Rowland said, and got up to refill his glass with ice tea. "I'm starving. How's it going at the grill? I'm going in to check if the wives need me to carry anything out."

On the way into the house Rowland stopped off at the bathroom. As he washed his hands under cool water, he puzzled about how this could happen. How did Cohen show up again, this time ushered in by Matt's story about a day in court? By sheer coincidence you meet someone whose path you've not crossed before. An interesting blip in the humdrum of life. And then, there he is again, back for another appearance soon after. Rowland didn't say anything about Cohen to Matt or the other neighbors. He tried to put it away for the rest of the evening.

Rowland did tell Polly about the two appearances of Cohen. They mused about whether this was the same person, and how unlikely it would be that a complete stranger would show up twice in such a short time. "You're lucky to have met an interesting person like Cohen with whom you have so much in common," said Polly. "You're both trying to figure out what you think of your fathers and what you expect of your sons. No wonder you picked each other out. It must be the energy fields we create by the things we brood about?" Polly paused to catch up with her own thoughts. "It's like your computer when you're working on an app. You have another one running in the background. It's there at the ready so that one keystroke can send it right up to the front again."

Cohen showed up again a few months later when Rowland went to get a blood draw. When he walked into the waiting room of the lab, who was sitting there but Cohen? Rowland did a double take.

"Cohen?" Rowland said.

"Arthur?" said Cohen. "Oh Geez, I've got that wrong! I recognize you, and I've got your last name, but I can't get to your first name." He pointed toward his head with a few quick rubs of the index finger, as if he were going through a filing cabinet. "Misplacing names is my specialty. Don't take it personally. Anyway, good to see you again, Barone."

"It's Rowland. Good guess, though. You were close, but you got the wrong knight."

Cohen responded with a hearty laugh. "At least I didn't call you Lancelot. Anyway, I'm sure you're not here to get time away from your kids." Cohen's grin shifted to serious. "Are you feeling okay?"

"I'm sound and healthy. Just checking out some routine stuff that will make my doctor feel better," Rowland chuckled at his own joke. "I'd think you could get your lab work done at your own office. How's your health? Are you okay?"

"Sometimes it's easier to get something done by going somewhere else. They fuss too much if I do a blood draw at my own office." Cohen looked across the small room at Rowland. "Let's get a beer sometime."

"I'm up for that," Rowland said, just as the phlebotomist called his name.

Rowland told Polly about meeting Cohen at the medical lab. "Do you think a complete stranger showing up three times within a few months means anything?" he asked. He rolled his eyes just a little to hint at irony, so Polly could brush his question aside if she thought he was getting too deep into fairytale thinking.

"The ancients never thought strangers appeared by accident," said Polly. "Strangers are messengers. Back in the day people didn't travel much, and there weren't many strangers in town. If one showed up in your village square, it was for an obvious reason, and if there was no obvious reason, then maybe he was there to announce something the Fates had in store for you. For better or for worse, the best move was to invite the stranger home for a meal because hospitality was the first line of duty when it came to the treatment of strangers." Rowland never knew how seriously to take Polly when she said things like that. She studied ancient literature, and it was on her mind all the time, so it popped up in conversations.

"That reminds me of what Dad used to say." Rowland paused for a moment to check if Polly wanted to follow his detour.

"And what exactly was that bit of wisdom from the lips of Ross Barone?" Polly asked. Rowland's father died before Polly joined the family, and she never developed fondness for him, not the way she did for Rowland's mother. She never met Rowland's mother either, but Polly spoke of Maggie as if they knew each other well.

"Nothing. Forget it," said Rowland. Going through his mind was one of his dad's warnings about wasted opportunities. *If it happens once, it's an accident. If it happens twice, it's a mistake to ignore it. And if it happens a third time, you'd better smarten up because it may be your last chance to get it right before it's too late.* Rowland went back to reading his book.

"By the way," asked Polly, "what are you reading? Would you rather read than talk?" She'd seen that he hadn't put the book down when she came into the room. She noticed things like that. He'd put his finger between the pages, clearly intending to go back to it when they were finished talking.

"*The Swerve*," said Rowland.

"By whom?" Polly asked.

"What difference does that make?" said Rowland.

"Well, if you're still thinking about your Cohen guy," Polly said, "it makes a huge difference. The swerve points to at least two possibilities . . . or maybe more. The ancients thought the swerve challenged the ways of the gods in determining Fate. Did they always get their way or could their intentions be bumped off course by human choices? How relentless was Fate? The modern swerve strikes the gods out of the picture completely, retires their team, and bans them from the league. Whatever happens is entirely by accident, and we get so panicked by the randomness of it that we try to see patterns in it even if there are none. It's like seeing dinosaurs and unicorns in the clouds." Rowland knew, the moment Polly mentioned seeing dinosaurs and unicorns, she'd been looking at patterns in the sky with a kindergartener, and he loved her for it.

"And your point?" Rowland asked. "Bring it home, baby! Is it an accident that means nothing or a swerve in which I've gotten caught up? Should I pay attention because this random guy showed up three times?"

"Maybe you should start by admitting that you'd like to go out for a beer with Cohen," said Polly.

"Should I call him or wait and see if he calls me?" Rowland spoke very slowly.

"Whatever! Rowland, don't make it so complicated." She had that look that sometimes made him think she would have been good at reading palms or tea leaves if she'd gotten her training in a circus instead of a university.

Chapter 6

ROWLAND FELT THE PHONE in his pocket, checked the screen, and saw the message.

"Watch soccer Thursday? 8 at Breakpoint?"

"C U there," Rowland texted back.

On his way out of the house Polly teased Rowland about Cohen, "a stranger thrown in your path by Fate." Rowland didn't argue with Polly when she said things like that. She was hinting that Cohen had stepped into Rowland's life for a reason, that sometimes events like that were more than a lucky spin of the wheel of fortune. Polly was also practical. She understood that an earnest guy like Rowland needed a friend with whom he could talk about weighty matters. "I can't be the only one with whom you toss around your answers to life's big questions," Polly had said.

Even though she hadn't met Cohen, Polly thought she'd like him, but Rowland felt ambivalent about having the two of them meet. Polly wasn't a strict feminist, but sometimes she complained about the way men dominate conversations so they can protect their own privilege. "For heaven sakes, Pol, give it up," Rowland had said after her most recent salvo. "Why do you have to be so judgmental? Women have had a say for decades already. It's not the 1950s anymore." Even as he was defending his buddies, he knew what she meant about the way men socialize.

Polly was a keen observer. She'd complained to Rowland about the rude remark Greg made to his wife, Brittany, when the neighbors were together for pizza. Brittany was explaining that the products we buy at the drug store are full of unhealthy chemicals.

She'd found a new hair color product that didn't have parabens or heavy metals. Greg rolled his eyes and said in a phony female voice, "I'll bet you guys are excited to know about that aren't you?" Then for good measure in order to be sure his wife didn't regain her composure and start talking again, he added in his confident male voice, "What do you know about chemistry anyway, Brittany? It's all marketing." Greg looked around the group to be sure he had their attention. "New bait; same fish," he said confidently, pointing his thumb in the direction of his wife. This was enough to silence Brittany completely so Greg could take over the conversation and treat everyone to a mini-lecture on the physics of his new tennis racket.

Polly told Rowland she regretted not stepping up and saying something to defend Brittany. "I should have asked Greg how much he knows about the physics of projectiles. He sells insurance." Polly sneered. "At least I could have asked Greg how much he paid for that tennis racket and whether his game has improved. It's all marketing. New racket; same score," she said.

Rowland was muddling these thoughts as he drove over to the Breakpoint Bar. He considered inviting Cohen and his wife over for dinner, but he had no idea what Cohen's wife was like. What if Polly got carried away and left Cohen with the impression that she's a ball-buster. Most people liked Polly once they got to know her. Her friends liked her because when it mattered most, Polly had your back. Her friends' husbands liked her mostly, except when she was too outspoken. Rowland wished she'd ease up a little and let smart men say a few stupid things once in a while, without needing to correct them.

That's my Pol. Honest and straightforward, Rowland was thinking. *She keeps me even.* It was no secret that Rowland could be arrogant. No one could bring that out in him quicker than his brother Will, although Rowland could bring that out in Will too. Recently Will had found a partner who was good for him, and that made him easier to get along with. It didn't smooth out all of his bad habits, but it made him less competitive. It occurred to Rowland that Barone men need good partners. *We need ballast*, he thought. *That's why I need Polly.*

Just that afternoon Polly had been telling Rowland what good times she had when she went out with her friends. "When women are together," she said, "we don't talk about all that stuff that amounts to nothing. We lean in and talk about personal stuff. We speak our own dialect, and we stick close to home. The things we share about ourselves would start getting really heavy if we couldn't share them with someone else."

"In other words, you complain about your husbands," Rowland said.

"You're such a knucklehead," she said and laughed, "but you're my knucklehead, so I forgive you." She reached down and squeezed his rear end. "Don't get me wrong, I like mixed company," and she gave him that certain look. "Especially the way you mix it up when it's just the two of us."

"Hey," Rowland said, "the kids don't get dropped off for another hour. What d'ya say?"

When Rowland got to the Breakpoint, he grabbed a stool at the bar straight across from a screen, and he put his jacket over the seat next to him to keep it for Cohen, who walked in a few minutes later. They shook hands, and Cohen said, "Let's get a booth." He stepped back, scanned the room, checked the screens, and pointed to a spot on the other side. "We'd like that one," he said to the server. "Better sight lines."

"Sure. Okay, help yourself," said the server. "I'll be right over to get your drink order."

As they walked to the booth Cohen said, "You think she knows what sight lines are?"

"You Neanderthal," Rowland chuckled. He was defending Polly *in absentia*. It's not that Cohen was primitive, but Rowland wanted to start out on the right foot and avoid the petty putdowns that he sometimes used to pump himself up when hanging out with the guys. He was hoping to have a serious conversation with Cohen.

When they were seated in the booth, Cohen looked across at Rowland, nodded slowly, and said, "So how are you, Barone?"

"Worried about my wandering lad. Zach's going to Iceland," Rowland said. "He wants to go where there's plenty of nature and not too much stuff. I tried to persuade him that the boundary waters of Minnesota don't have much stuff, but he told me it's too close to home. He wants to get away for a while."

"His timing's right," said Cohen. "Isn't he about the age we were when we would have said something like that to our parents? We let them know when we didn't need them anymore, and now it's our turn to be put out to pasture, but we don't like it."

"A few differences. Zach texted me and asked if instead of me paying for his tuition by electronic check through the online portal, it would be okay if he paid it with his credit card. He has a plan."

"He's going to pay his own tuition? Go Zach! Things are progressing." Cohen nodded his approval.

"No. On the contrary. He thinks I'm going to pay his credit card bill when the charge shows up on it," Rowland said.

"Plot thickens," said Cohen. "What's that about?"

"He wants the flyer miles. Zach wants to add a little junket to Greenland before he returns home, and the flyer miles he gets on his card are the only way he can afford it."

"What did you tell him?" Cohen asked.

Rowland took out his phone and found the message thread in his texts. "Here," he handed the phone to Cohen, "read it for yourself."

In response to Zach's request, Rowland had written, "Tuition through a credit card has a 3% upcharge to cover the credit card fee. Smart, but not smart enough to scam your dad. Furthermore, in view of cost for tuition, I deserve to use the flyer miles for a vacation."

"Chill," Zach wrote back. "Still worth it to get the miles."

"Don't think so," Rowland responded.

Cohen was still reading the texts, but Rowland interrupted him. "Do you notice the absence of pronouns in text messages? Is that arrogance or humility?"

Cohen smiled and went back to the text message Rowland had written to Zach. "Clear about not using the credit card for tuition, right?"

The message he got back said, "UR paying U pick."

"Junior sets Pops straight and gets the last word," said Cohen as he handed the phone back. "Only difference between us and them is that we had to talk on the phone, or worse yet, we had to look Pops in the eye and have a face-to-face conversation."

"Tuition was cheaper back then too," Rowland said.

"Speaking of overpriced universities," said Cohen, "how's your work going?"

"Speaking as an underpaid professor to an overpaid doctor," Rowland replied, "it's going well. I'm still comparing texts using computer programs. I have a young guy who's whip smart at writing code. I give him ideas, and he makes a computer do the work."

"What texts?" Cohen asked.

"I'm comparing *Don Quixote* and *The Wizard of Oz*," said Rowland. "We're building a program that analyzes sentence length and word choices."

"What about content?"

"We leave that to the consumer. Some people still read books. The rest of them look up plot summaries on the internet or watch film versions of the classics." Rowland chuckled.

"I read *The Wizard of Oz* when I was a kid," said Cohen. "I don't mean I watched the movie. I read the original. I wore out the pages about Oz the Terrible. When I discovered that he was nothing more than a humbug, I felt ready to grow up."

"I read *Oz* too," Rowland said. "It may have been part of what inspired me to study literature when I went to college. I just read it again several times. I can't believe the book I read when I was in high school is the book I'm reading now."

"Maybe it isn't," said Cohen. "In the final analysis, isn't the book in the mind of the reader?'

"You should read it again," said Rowland. "I wish my kids would read it."

"They won't. I never read a book my dad suggested," said Cohen. "That's why I'm not surprised that my kids don't take my recommendations." Cohen looked pensive and Rowland didn't interrupt him. "Sometimes I wish I'd read the stuff my dad suggested, and I wish I'd talked with him about it. I missed my chance."

"That's all water under the bridge now," said Rowland. His tone matched the look on Cohen's face.

They paused to let their conversation sink in, but also to look for a new subject for their banter. They knew when enough was enough. They weren't quite ready to talk about their dead fathers or their memories of them.

"How's your work going?" Rowland asked Cohen.

"Well, as they say, genetics is the new frontier." Cohen smiled a knowing smile. "No end to the questions. It's interesting that you and I both instruct computers to break down messages coded in letters. The only difference is my alphabet is smaller. DNA has fewer letters, but spelling mistakes can kill you."

"It may have taken millions of years for your book to be written," said Rowland, "but in the end, at least you've got something. I mean, you do, don't you? I don't really know anything about genetics. How dependable are the results?"

"More dependable than you'd think; less than you'd like." Cohen was serious. "You start out thinking you're going to solve the riddle of diseases, but it takes years to track down something significant. You try to get enough samples to carry out comparisons so you can determine if there's a marker. Now and then your guesses are good. You've devised a new diagnostic tool, but you haven't even begun to figure out how to cure the disease."

"Well, at least in your field, once in a while, you find something worthwhile that might change the future," Rowland said. "In my field, things fade as soon as we publish them. Everything's socially constructed and temporary. Ideas have a short shelf life, and our products are consumables. I go to the annual convention to see who the new stars are in the field. A year later I can barely remember who last year's stars were."

"We can complain all we want, but what choice do we have other than to stay with our work. It's the only thing we're good at." Cohen looked at Rowland. "If we give in, Barone, if we can't stand up to the reality of the work we do, soon we'll be watching sports full time. We won't have anything to talk about or complain about.

We'll be taking golf lessons from the pro at the course, or getting a fitness trainer and going to the gym every day so we have something to do while we stretch life out as long as we possibly can, chasing after every new idea for how to stay healthy and fit. Meanwhile we'll be ambling our way through the valley of the shadow of death, realizing that no matter what we do to stop it, mortality is slowly overtaking us. If that's the alternative, I say it's better to have distraction, even if the distraction is work."

"That's some speech coming from a geneticist whose field is supposed to be the field of the future. And that's some old-fashioned prose you're dressing it up with. You're right about one thing, though; you and I both will go back to work tomorrow. What if we complain to each other a little over beers? No harm done, as long as we decide at the end of the day that a little island of meaning in an ocean of uncertainty is better than no meaning at all."

"Barone, if you could do any sort of work you wanted, and you didn't have to make a living, what would you do?"

"Oh, I don't know," Rowland replied carefully. "Maybe collect art. Become an expert on ferreting out forgeries. That was pretty interesting in a novel I just finished. And you? What would you do?"

"Maybe I'd do cryptography," said Cohen. "In the Yale library there's an old scrap of faded parchment that no one has been able to decipher. I'd work on it until I figured it out. Anything else you'd like to do?"

"Write a novel," Rowland said, "about a guy who's writing a novel but can't find the right ending, so he ends up with a whole set of great starts to a story he never finishes."

"Is that what they call post-modern?" asked Cohen.

"Close enough." Rowland grimaced. "In truth we've already moved way past that."

The server came and removed their plates. The burgers were finished except for some drips of ketchup and mustard and a few pickles that had escaped. That and crusty overdone fries was all that was left on their plates.

They turned their attention toward the screens. Rowland watched the one just over Cohen's left shoulder. Cohen watched the one across the room above the bar. On the glass screen were teams of guys in identical uniforms except for the colors. Tireless guys running in circles after a black and white orb. Every so often one of them got knocked on his butt, or dove for the ball as if nothing else in the world mattered. When their shots missed, they wiped sweat on their sleeves, stooped over to catch their breath, and started running again. They didn't seem to tire of what they were doing, even though most of their shots missed. And their spectators, the fat guys who couldn't run the length of a field, the clownish young guys who'd shaved their heads and painted their bumpy pates in team colors, cheered them on. From a distance and through a glass screen it all seemed so easy.

On an impulse Rowland broke the silence of two middle-aged guys watching soccer. "Did I ever tell you I'm a twin?"

"No. Identical?"

"Not at all," Rowland chortled as he replied. "Far from it. We couldn't be less similar. Sometimes I imagine that day back when two ready eggs were hanging around waiting for two eager sperm. I have this bizarre fantasy that one sperm was headed toward the egg on the right and the other sperm toward the egg on the left. Then at the last moment one of them flicked his little tail, shot ahead, and decided he wanted the egg toward which his buddy was headed. He cut in and made his move. His buddy just figured, 'what the heck, what difference does it make? I'll just take that egg over there then.' And that has made all the difference. Except for that one little flick of the tail, we wouldn't be Will and Rowland; we'd be 'whoever' and 'what's-his-name' instead. It's not impossible, is it?" He looked at Cohen.

"Not impossible at all," said Cohen.

"C'mon, Cohen, you're the DNA man. Is that all you can say? In the end it's accidental?"

"My Dad used to say about such questions that they deserve to be put in the box and tucked away with all our other musings about the ineffable," said Cohen.

"Ineffable? Rare word." Rowland wondered if it appeared in the word lists for the texts he was studying.

"It is an odd word choice," said Cohen. "When I was a smart-assed teenager, I thought my dad was trying to belittle my questions when he responded like that. Later I thought he was hinting that some questions don't have answers yet, but we should keep searching 'til we get them. My assignment was cut out for me when I entered medical school. After Dad died, his closest friend, who also happened to be a rabbi, said to me. 'My son, your father was a good doctor and a solid scientist, but he never gave up his reverence before the ineffable.' Still think it's an odd word choice?"

"Now I think it's an odd sentence structure," Rowland said. "Why did he say 'reverence *before* the ineffable' instead of 'reverence for the ineffable?' And why did his friend repeat it to you exactly that way?"

"See, what I mean?" Cohen said. "We get hung up on a single word. If I'd thought about it earlier and asked my dad what he meant, he could have told me. Now both my dad and his friend are dead."

Rowland didn't' say anything in response to Cohen's comment about his dad, because he was still thinking about competing sperm. He was wondering if they had something to do with the ineffable.

Cohen glanced at Rowland. "You know the thing about cryptography? That's my second choice. Sometimes I think of giving up medicine and becoming a rabbi."

"Seriously? A rabbi?" Rowland asked. "What stops you?"

"What stops me?" Cohen repeated the question and paused long to surface his answer. "Maybe it's because, as it is, I can have a conversation with a guy like you at the bar, but if I were a rabbi and you knew it, you'd close me down. It would be the end of our conversation."

"Not fair. I'm not like that. I'm not a religious bigot. I'm open-minded. I'd still hang out with you at the bar doing late-night philosophy, even if you were a rabbi. I'd still be interested to hear what you have to say."

"Of course you would," said Cohen. "But now you hold it against *me* that I don't have the answers. If I were a rabbi, you'd hold it against . . . as we say . . . HaShem . . . for not giving me the answers."

Chapter 7

ROWLAND HAD A CHANCE to talk with Cohen again, but it wasn't until weeks later. This time Rowland texted Cohen. "Time for beer, 8 Wed, Breakpoint?" The message to Cohen was written at Polly's suggestion because Rowland had been talking to her about his dad's family, especially after he was on the phone with his sister Jenna. She'd been visiting with Aunt Lillian at Laura's urging, and Aunt Lillian had been loading Jenna up with family stories. Sometimes the conversations with Jenna were like a series on cable TV. Every episode began with an answer to a previous question, but then ended with a new and bigger question.

Rowland talked with Will about the family too. "Don't get tangled up in this thing," Will said. "If our sisters like chasing down information, leave it to them, but be nice about it. They're your sisters. These things have a way of sorting themselves out. Give it time. It might just disappear. Or when you least expect it, with a little help from the universe, the most important answer will find its way to you."

"What is this, California spirituality?" Rowland asked his brother. "Have a little patience? Wait for the universe to send you what you're looking for? Has someone sold you a program, and now you're getting your consciousness raised? Are you finally getting in tune with the universe?" Rowland tried to shift his tone of voice away from aggressive and more into the range between sarcastic and light-hearted, but he felt agitated. He had that old impulse to trim Will down to size and show him who's smarter.

"Get over it," Will said. "Spirituality never hurt anybody. Maybe I'm a late bloomer when it comes to that, but you should talk. Do you have all the answers? No more puzzles you're working on? Done thinking already? Clarity, Row. That's what I'm searching for. Clarity. Unless you have something to offer there, let's not get into it."

Rowland told Polly what Will said. It was uncharacteristic of his practical brother. The clarity Will usually pursued was connected to dollars and cents, or good real estate, or flashy high-tech cars, or legally solid construction contracts. What was this about?

This thing about spirituality got Rowland thinking about all the people he knew who lost interest in religion after they graduated from Sunday School. When it came to church membership, a few of them dipped in for a short stay so they could have their children christened, but other than that they spent their Sunday mornings golfing or going to their kids' soccer games. In some cases, they kept their names on church rolls so they'd have a place to turn for help when they needed to bury their parents. For the rest they didn't give it much thought until they got cancer, or lost a job, or one of their kids got in serious trouble with the law. These were the circumstances that lined them up for a head-on collision with the big "WHY's?" Why me? Why now? Why this? Even in the best of times they felt that life falls short of fulfillment, but when the bad times hit, they got desperate to find a way to fill the emptiness and dread.

Rowland thought about his parents. His dad dropped out of religion once his children were grown. Ross credited the church with providing moral formation for kids, but he concluded that when it came to his own morals, he'd already made up his mind and talking about it again and again was a waste of his time. "Most talk about right and wrong is a search for excuses," he'd said. "Why not just do the right thing? What's so complicated about that?"

Maggie, by contrast, drifted around to a few different churches, but she never dropped out completely. She was a great defender of repetition. "When I go back to the old favorites, like the Lord's

Prayer, a hymn, one of the Psalms, I find it comforting. Not necessarily something new. Sometimes I find something old, but I always find something," she'd said when Rowland pressed her for an explanation.

"Could you be more specific?" Rowland asked.

"No," she said. "It is what it is."

Eventually Maggie went back to being Catholic and attended Mass regularly. Rowland asked her why that church. "It's deep in me," she said, "It's where I was before I learned to doubt, and it's where I want to be when I'm done asking questions." There was something about her simplicity that needled Rowland.

"I think of myself as spiritual," Rowland told Polly. "I muse about why we're born and why we die. If it's so wonderful that we're born, why does it have to end on such a dark note? Who doesn't think about these things? Have you ever met anyone who says 'I'm getting in touch with my un-spirituality?' Besides, I try to be a good person. That's spiritual too. And who's ever met anyone who says they're trying to be a bad person? Even bad people don't go that far. So, when it's all tallied up, it looks like everybody is spiritual."

"Like your mom?" Polly asked.

"No. Not like Mom. She was more trusting than I am. Simpler, maybe. She'd made up her mind. My dad had made up his mind too, but what Mom had was different. She seemed to get more out of it."

"Do I detect some spiritual envy? You seem to be working through a lot of heavy stuff," Polly said.

"Oh, so now it's spiritual envy? You're always good for a new term, but that's not the same as an answer." Rowland realized he was being unfair to Polly. He was the one who'd pulled her into the conversation. She was trying to be an active listener. "Well, at least thanks for not accusing me of having a flare-up of my Oedipus complex." Rowland laughed. He often laughed in an effort to lighten things up if they started getting too serious. His most habitual laugh points had to do with religion, death, and anger. Get in range of any of these and you could count on Rowland to crack a joke or make a sarcastic remark and then excuse himself by saying he didn't mean it.

"It's okay, all those feelings about your mom," Polly reassured Rowland. "She probably was spiritual, and now and then you got a glimpse of it. Be grateful. She was in a boat that got rocked pretty hard sometimes, but it never sank. What's not to admire about that?"

"You think she had something?" Rowland asked.

"I didn't know your mom, so I don't think I can comment. Besides I can't get into that too deep with you right now," said Polly. "I've got work I need to focus on so I can get it finished before summer's over. I need to arrange activities for the kids, and somewhere in our schedule I need to carve out a week to visit my mother. That's a heads-up, by the way. I'm counting on you to be here for the kids while I'm gone. Don't take this wrong, Rowland, I know you're hungry for talk, and you need someone to listen. We all need that sometimes, but, honey, I'm really busy. Could you talk it over with Cohen? The stuff you're mulling over isn't particularly time sensitive, and he probably wouldn't mind."

When Rowland met Cohen at the Breakpoint Bar, they grabbed a booth away from the large table of young guys who were making noise. Five minutes into their conversation Cohen asked, "How did Iceland work out for Zach?"

"Good," said Rowland. "A young guy should have leeway to pursue happiness before all the heavy responsibilities set in. He's stayed in touch."

"That helps," said Cohen.

Rowland told Cohen about Zach's last message. He was off hiking with some guys he met in Iceland. He wrote about waterfalls, rock formations, and good areas for setting down tents. The highlight of his trip was white-water rafting. "The rivers are terrific," he wrote. "I think you would find Iceland interesting. Maybe not the river-rafting, but the rest you would like."

"All positive," said Cohen.

"It is," said Rowland. "He mentioned I might like Iceland even better than finishing the Appalachian Trail. The summer when he was fifteen, we walked part of it, and we promised we'd do the rest before I'm too old to hike."

"Is he inviting you to Iceland?" Cohen asked.

"No," said Rowland. "We used to make jokes about my bucket list. This time Zach didn't mention the bucket list, and he didn't say anything about hiking together before I'm too old. He definitely didn't invite me to Iceland. I think he was hinting that I should bow out of the plan for the Appalachian Trail."

"Maybe he's staying in touch just to be in touch. No plans. No requests. No loans. All good signs."

"I guess so," said Rowland. "That's a good way to see it."

"Once these kids go out beyond where we can see them, and once they get a taste of freedom that proves they can manage life on their own, it changes them." Cohen took a deep breath. "That's what happened when Ben went to India for a semester. We didn't hear from him for over a month, and I was going crazy. I thought about getting on a plane and going to India to see if he was okay, as if in India I'd know right where to find him."

"I worried about Zach too when he first went to Iceland," said Rowland. "He's a smart hiker, but I had no idea if the trails are well-marked or how rough the terrain is. I called him to remind him to carry enough water when he hikes areas he doesn't know, but he didn't answer his cell. He was out of range of a tower. It's hard to explain how uncomfortable I was waiting for him to call me back. What is this animal instinct? We don't want our kids wandering into spaces with which we're unfamiliar?"

"When Ben finally called from India, everything was fine," said Cohen. "He seemed older and nicer. When he returned home again, he was comfortable enough, but he didn't think of our house as his home anymore. It was like a dagger in my heart when he said 'Where do you guys keep your tape and your scissors?' It wasn't his tape and scissors anymore. He's become a turtle, taking his home with him wherever he goes. If there's anything he needs, he borrows it, but he doesn't want to own it."

"How different was it when we left home?" Rowland asked.

"We tethered ourselves to new things much more quickly than our kids do," said Cohen. "They have a different sense of the future and don't want to be tied down. They figure the world's their oyster." Cohen caught the puzzled look on Rowland's face. "That's what we think they think, even though that might not be what they think at all . . . if you can unravel that," said Cohen.

"What if it's only us thinking the world's their oyster? They're worried that the world is going to end in fire and ice. Our kids are the post-Icarus generation. We warn them that everything's possible for them as long as they don't fly too close to the sun where their wings will melt. Meanwhile we hint that it's okay to dream of traveling to Mars. That makes them angry. They can't get through to us that our wax wings can and probably already are melting at sea-level because we're destroying the atmosphere and heating up the world. No matter what they say, though, we feel that *we* are responsible for *them*. At least I do. I still feel responsible for Zach."

"Of course," said Cohen. "We'll feel responsible for them 'til we die."

They were silent for a bit. Finally, Rowland said, "I wish I'd done a better job of being Zach's dad. If I'd gotten my head on straight, could I have made a marriage last with his mom? Could I have saved my kids from divorce, and would they be better off and more attached to us if I'd kept our family together?"

"That's how it looks in the rearview mirror," said Cohen.

"I could have tried harder." Rowland caught Cohen's direct gaze. "I know that now, but I couldn't admit that then."

"Probably not a good idea to tell Polly that," Cohen said.

"I have told Polly that. When she first met me, we broke up for a while. She figured out that I wasn't good marriage material, and I had a hard time persuading her to give me another try. She understands that I was a good share of the problem in my first marriage."

"Looks like we each need at least two marriages before we have a hope in hell of getting it right?" said Cohen.

"I didn't know you've been divorced too."

"We never did divorce," said Cohen. "But our first years were a mess. I went through medical school thinking it was all about me. Rachel had to take what she could get. I graduated believing all the wonderful things my mother said about me to her friends, and I didn't hear anything that Rachel asked for or complained about."

"How did you pull it out of the bag?" Rowland asked.

"We were close to quitting," said Cohen. "Then my dad died, and that bought us a little time. I saw how bereft my mother was, and it surprised me because I never thought they got along well. She nagged him. He complained about little things, and he complained often. He thought his home should be like his office where he was boss."

"And? That's what put you on the brink of divorce?" Rowland asked.

"When my dad died it delayed our divorce. It seemed in poor taste to add to the stress of a death by announcing the failure of a marriage. My mom was woebegone after my dad died, and it wore on me. I told her straight to her face that her grief didn't make sense to me. If she didn't love him that much when he was living, why was she so devastated by his death? I meant it. I thought she was playing on Dad's death to get sympathy."

Rowland looked at Cohen to see if he was joking. "You said that to your own mother?"

"Remember, we're talking family," Cohen said. "I can say anything I want to Mom, because she's stuck with me. I'll always be her son, and she'll always be my mom. Don't get me wrong, though," said Cohen; "it wasn't easy to confront her. She's no pushover."

"How did she take it?" Rowland asked.

"You stupid little boy," she said. "What makes you think you know what love is? It's not what you think at all. Your father and I lived side by side all those years. We knew every ugly thing about each other, and we didn't walk away. That's love. You can't tear that apart and throw half of it out."

"Stupid little boy, huh? She knows how to hit back."

"It made me think," said Cohen. "I'd have to put up with things I didn't like, whether Rachel and I were together or apart."

"From which you concluded what?"

"Six of one and a half dozen of the other," said Cohen. "I decided I had to give it another try with her. I think of that as my second marriage. Not Mom's way exactly or Dad's. I didn't want the nagging and complaining."

"Did you make a deal with Rachel?"

"No," said Cohen. "I told her I was going to try harder."

"What did she say?"

She said, "Well, we'll see what comes of that."

"Has she ever admitted that you turned it around?"

Cohen, who wasn't usually at a loss for words, didn't say anything. He was pensive. Finally, he said, "Rachel's good enough for a guy like me." He paused again before he continued. "Here's the point, Barone, we both know that whether we stay together or we leave, our kids are not going to have perfect lives because they don't have perfect parents. That was true for us too. We didn't have perfect parents, and the people we married didn't have perfect parents. There's no way to winnow a good excuse for ourselves out of that setup. We all face disappointments, and so do our kids. Some people sort it out, and some people give up."

"That's the big question," said Rowland. "What determines who goes which way? If we could hedge our bets, put money on our futures like we do in the stock market, we'd risk everything we have to save our kids, but we don't have a clue about what sorts out the winners from the losers. It's such a gamble."

As he spoke Rowland felt a shudder of self-doubt. Would he really sacrifice everything for his children? During his first marriage he left most of the work to their mother and made a big show now and then of how much he cared about them. Now his older kids didn't need him anymore. Time would pass quickly, and the little kids he and Polly had together would grow up and leave before he knew it.

Rowland wondered if anything really lasts. Rowland had to admit the truth to himself. Maybe he was always missing out because he didn't make the present his priority. Maybe he didn't think anything was important enough to matter more than he did. Maybe he was locked up in a preprogrammed agenda for manhood that was just like his dad's. And then the boom fell. Maybe when all was said and done, he was no different than his Grandpa Willard.

"In a few years, what are we going to look like to our kids?" Rowland asked Cohen. "If they're messed up, they'll think we did it. If they're doing fine, they'll think they achieved that despite our interference?" He noticed Cohen's grin, but Rowland was serious and he didn't cover it up with a joke.

"For better or worse we hope our children will feel some regard for us," said Cohen. "We hope they'll value something they learned from us, and we hope they'll relinquish their disappointments. If that's what we're hoping our children will do, doesn't that pass the buck back to us? Shouldn't we be figuring out how to honor our parents rather than busying ourselves with impressing our kids, so they won't take note of our screw-ups?"

"Did genetics teach you that?"

"No," said Cohen. "I learned it from my dad."

"Seriously?"

"Yes, seriously," said Cohen, "but he didn't live long enough to see it take."

"It took, finally?" Rowland asked carefully.

"It's not that simple," said Cohen. "When I was getting close to the age for bar mitzvah, my dad wanted to start the study and get ready for the big event. I refused. I wasn't the first one to do that. My parents had friends whose sons had refused. It was blowing in the wind. Resist your parents! Be revolutionary! Grasp the future; ditch the past! Claim your own life for yourself! Never trust anyone over 30! I know it hurt my father, but he took me aside and told me he wanted to discuss it once more, and then he would let it go."

"How old were you?" Rowland asked.

"Just starting high school," said Cohen.

"You are bar mitzvah whether you like it or not," my dad said. "Until now I've been responsible for what you do, but you're at the age when it shifts over to you. Refusing to take responsibility doesn't mean you get to change the laws of the universe, and it doesn't mean I'm stuck with responsibility for you, while you have all the freedom to make bad choices. Those choices are yours. So, I'm asking this: read the commandments and consider from which of them you think you're exempt. At least then I'll know the kind of man I'm dealing with. Once you've done that, our conversation is over, and I won't bring it up again."

"Do you think he was serious, or was this a setup to get you to change your mind and have a celebration?" Rowland couldn't imagine having a conversation like that with his own dad.

"My dad handed me the commandments, and to indulge him I read them," said Cohen. "I pointed out he wasn't exactly stellar in observing sabbath. I told him that single people my age considered preoccupation with adultery old fashioned and small minded. Values had changed. I reminded him that if he knew me at all, he would know that most of the other laws weren't even a challenge. By character I'm not inclined to lying and stealing. And I told him that the commandment about honoring parents pissed me off, because it's up to them to earn it. Dad took it all in, and he didn't say a word."

As Cohen went through the list, Rowland was clicking off items on his own list. He was surprised how closely his matched Cohen's. He nodded along as Cohen spoke.

"My dad didn't argue with me about any of it," Cohen continued. 'I know now where you stand,' he said, 'and my work is done.' He kept his word, and he didn't mention it again."

As he spoke Cohen looked sober. "I didn't think about it for a long time, but recently I ended up in court with my own kid. He did some vandalism, and I ended up paying for it. He didn't feel guilty. On the contrary, he accused me of not understanding him. What can I say, though, because I did that to my dad and mom. I'm old enough now to be on the other end of that stick. My kids are judging me."

"Is that the best we have to offer our kids?" Rowland asked.

"You mean another generation of judgment without honor?" Cohen said.

"Back up a step," said Rowland. "I don't mean to get too personal, but do you think you still have to find some way to honor them? They're dead."

"What's the alternative? If I choose not to honor them, I lose the past. To keep the past, I don't have to accuse and forgive them, I don't have to cook up good stuff and aggrandize them. I just have to remember them. The point is to stop being indifferent."

"Maybe you *should* become a rabbi." Rowland tried not to sound ironic. And he could tell that Cohen noticed he wasn't joking.

They finished their drinks in silence. "Time for a beer next week?" Cohen asked.

"I'm heading to Chicago to see my sister Jenna."

"Going to catch up on the family stories?" Cohen asked.

"Yeah. My brother Will might come from California, although it's his busy season. I'll know he's joining us when I see him walk through the door. This is the guy who thinks that if you keep chipping away at it, the universe will bring you answers. Did I tell you he's getting sort of spiritual?"

"Try not to trip over your brother," said Cohen. "That won't make it simpler. You're stuck with each other. Your stories are his stories too. I wonder why there's no commandment to honor your brothers and your sisters. Or maybe there is, and I didn't pick it up. Give me a call when you get back."

Cohen checked his phone and put it back in his pocket before he got up and put on his jacket. Together they walked out through the glass doors and into the parking lot. Rowland reached out his hand, and when Cohen took it, he pulled Rowland into a bro hug.

"Good luck," said Cohen, "and bon voyage!"

"I'm only going to Chicago."

"Of course, but you'll be time traveling," said Cohen just before they each headed off across the parking lot in different directions.

Part Two

Lillian's Story

Chapter 8

WHEN JENNA WAS a little girl, her Gramma Jeanne and Grandpa Willard lived in a big house in Evanston, and her Aunt Lillian lived there with them. Lillian had polish on her toenails and wore mule pumps with kitten heels that clicked like castanets on the tiles in the foyer and on the hardwood floors. Her hair was long, and her voice had a smile in it. Little Jenna thought Lillian was glamorous, and she wanted to be like her. She tried to walk the way Lillian walked, and sometimes Jenna talked to herself in front of the mirror and smiled the way Lillian did or used the words "groovy" and "hip," even though she didn't know what they meant.

Memories of Aunt Lillian stopped abruptly when Jenna was still in elementary school. Much later she saw her aunt again at Grandpa Willard's funeral. Before the funeral Lillian was gone, and after the funeral she was back again in Chicago, where she lived in an apartment north of the loop on Lakeshore Drive. It had huge windows that looked out over Lake Michigan. Aunt Lillian was her dad's sister, but Jenna had no memories of visiting Aunt Lillian at her apartment with him. She visited with her mom, and she could tell that the two women were fond of each other. At the door they greeted each other with a hug that wasn't one of those careful, barely touching hugs that Jenna knew adults offered when good manners required it. When Jenna's mother hugged Aunt Lillian, it was a warm hug that folded the two women together. "Darling Maggie," Aunt Lillian would say, "it's so good to see you."

"It's good to see you too, Lillian," Maggie said. "You'll never know how much you were missed during those years you were hidden away." Jenna wondered if somebody could be kept in hiding for years at a time. It wasn't likely that Aunt Lillian was locked in an attic somewhere, but was she in jail or in an institution?

After Aunt Lillian wrapped Jenna in her arms and kissed her cheeks and forehead, the scent of her perfume would linger on Jenna's clothes. At the end of their visit, before Jenna and Maggie disappeared through the door of the apartment, the women hugged again, and as Jenna and Maggie descended in the elevator to the street the fragrance of Aunt Lillian's perfume floated with them.

Jenna had clear memories of Aunt Lillian's presence at her dad's funeral too. One scene in particular stuck in her mind. At the graveside, while the preacher was reading out of a book, Jenna glanced over at Aunt Lillian and saw her dabbing her eyes with a lace handkerchief. Jenna couldn't imagine why Aunt Lillian was so sad, because Lillian and Ross never seemed close. But there she was at Ross's funeral, reaching up under the edge of her sunglasses to wipe tears away. Aunt Lillian was the only one wearing sunglasses on that overcast day, big and glamorous sunglasses like movie stars wear.

Jenna asked her mother about this distance between Ross and Lillian. She also shared her observation about the tears at the funeral. "We cry for different reasons," Maggie said with a sigh. "Nothing brings that out as obviously as a funeral can. Sometimes we cry for what's lost, and sometimes we cry for what's broken. It's not fair to say there was no love between Lillian and Ross, but they did keep their distance."

By the time Maggie died, Jenna was a grown woman with grown children of her own. At that visitation, when Jenna and Aunt Lillian sat together to share sweet memories of Maggie, Jenna began to cry, and Aunt Lillian comforted her like she was a little girl, stroking her hair and drying her tears. "Oh, Darling Jenna," she said as she took her niece in her arms, "your momma was a sister to me, the only sister I ever had, and when dear Maggie came into our family, it meant the world to me. You and I are going to miss her terribly, but we'll get through this together." Aunt Lillian was crying, not sobbing exactly, but she breathed in short gasps as if she were in pain.

At first it was hard for Jenna to go to Aunt Lillian's apartment without her mom. She liked being with Aunt Lillian, but Maggie's empty chair made Jenna's heart ache and reminded her that a warm routine had been broken. She and her mom had made a fun day of it when they visited Aunt Lillian together. On the way, Maggie and Jenna would stop off to pick up lunch for the three of them at the deli just off Roosevelt. For themselves they bought sandwiches, but for Aunt Lillian they got soup and a strawberry milkshake. The soup Aunt Lillian stowed in the refrigerator for later, but while Maggie and Jenna ate their sandwiches, Aunt Lillian sipped her sweet pink drink.

On occasion Aunt Lillian drank the milkshake way to the bottom, and her last sip through the straw made a slurping sound. She'd laugh and say, "Straws be damned. This is why it's only permissible to use them at home or in hospitals." In a restaurant she would never have used a straw. Once when Jenna was chewing gum, Aunt Lillian whispered to her that "ladies don't chew gum. It's okay in private, but in public it's *coarse.*" Her aunt was the only person Jenna ever knew who used that word or was particularly concerned about being coarse. Maybe she'd picked this up from Grandpa Willard, because he too was concerned about women being refined.

Aunt Lillian didn't cook when they visited her. Jenna wondered if there were pots and pans in her kitchen. Treats were another matter. For tea they sat at the small table near the window, where Aunt Lillian poured Queen Mary Blend into thin china cups on pretty saucers. In the center of the table, she set out a small pearly white plate with fluted edges on which she'd arranged tiny macaroons that Maggie brought from Marshall Field. They were favorites. As a backup, if Maggie didn't bring macaroons, Lillian offered cookies she kept in a fancy metal box. The box was orange, and in a circle on the front, it said Lazzaroni and Saronno. The cookies had a very special fragrance, and each one was wrapped in its own tissue paper.

Jenna didn't think of Aunt Lillian as an eater; she thought of her more as a nibbler. She was the kind of woman who went to a restaurant alone for lunch and ate small salads, but lingered long at the table. Soon after Maggie died, Jenna called Aunt Lillian and said, "Let's do something different. Let's go out for lunch." Lillian accepted the invitation, but when Jenna picked her up, she asked to go to the restaurant near her apartment where she felt most comfortable. At the restaurant Lillian left her fur coat with the woman who tended the coat check, but she didn't take the numbered tag with her. "I don't need a tag; they know me," she said.

When Maggie died, Jenna determined to keep visiting Aunt Lillian. It seemed like the right thing to do because she didn't have a husband or children. While they drank tea together, Lillian told stories from the days when she worked for Maison de Mode in Montreal as a buyer of women's fashion accessories. Her favorite buying trips were to Paris, and her favorite meetings were with the glovemakers, from whom she ordered a variety of styles. "An excellently crafted glove flatters the hand," Aunt Lillian told Jenna. "It's perfectly stitched so the seams hide between the fingers and the top surface is smooth to the touch. Perfect gloves are mysterious; like all women's fashions, they both hide and reveal what is underneath."

Lillian kept gloves in shallow drawers of a small chest next to the coat closet by her front door. On one visit she took out a pair to show Jenna. The way she slid her hand into the glove was elegant, sort of sexy, and she extended her hand to Jenna like a ballerina. The glove was cream-white leather, perfectly fitted, and it extended to just below her elbow. On the underside of the glove was a row of tiny pearl buttons that fastened so that the glove showed the contour of her wrist and arm. Jenna told Aunt Lillian how beautiful it was, and then admitted that the only gloves she owned were the ones she wore to keep her hands warm in winter.

"Dear Jenna, that is a glove of an entirely different sort," Aunt Lillian replied. "This pair is from the best *gantier* in Paris, and it was a gift from a gentleman. Someday I want you to have it."

"Thank you," Jenna said, "but I don't think it'll fit my hand. My hands are bigger than yours."

That Jenna wouldn't be able to wear the gloves didn't seem to trouble Aunt Lillian. She went on describing the years she lived in Paris before she came back to Chicago. It was a fashion-conscious time when men and women dressed up to go out for dinner or to the theater. A man in a well-cut suit with a perfectly pressed shirt, a fine silk cravat, and the right gold and onyx cuff buttons, naturally carried himself like someone of importance. The woman sharing his company attended to her shoes, her dress, and her evening wrap. Together as a pair they cut a striking image.

In Paris, according to Lillian, a woman wore a good coat and gloves to do her shopping or to go to the museum in the afternoon. She didn't carry things in her pockets even if her coat had them. She carried what she needed in a leather purse, not one of those shapeless bags in which women tote all sorts of clutter everywhere they go. "We weren't like the crowds that mob the Art Institute now," Aunt Lillian insisted. "The last exhibit I went to there drew such a motley crowd, I couldn't enjoy the art. It was like being served in a fine restaurant by an unshaven waiter with dandruff and bad breath. It ruined what was meant to be a beautiful experience."

Jenna thought about the field trip to the Art Institute that she made with her daughter's class. The girls wore blue jeans with holes in them, and the boys wore puffy down vests and hiking boots. Jenna tried to imagine Aunt Lillian in her fur coat mingling with a crowd like that. She would have been an eye-catching exhibit in her own right, all decked out like an actress in old movies.

Aunt Lillian took another pair of gloves out of the drawer. "These are day gloves," she explained. "Of course, most people wouldn't notice if you wore them now, any more than they would notice if you were wearing gardening gloves. In my time in Paris, however, a pair of gloves like these was as good as a business card. In the establishments where I bought for the store, good gloves were the signature of a smart dresser. Just look at them!"

The leather was soft chestnut brown. The cuff at the wrist turned back and revealed a checkered brown and white pattern of woven leather, and the glove was closed on the underside of the wrist with a small round button the exact color of the leather. "Put it on," said Aunt Lillian.

"My hands are bigger than yours, and I don't want to stretch your glove," Jenna said.

"It'll fit your hand," Aunt Lillian said. "You learn to estimate the size of a hand when you work in the accessories department of a good establishment." She reached for Jenna's hand and smoothly pulled on the glove. Deftly she pressed the button on the underside of Jenna's wrist through the dainty buttonhole, without even needing to look at it. "When I saw this glove years ago, I had to have it, even though it wasn't my size," said Aunt Lillian. "It was so exquisite. I've enjoyed having it in the drawer ever since, but now I'd like you to have it."

Jenna stroked the glove. It felt like skin. "The finest quality lambskin is both soft and durable," Aunt Lillian explained. "Like your own skin, if you care for it properly, it ages well." She pointed out how the seams fell perfectly between Jenna's fingers. It was an odd contrast to the worn and puckered cuff of the fleece Jenna was wearing, but Aunt Lillian appeared not to notice.

"Drawing a glove like this onto your hand," Aunt Lillian purred, "invites you to admire the skill of the person who made it. It also can bring out the worst in you, if it makes you vain or if you reduce its value to money. That's why a woman of elegance would never reveal what she paid for her gloves. She's most fortunate if she receives them as a gift, so she knows their value, but not their price."

"Thank you, Aunt Lillian," Jenna said. "I'll cherish them. When I see them in the drawer or put my hand into them, I'll always think of you."

It was a strangely tender moment, especially because it transported Jenna back in time to the big house in Evanston where she used to visit her grandparents. That was when Aunt Lillian was her gorgeous young aunt, and Jenna was a little girl who wanted to grow up to be just like her.

Lillian enjoyed telling stories about her life in Paris. It was as if the old woman was asserting, "Maybe the family forgot about me, but I went on living!" When Maggie and Jenna began visiting Lillian again after Grandpa Willard died, Aunt Lillian didn't seem like someone who would go away and not care about the people she left behind. The opposite was true. When their visits were over, and they were preparing to leave, Aunt Lillian would say, "Come back soon. You know how much your visits mean to me. Don't stay away too long."

On one of the visits after Maggie had passed away, when the time seemed right, Jenna asked Aunt Lillian if she remembered when Maggie and Ross along with their children came for visits to the big house in Evanston. "Oh, how I remember," Aunt Lillian said. "You were young when I left, but I often recalled the energy your big family brought into that dark old house. Sometimes the thought of it made me homesick, but other times it was the most comforting memory I had of those years."

"I was scared of Grandpa Willard," said Jenna, "but when the other cousins were there and we played together, that big old house was magical. There was a huge room at the top of the house. Do you remember that? It was up steep stairs. The ceilings were slanted, and there were dormers that had curtain rods with sheets hanging across them. We could divide up the space so that it was like a house with lots of rooms, and we played there with our dolls. Sometimes we played school. My sister Laura was always the teacher, and the cousins and I were the students."

"Long ago, in the days when liquor was illegal," Aunt Lillian said, "those big houses in Evanston had finished rooms in the attics where people played cards and drank. Some of the houses were large enough to have a ballroom on the top floor."

"Did Grandpa Willard and Gramma Jeanne have that?" Jenna asked.

"No, they moved to Evanston much later," said Aunt Lillian. "In my time the large room at the top of the house was used to store winter clothes in summer and summer clothes in winter. They also kept extra furniture up there. The sheets hanging across the dormers blocked out direct sunlight and kept the clothing and furniture from fading. We children weren't allowed to play there, but by the time you came along your Gramma Jeanne had loosened the rules. It was a good space for grandchildren while adults visited downstairs. Your gramma didn't want you to get on your grandfather's nerves."

"My very best memory of those visits," Jenna told Aunt Lillian, "was the time you bought me a pair of peep-toe patent leather shoes with tiny heels. I thought I was unbelievably fashionable."

"You were fashionable," said Aunt Lillian. "You were one of those naturally pretty little girls who only needed to be taught good taste. You had stunning eyes and wild curly hair. Best of all you had no idea how pretty you were. So instead of being vain or spoiled, you were sweet. Adorable really. I always thought you were your father's favorite." Aunt Lillian smiled as she spoke, and then as if to be fair she added, "Your sister and your brothers were darlings too. Your mother and father were very fortunate."

"Did you ever know Steven, my brother who died?" Jenna asked. "He must have been very little when you left. He was a sweetheart who went sour." Ross and Maggie's family talked about Steven more after he died than they did while he was alive and using drugs. Before he died, they worried about him, but after he died, they missed him, and they rarely talked about the gun or the drugs. Instead, they talked about Steven the way he had been before he started to fall apart. On his birthday they remembered how old he would be, as if he'd grown up normally, but was absent because he was off on a trip somewhere. When they were all gathered for the holidays, Maggie recalled sweet little things about Steven, as if by remembering him she could give him a seat at the table. She was determined never to let him die out completely.

"Your mom didn't stop loving Steven when he made a mistake," said Aunt Lillian. She looked at Jenna waiting for a response. When Jenna said nothing, Aunt Lillian went on. "Sometimes love survives the pain, and sometimes it doesn't. There are people who aren't strong enough to keep loving after disappointment. Life never turns out exactly the way it's supposed to, and some people can't bear that letdown." Jenna was holding back tears, but Aunt Lillian's eyes were clear, and her gaze was steady.

"Do you know why grown women cry at weddings?" Aunt Lillian asked. "They cry because the bride is hoping to live happily ever after, and the older women know she won't. No one ever does.

That story repeats itself every time a hopeful mother and father have a baby. The grown women cry again at the christening for the same reason they cried at the wedding. They're hoping this fresh little infant will have a perfect life. It's their obligation to wish that, because it would be cruel to expect anything else. But deep down they know this wish won't come true. It never does. It can't. Life isn't like that."

Jenna blurted out the question she hadn't planned to ask. "Aunt Lillian, why did you disappear? At first you were there, and then you were gone for a long time, and then I only visited you at your apartment with my mother, but you hardly ever came to see us at our house. What happened to you? What went wrong?"

Lillian fussed with the cuff of her silk blouse as if she were getting ready to pose for a portrait. "I was a sore spot for my parents. I was driven out."

For a moment Jenna tried to picture what that could mean. Driven? Sore spot? And then she gave up and took the obvious course. "What happened?" Jenna asked.

"Well. Where to start. Let's begin here. Do you remember that your Grandpa Willard had stores?" Aunt Lillian asked.

Jenna could remember. He had clothing stores with hats and shirts for men. She loved the wall on which there were special racks with ties in all sorts of colors. She like the pocket handkerchiefs too. They were squares of beautiful silk, especially enticing because children weren't allowed to touch them. There were other racks with suits and big overcoats. And she remembered a very short man who had a measuring tape around his neck. He had one very thick shoe, and he leaned over to one side as he walked. After the customer tried on his new suit, the short man marked it with a chunk of white chalk to show where it had to be altered. He was Grandpa Willard's tailor.

"That's the way good stores were when not all clothing was ready-made," said Aunt Lillian. "Your Grandpa Willard set up his first stores in Chicago and then branched out to Indiana and Wisconsin. The young man who was the store manager in Wisconsin was Harold, handsome and charming Harold," said Aunt Lillian. "He came to Chicago from time to time to pick out merchandise and talk with your Grandpa Willard about setting up additional stores." Lillian paused and gazed out the window. She shook her head in a way that made no sense to Jenna, and she cleared her throat.

At last Lillian continued. "On some visits Harold stayed overnight, and after doing business with him all day, Grandpa Willard was happy to turn over responsibility for evening entertainment to Ross and Charlie. "Your dad and your Uncle Charlie liked taking Harold out when your Grandpa Willard was paying for it. As they went out the door your Grandpa Willard would say, 'Run a tab Ross; they know me at the restaurant.' It wasn't necessary for him to say that; the boys knew the routine, but it made your Grandpa Willard feel important, and he never missed an opportunity to remind his children that he was somebody."

Jenna nodded. She remembered that everyone treated Grandpa Willard as if he were important. She also remembered that she was scared of him.

"Sometimes when my brothers took Harold out for entertainment, they invited me to go along with them," said Aunt Lillian.

"How old were you?"

"At first I was only seventeen, but when I was dressed up, I looked older." Lillian had a dreamy smile of someone thinking about events long ago. "We'd go to a restaurant where there was a bar and a dance floor. Harold was an exceptional dancer, and I loved dancing with him. He'd escort me out onto the floor and the band would strike up popular tunes. When we finished dancing, the patrons who'd been watching from their tables clapped. Sometimes they sent over a round of drinks, or the host offered the boys expensive cigars."

"Were you old enough to drink?" Jenna asked.

"It didn't matter," Aunt Lillian said. "We weren't rowdy teenagers. We were fashionable young adults who knew how to behave in a restaurant and leave a generous tip on the table at the end of the evening, courtesy of Willard Barone."

"Your brothers went along with that? Even my dad?" Jenna asked. Her dad had never been easy-going with his own children about smoking or drinking. In fact, he made a huge issue of it when he caught them with cigarettes, and he wouldn't allow the children to have even a sip of wine at home when they were under age. A few times at dinner when Ross was serving wine for the adults, Maggie had suggested, "Pour the children a little taste, Ross." But he wouldn't. "They'll have time enough for that later," he'd say.

Only Grandpa Willard could get away with serving children a few sips of wine in a proper wine glass at dinner around the big table in the dining room in Evanston. Along with the wine there came long instructions about how to hold the wine glass by the stem and not hold it with your fist around it like it was a beer glass. Grandpa Willard instructed the children about sipping, not gulping, and not leaving smeary mouth prints. By the time the lesson in etiquette was finished and it was time to drink the wine, it felt like taking medicine. Ross would say nothing, but Maggie would roll her eyes.

"Children raised by overly strict parents know how to test the limits a step at a time," said Aunt Lillian. "That's what we did. Once he'd become a familiar visitor in the family, Harold invited me for a Saturday matinee at the movies and dinner. Grandpa Willard didn't object because the business in Wisconsin was going well, and he trusted Harold. 'A smart owner keeps a good worker motivated' the boss liked to say."

Jenna watched as Lillian spoke. Her face seemed calm, but she kept fussing with the edge of the table cloth as if it wasn't fitting quite right on the table. Jenna looked into Aunt Lillian's eyes as she spoke. They had grown old around the edges with the typical creases at the corners and slight sag of soft skin underneath, but the eyes themselves were sharp. They were looking into the distance, and were unflinching.

"On one of Harold's trips to Chicago, he stayed at the Palmer House, a grand hotel with a dazzling lobby and a sweeping staircase perfect for a romantic scene in a movie. The boss didn't know his employee booked a room for himself there, because Harold knew better than to press his luck. In any case, on that Saturday afternoon instead of going to the matinee at the movies, Harold took me to the hotel to show me around. As we arrived, the uniformed doorman helped me from the car, and he called Harold 'sir.'"

"Did you look old enough to be his wife?" Jenna asked.

"Probably not. There are occasions when men don't question other men. It's obvious it was planned, because waiting in Harold's room was champagne on ice." Aunt Lillian paused. "Are you okay with this? It's not too much?"

"I wasn't born yesterday," Jenna said.

"Of course, you weren't, but I don't want you to be uncomfortable."

"I'm fine," said Jenna.

Aunt Lillian took a deep breath. "When we got to the room Harold was very charming. We sat side by side on a love seat, chatting while we sipped our bubbly. He kept refilling mine, and I felt like Cinderella being singled out for attention by the prince. After several refills to my glass, he kissed me. It was an ardent kiss. Not like those urgent kisses of the boys at the school dances. He tangled his fingers into my hair and told me how beautiful I was. One step at a time he became more daring, and before I knew it, he was waltzing me across the room to the bed and my buttons had been undone. Harold was as deft at courting as he was at dancing. There was nothing crude or clumsy about his advances, and I found him irresistible."

Jenna hadn't told the truth about being perfectly comfortable with Aunt Lillian's disclosures. The details her children dropped about their sexual adventures sometimes worried Jenna, and occasionally she and her friends chatted indiscreetly about themselves, but never in her wildest imagination had she expected to be told a story like this by someone as old as her mother.

"After we'd taken the first steps, we found ways to repeat those fantasy afternoons when Harold was in town. We never went to the Palmer House again, but Harold was good at organizing his business trip so there was enough time for me in it. Rarely with champagne, and no longer to the movies, but there was always time for an interlude at his hotel. Our meetings together were never reduced to those steamy, groping encounters some young people were having in cars. Harold was a gentleman, and he was always considerate of me."

Lillian's voice wasn't easy like someone describing a picnic in the park, but it wasn't defensive either. That's what surprised Jenna. No embarrassment and no excuses. "Harold assured me we would be okay, because he knew how to take care of these matters. He seemed so expert in these things, I took him at his word," said Lillian. "I was bedazzled. Several times I told myself this had to stop before we were found out, but then when we were in his hotel room again, my judgment went on pause and another force took me over. You know what I mean?" She blushed slightly, but just as quickly Lillian's blush faded, and another look took its place. "The rest is history," she said and looked out the window wistfully.

Of course, it happened. Lillian had to go to her parents and tell them she was pregnant. Her mother was surprisingly kind. Even though she was an observant Catholic who knew how the church would view this, she didn't scold Lillian. By contrast her father was enraged. He insisted he'd counted on her, and she'd violated his trust by getting involved this way with an important employee. Harold was running a good business in the Wisconsin stores, and now Lillian had put that in jeopardy. "What healthy man away from home wouldn't be tempted when a beautiful young thing throws herself at him. Why did you do this to me?" her father asked. When he discovered that Harold had a wife and child at home in Wisconsin, his view of Harold changed, but he never apologized for blaming Lillian.

"I don't know how I would have gotten through this, except for my mother's help," said Lillian. "She neither blamed me nor excused me. Instead, she turned her attention to helping me figure it out."

This didn't surprise Jenna. She remembered how Gramma Jeanne treated her grandchildren. She never raised her voice, and she didn't get upset if one of the children tipped over a glass of milk at the table or left tracks in the entryway when they came in with wet shoes. She didn't even get upset the day Will chose the dining room in the old Evanston house for a place to practice some new moves with his yo-yo. His effort to shoot the moon broke two of the globes on Gramma Jeanne's chandelier, and she didn't make a big deal of it. Jenna understood that Lillian's problem was of a different scale, but she could imagine Gramma Jeanne handling it calmly.

Grandpa Willard was a different story. Jenna had always been afraid of him. He was like a slumbering pit bull, and clearly Aunt Lillian had roused his fury. Jenna could easily bring to mind the look of rebuke on his face, and it took nothing at all for her to recall the sound of his voice when he was furious. "How did my dad react?" Jenna asked. "And what about Uncle Charlie? They were in the business too. They must have known what was going on."

"They did what we all had been trained to do; they looked the other way and remained silent. They went on with business as usual as if nothing outside the ordinary had happened."

Meanwhile Gramma Jeanne turned to the priest of the local parish for help. She was able to do this without compromising the priest's relationship with Grandpa Willard, because the two men had never met. Grandpa Willard was Presbyterian and Gramma Jeanne was Catholic. They had what some people called a "mixed marriage." The priest arranged a place for Lillian to stay until the birth of her child, and under the guise of going off to school, she left for Montreal. "As you can imagine, it wasn't a school like other schools," Aunt Lillian said. "The disgraced girls finding refuge there called it 'the school of hard knocks,' and it lived up to its name."

Well before the end of Lillian's pregnancy, her mother arrived in Montreal to be with her. She had no trouble getting Lillian's father to agree with this plan, as long as she kept his embarrassing daughter far away. There was something strange about the way Aunt Lillian told Jenna this part of the story. The baby was a girl whom Lillian named "Margot." That's all Aunt Lillian said about the baby, and Jenna didn't dare to press her for more. Instead, Jenna asked, "Did Gramma Jeanne return to Chicago?"

"She stayed with me for a time, but then she had to go," said Aunt Lillian. "I found employment and poured myself into my work."

"Did you come back to Chicago to visit the family?" Jenna asked.

"It took a long time, and I vowed never to go back to the house in Evanston. It was a place of so much pain, and I couldn't forgive my father for being merciless." Aunt Lillian flicked away a tear, cleared her throat, and wrapped up her story. "Never is a long time, and here I am back home in Chicago."

Jenna couldn't help wondering how her mother handled the secrecy of the family into which she married. When Jenna was a child, she picked up tidbits of gossip about other families in the neighborhood or at their school. When she asked her mother to explain, she was told, "Honey, that's not my story to tell. When families go through hard times it doesn't help them if others chat about it behind their backs." Maggie Barnes was no fan of gossip, and she didn't work over other families' business in front of her children, but Jenna wondered why her mother never explained to her own children why their dear Aunt Lillian disappeared.

Whatever reasons Jenna's parents had for hiding the truth, Aunt Lillian lived by a different standard. "It's better to know," she said. "At first, it's shocking, because you have to repaint the family portraits. But once you face the truth, something else happens. You discover that the capacity for love is bigger than you knew. How much healthier families would be if they gave children space for learning that. I'm going to tell you the whole story, and you will have to decide what to do with it."

Chapter 9

WHEN GRAMMA JEANNE joined Lillian in Montreal before the birth of baby Margot, the ease with which her mother found her way in this foreign city surprised Lillian. It fascinated her to hear her mother chat in French with people she met in shops or visit with other patrons in the cafe where they ate their lunch. In Chicago her mother rarely spoke French. Lillian did remember her making phone calls and speaking French around the holidays, but her father scowled as if what she was doing were objectionable. "Keep it short. It's expensive," he'd say.

Grandpa Willard had been persuaded to send Lillian to Montreal during her pregnancy, because he also assumed the baby would be placed for adoption soon after birth. Once Gramma Jeanne arrived in Montreal, however, it was clear she had no intention of following through with that plan. "We'll find a way," she said. "We've had enough loss in this family, and I can't tolerate any more. If death comes knocking at your door you may be helpless, but when life comes knocking at your door, you must invite it in. Leave it to me." She seemed oblivious to the difficulty of what she was suggesting.

In the afternoon while Lillian rested, Grandma Jeanne went out. Lillian assumed she was looking for an apartment suitable for her and her baby. She tried to imagine how she'd manage with an infant; she had no experience taking care of babies. Even if she gave her baby up, how would she manage living alone, because she'd never been responsible to provide for herself? Lillian passed her days in a cloud of angst.

On one afternoon when Gramma Jeanne returned, she announced that as soon as the baby and new mother were fit to travel, the three of them would fly to Paris. "I'm not up for it," said Lillian. "It's a terrible idea. I don't want to go on vacation right after I have a baby. Besides, how can we afford it?"

"I've sold my jewelry," Gramma Jeanne said with a look of satisfaction. "I made an agreement with a jeweler to sell my ruby bracelet and my good pearls. I brought them with me when I came because I knew I could use them to get money if we needed it. They brought a good price; the jeweler found a ready customer for them. Today when I went back to pick up the money, I decided to cash in more of my jewelry. I can't see a reason to hold any of it back. I don't need jewelry. I need my family." Lillian noticed that her mother's large sapphire ring was gone, and in place of the large diamond studs her mother usually wore in her ears, Lillian saw two tiny diamonds.

"Your watch?" Lillian asked her mother.

Willard Barone had been generous giving gifts to his wife, and he liked telling those who admired the gifts how much they had cost and where he'd purchased them. He especially liked to brag to other men. Embarrassed, Gramma Jeanne would say, "Willard . . . please . . . enough!" The watch with its circle of diamonds was the item about which Grandpa Willard bragged most. He was proud of how expensive it had been, and he was equally proud that he had gotten the price down by driving a hard bargain with the jeweler from whom he bought it. Lillian had always thought of the watch as Dad's watch on Mom's wrist. She thought of the other jewelry that way too. Dad's earrings in Mom's ears. Dad's necklace around Mom's neck.

"The watch is gone," her mother explained to Lillian. "These little diamonds for my ears I've kept. They were given to me by my mother when my first child was born, and I'd planned to give them to you to mark the birth of your baby, but you'll have to wait for them, because I need to wear them for a while. After all, I can't go around with nothing but holes in my ears." She chuckled as she spoke. Lillian had never seen her mother so sure of herself.

"You got those diamonds when Ross was born?"

neighbors moved in and out of the house freely, as if they were family."

"This is what families do," Gramma Jeanne told Lillian repeatedly. "You must trust me with this." Gramma Jeanne was resolute. She never backed off her decision for one moment.

Lillian and Gramma Jeanne returned to Montreal, where they found a tiny apartment for Lillian. As they sat down to their first small meal at a table in the corner of the room, the shock of it hit her. Lillian's new life was nothing like the life she'd lived in Evanston. She wasn't the princess anymore, but her mother didn't seem shocked by that at all, and Lillian wondered how this could be. Didn't she see it? Didn't she care? "I'm going mad," Lillian said as she got up and paced around the room, pounding her head with her fist. "Seriously, I'm going to completely lose my mind."

"You'll find it again," her mother said.

"Sitting at that table, thinking about my life, I was filled with hate," Lillian told Jenna when she recounted the story of that painful day. "I hated Harold. I hated my mother and father. I hated my brothers who acted as if they didn't care about what was happening to me. I hated the nuns who took care of me at Margot's birth, and I hated Camille and Leo for stealing my baby from me. 'You can't just hand a child around for convenience,' I screamed at my mother. Margot was the only speck of love left in my heart, and I felt sick with longing for her. I wondered if mothers die of this agony. I truly didn't know if I would survive."

"Did you tell Gramma Jeanne how you were feeling?" Jenna asked. "Did she know how scared and depressed you were?"

"There was no use. I didn't want to hear what she had to say. I wanted to blame her. We had tense words with each other, although they were mostly about unimportant things. Everything she did annoyed me. I couldn't stand how she chewed her food. I couldn't stand how she sighed before saying she was tired and going to bed. I felt trapped in that little apartment with her, and at the same time I felt abandoned by her. When she left to return to Chicago, I was eager to see her go, but within hours after she left, I was desperate.

Mama wrote me letters and called me on the phone. I didn't write letters back, and I wasn't friendly on the phone, although I would have been terrified if she hadn't kept calling. I went through hell."

"How did you survive? What got you through it?" Jenna asked.

Tears welled in Aunt Lillian's eyes. "Your mother," she said, and her voice was thick. She put her hand to her forehead and looked down. "Maggie helped me get through it."

"My mother?" said Jenna. "My mother was in Chicago, and you were in Montreal. What does my mother have to do with it?"

"Soon after your Gramma Jeanne returned to Chicago, Maggie called me. From the very start she was honest with me. 'I can't imagine how angry you must be,' she said. 'How could this happen? You must be fed up with this sick family and its secrets. I want you to know that I understand.' I was stunned. The call was completely out of the blue, but I could tell Maggie was sincere. We talked often on the phone. Sometimes the calls were short, just enough to hear each other's voices. When I had to make decisions, I called her and asked her advice. Before the first year was up, she visited me in Montreal. It was a very short visit, but it meant the world to me. And when she knew I would be having hard times, like Margot's birthday or holidays, she always called to tell me I wasn't forgotten."

"When did you come back to Chicago?" Jenna asked.

"I didn't move back, but within the first year I made a visit. I stayed in a hotel where Mama and Maggie could come to see me. I couldn't stand the thought of going to the house in Evanston, and I didn't want to see my father."

"Did you see my dad and Uncle Charlie?"

"No. I didn't want to see them either. They blamed me for what your Grandma Jeanne had done. They thought I was the one who persuaded her to sell off her jewelry. They didn't understand why I bailed out of the plan to give my baby up in Montreal, and they thought it was messy to involve some distant relatives in France. When embarrassment happened in our family, they were the kind of civilized people who did everything they could to make it disappear. They thought I had made the whole business more complicated than it needed to be, and I had made our family look bad.

That's the way my brothers had been trained to think. They were totally bound up by my father's view of manhood."

Jenna listened carefully, searching her memory for any clues about that time. It was an event that had passed her by. It also hurt her to hear Aunt Lillian speak of Ross this way. It didn't fit the father Jenna had known; he was protective of his own daughters. "I have no memory of that time at all," said Jenna. "I don't remember my mom being away to visit you, Aunt Lillian, and I don't remember that you visited us."

"Why would you remember that? You were little and it wasn't important to you." Aunt Lillian was matter of fact and went on with the story. "Maggie was loyal, and she disliked conniving. During her first visit she said to me, 'I need to put the cards on the table with you, Lillian. Your mother asked me to call you when you first returned to Montreal after leaving your baby in France. Also, you deserve to know that Leo isn't Gramma Jeanne's nephew. Ask her to tell you the whole story. It's not really mine to tell.' That was so like Maggie. Always trying to find the sweet spot between honest and fair."

"You can talk about anything you like," Gramma Jeanne had told Maggie. "You can tell Lillian all the family secrets if you think that will help. You can be critical of me if that's how you feel. You don't have to defend me if Lillian wishes she could tear me limb from limb. All I ask is that you not abandon Lillian. She's so alone; she needs someone. I try my best to be there for her, but it doesn't work because she needs me to blame. It's hard to accept comfort from someone with whom you're angry. Her anger crops up at the sound of my voice. My phone calls to her don't do much good. I'm too close to her hurt to be able to offer her comfort, but I'm not going to give up on her. I need your help, Maggie."

"I'll never forget that," Aunt Lillian said in a whispery voice. "My mother wasn't willing to give up on me even though I'd given up on her. She kept calling me, and I kept being ornery with her. A few times I swore at her. She pushed back a little and told me I had no right to be rude with her, but she didn't let go. I'll never forget either that Maggie stepped up to help me exactly when I could've drowned in my sorrows or burned up in my resentments. Your mother and my mother understood each other. It seems they both understood me too, although I couldn't see it at the time. Maggie was the closest thing to a sister I ever had, and she was a very loyal daughter-in-law. Your Gramma Jeanne loved her dearly."

"What was your life like, though?" Jenna asked. "You were all alone in Montreal. I can't imagine what that was like for you."

"I poured myself into my work," said Lillian. "At first, I mostly served English-speaking customers, but the store was a perfect place to learn French. I worked so hard there wasn't room for the sorrow that came oozing up whenever I was idle. I hated holidays. I didn't want vacations. I didn't make friends either, because if you have friends you have to talk about yourself, and that's the last thing I wanted to do. Maggie and Mama were my lifeline. You know something strange, Jenna? Sometimes I didn't like either of them very much. I can't remember being grateful; that only came later. I needed them, and that made me angry. That's a hard spot to be in. I was rude to them when I was most distressed. I wonder, why did they stick with me?"

Lillian was a model employee. She stayed on after hours to tidy the displays so they would be ready when the store opened the next day. She filled in for other employees who asked for days off. Within a year she was asked to manage a small department with hosiery and lingerie, and proudly wore a key on a band around her wrist, which marked her as the employee who could open the locked cabinets where the most expensive items were kept. When a position came open in fashions, she was promoted to the position that was the dream of all the young women who worked in the store.

Lillian lavished attention on her customers, although some of her best customers she rarely saw. They were women who sent their maids or assistants to pick up items for them, and Lillian was skilled at selecting styles that flattered them. She prided herself that only a few of the items she sent out for fitting came back. With each sale, she took notes in a small notebook so she could refer to it later when making future selections. As a personal shopper, she was in demand.

Lillian loved telling Jenna about her work as a shopper, but sometimes Jenna found the details tedious. "I took new customers selectively and only by referral," Aunt Lillian said. "I needed to be sure they had the resources to pay for the things I selected, and I wanted to know that if they bragged about their shopper, it only would be in good company. I didn't need customers who had bad reputations or would create bad debts for the store. There were gangsters and questionable characters in Montreal at that time, and some of them had lots of money, but no class. I wanted to avoid them."

Aunt Lillian went into considerable detail telling Jenna about a fashionable redhead for whom she made selections. Lillian knew exactly the color palette that would showcase the woman's striking hair, and the customer was delighted because her normally critical husband thought she was finally dressing well. Not long after, another new customer requested Lillian's services, but she adamantly refused to identify who had referred her. She already had a long buying history with the store and no bad debt, so Lillian had to take her. Gradually it dawned on Lillian that this second customer was the mistress of the fashionable redhead's husband. His tastes dictated the choices of both women.

The wife and the mistress were returning to Lillian with identical compliments. The husband liked the low neckline of his wife's dress because he thought it was "sassy." Not long after, the mistress told Lillian that the man she was dating liked her new dress because he thought a show of cleavage was "sassy." He'd also said to both women about very dissimilar dresses that it didn't concern him to spend large sums on their wardrobes, because being the escort of a "knockout" made it worth it to him.

Lillian took note of important social events the mistress skipped because she knew better than to embarrass her man by showing up at the events he attended with his wife. When the wife told Lillian her husband was traveling, the dates lined up perfectly with a request from the mistress for a good traveling ensemble. "You see," said Lillian, "everyone has secrets, and if you pay attention, sooner or later they'll reveal them to you. Knowing people's secrets gives you power." And with this little sidebar, Aunt Lillian revealed a secret of her own of which Jenna took note.

Eventually the manager at Maison de Mode approached Lillian to ask if she would accompany the buyer to Paris and Milan to place the orders for spring fashions. The buyer was an experienced older woman who welcomed a travel companion, and they both understood that Lillian was being groomed for the position from which the older woman would soon retire. "The trips back and forth to Europe to buy for the store were happy times for me," Aunt Lillian explained to Jenna, "because I finally knew I was really good at something." It also gave her opportunities to visit Beauvais and see Margot.

Sometimes Aunt Lillian's stories went long, and Jenna was bored, but she also discovered the kindness of listening. How better could she love this lonely old woman than by letting her feel that finally she had found someone who took interest in her lost years. It also helped Jenna understand the mysterious gift of Aunt Lillian's gloves.

In Paris Lillian met Raymond, a restaurateur in whose establishment many Canadian business people gathered. He was well-suited for his job because, in addition to being gregarious, he hailed from Montreal, and his patrons found him more welcoming than they found the restaurant managers who looked with suspicion on foreigners who crowded their establishments and were ignorant of French customs.

Raymond liked to have Lillian spend time with him at the restaurant, where he'd escort her through the maze of tables and seat her at his own booth. He had to continue with his work, but he would return for short breaks, during which he would have a cigarette and a drink. Sometimes he'd collect Lillian from the table where she was seated so he could bring her to meet his favorite patrons. The admiring glances as he escorted a well-dressed, well-mannered young woman on his arm pleased Raymond. He also liked to instruct Lillian how to behave. "Oh, no," he would say about the smallest thing. "Let me show you how that's done properly, Lillian." Like a good piece of silver or a prize bit of jewelry, Lillian was his to polish, and her role was to make him look good.

Sometimes, to take the edge off his criticism, Raymond would add that he was only correcting Lillian because he didn't want her to feel awkward among people of a certain class. She resented his comment, because she didn't feel awkward; she had been brought up with all the manners of a certain class, and the work she was doing with people of that class had made her confident.

"Then it was hard to see what was happening to me because I was so desperately lonely," Lillian admitted to Jenna as she recounted those times. "Later it became clear that I was giving myself up for him. Raymond hinted often that if I could conform a little more to his expectations, he'd like me more. What foolishness that was, because once I was completely made over to his specifications, he became indifferent. I should've known better. A good personal shopper knows that the new coat, this year's fashionable favorite, eventually hangs in the storage closet with moth balls."

Raymond asked Lillian to marry him, but marriage meant giving up her job with the department store in Montreal and moving to Paris permanently. It was a huge sacrifice for her; she loved her work. No one else seemed to notice that she was giving up something of value; it was expected of a married woman. Along with congratulating Lillian on her engagement, people complimented her for finding a man who was such a generous provider.

After marriage and her move to Paris, Lillian missed her work, but when she mentioned it to Raymond, he said, "Look at the hotel maids and household workers you see walking home on tired feet at the end of the day! They would gladly have your life. You don't know how good you've got it. I worry, my dear, that you're spoiled, and that's not attractive."

At first Raymond carved time out of his work to spend with Lillian, but that quickly diminished. He'd apologize half-heartedly. "What can I do? I have work," he'd say. "It isn't easy to keep a premier establishment running smoothly. You must understand." Lillian did try to understand, and she did her best to occupy herself in his absence. Lillian visited the family in Beauvais as often as she could. It was painful when she heard Margot calling Camille "Mama," and being called "Aunt Lilli" by little Margot was painful too. Lillian didn't let on to the child about her identity, but in her heart, she never gave up thinking of Margot as her own.

Raymond rarely went with Lillian to Beauvais, and when she returned from one of her visits, she noticed that Raymond had not slept in their bed while she was away. When she was home, Raymond was often at his work until very late, but he always returned to sleep next to her by morning. This was different. She asked him if there was another woman, and he denied it.

Meanwhile, Raymond was nervously avoiding Lillian's affection. Among his toiletries she noticed new medications, and she went to the pharmacy to inquire. After some arm-twisting, the pharmacist told her she should be grateful if Raymond was distant, and she should avoid intimacy with him. Lillian confronted Raymond again, and he admitted that he had contracted a disease from a careless encounter, but that it was over and wouldn't happen anymore. "Give the medicine time to work, and I'll be a gentleman. I don't want to expose you," he said, as if she should be grateful for how considerate he was.

"I don't feel I can live this way. I'm not designed to be the shamed wife," Lillian told Raymond. "I'm going back to Montreal, will try to get my old job back, and will make a life for myself in which the mention of you and your work doesn't make me blush." This was not bluff. Immediately she began with letters to her colleagues at Maison de Mode, thinking that contact with them on a purely social basis would give her an opening to explore employment when she could meet with them in person.

It dawned on Raymond that Lillian was serious about leaving, and he confessed to her that the life he was leading in Paris wasn't good for him either. He was drinking too much, and he was using drugs both to help him sleep and to stay awake. "I need to leave Paris too," he said. "Let's leave our problems behind, go home to Montreal, and make a good life for ourselves there." He had debts he could escape by handing over both the debts and the restaurant to his partner.

Raymond had another motive, and Lillian had uncovered it. "He couldn't live without me," Aunt Lillian told Jenna. "Realizing that put our relationship on an entirely new basis." Aunt Lillian smiled knowingly as she said this to Jenna, and without even the slightest smile Jenna thought to herself, *Knowing people's secrets gives you power.*

In Montreal, Raymond used what he had learned about restaurants in Paris to find a position managing a fine establishment in the center city. He worked hard, but he also arranged his hours so he could spend time with Lillian. "The trick to being a good manager is to have good assistants," Raymond said to justify an evening or two each week away from the restaurant. "Life is more civil here than in Paris."

Their income was finally sufficient to allow Lillian to furnish their apartment handsomely. They made new friends, sometimes entertaining at home or going out to clubs where they could listen to music. Lillian revived her love of dancing, and together she and Raymond were often the eye-catching couple out on the floor. She found students and taught French. It was a good time for both of them.

One evening while waiting for Raymond to return from work so they could go out to meet friends at a club where there was a new singer, Lillian was paging through magazines and listening for the sound of Raymond's key in the door. The phone rang. It was a call from the hospital. Raymond had been admitted. She went immediately and was told he'd had a heart attack.

Raymond had an oxygen mask over his face, and he looked gaunt. As she took his hand, he opened his eyes and looked at her uncertainly. He gazed up like a trusting child when she leaned over to kiss his forehead. A priest arrived, and Lillian left the room to give them privacy. The extremity of the situation sank in when Lillian realized Raymond was being prepared for death. Through the window in the door of his room, Lillian could see the priest administering last rites. After the priest left, Raymond was calm.

"Are you going to be okay?" Lillian asked him.

"Don't be afraid. But you . . . " Raymond gasped a deep breath " . . . go home to your mother."

Lillian called her mother, and she called Maggie, but she didn't leave the hospital. Early in the morning, the attending physician came into the room. After a very brief exam, he told Lillian that Raymond's condition was deteriorating rapidly. "There's nothing more to be done except keep him comfortable. His uneven breathing is what we expect as the end approaches, but he isn't in pain, and your presence seems to reassure him. Call for the nurses if you need them." Lillian was at Raymond's side when the nurse listened to his heart, touched the side of his neck, and pulled the sheet up over his face.

At the visitation before the funeral, Lillian asked his fellow workers who had called the ambulance and accompanied Raymond to the hospital. She wanted to thank the worker who assisted him. His coworkers were sheepish and didn't give her straight answers. "Everybody helped," one said. A few days after the funeral a woman who worked in the kitchen came to Lillian and told her that if she were in a wife's shoes, she'd want to know: Raymond's heart attack occurred in the bed of the assistant with whom he'd been working closely at the restaurant. "I'd wondered," said Lillian, "why she didn't appear at the visitation. You'd think that courtesy would be expected of his assistant."

Jenna listened quietly while Lillian spoke. Finally, when there was a pause, she said, "I'm so sorry your life has been hard. You were so brave. You're still brave because it takes courage to tell a story that has so much pain. Thank you for trusting me."

"Pain, yes. You're right about that. But why would I apologize for my story?" There was an edge of defensiveness in Aunt Lillian's voice, but when she saw the hurt on Jenna's face, she paused. "The first time I had to tell it, maybe then it was hard. Yes, then it took courage. But each time I repeat it, I discover that my story is everyone's story. Love is imperfect. The tale of Cinderella is a lie." To her words Aunt Lillian added a small shrug. "Why sweep away imperfect love as if it's trash? Hiding the flaws doesn't change anything. Love is love. I know what I had was real."

Aunt Lillian had Jenna's full attention. This was not one of the rambling stories about Maison de Mode. "At first I thought I was Raymond's victim," Lillian said, "but once he was gone, I understood how much I'd needed him. I missed him because he was my true love. I was wounded by a cold father. Harold was a shallow trickster, that bastard. My brothers were too caught up in their own lives to care much about me. But Raymond actually loved me. He had weaknesses, but so did I. He was damaged, but look at the family I came from. I was damaged too. Sometimes Raymond was careless, but above all he was loving. I don't care what others think. Let them call him a Lothario. He was my Romeo."

"I know what you mean," said Jenna. "I've only been in love once. I've liked other men and enjoyed them, but I've only ever been in love with Jak. Nobody wants to hear that. They want to convince me that Jak was a loser, that somewhere there's a better man for me. Let them think whatever they want. I know Jak loved me. One day I couldn't imagine living without him, and the next day I couldn't stand to be around him anymore. His impulsiveness drove me crazy. I went around that stupid circle over and over until I thought it would drive me insane. After I divorced him, that's when I could see that he loved me, and he loved our children. But the chaos . . . honestly, there was some new craziness every day . . . it was more than I could handle. That matters too, but it didn't erase all the love. It just made it messy. No one seemed to understand that. They didn't understand how hard it was to end it, and how much I missed him once we weren't together anymore."

"We aren't talking about some silly form of puppy love," said Aunt Lillian. "We're talking about our own lives. Yours and mine. We're the only ones who really know what happened. That's why it doesn't matter what everyone else thinks."

"What about Gramma Jeanne?" Jenna asked. "Why did she stay with Grandpa Willard? She had to sneak around behind his back in order to do what she thought was right. He was a miserable man. Why did she stay with him?"

"Mama had a different way of loving, and it was a different time," said Aunt Lillian. "She didn't stay with him; she stayed with the family. She understood the risks and loved her children by being tough. She could be as tough as she needed to be once she decided what mattered most. Sometimes I hated her for that toughness, but something happened to her long ago that took away her expectation that love would be easy or sweet. She was sweet to children, and she was fiercely loyal to her boys. Underneath her kindness was something invincible."

"Do you think she had a good life? Was she satisfied with it?" Jenna asked.

"When she was very old," Aunt Lillian said, "I asked her that same question."

"Probably someone looking at me would say my life was tragic or that I was weak," Gramma Jeanne said. "But my life is like my hands with scars and wrinkles and crooked fingers. They have held what is dear to me. The scars aren't what's most important."

Chapter 10

THE DAY AUNT LILLIAN talked to Jenna about Lennie, she prefaced it with, "I don't know where the notion came from that the Barone family is different from other families, or that it doesn't have any soiled linen. The worst thing that happened in our family was what happened to Lennie."

Ross was the firstborn, followed by Charles five years later, and then came Leonard soon after. Lillian was the fourth child, the only daughter and the family's princess. When Lennie was little, he was desperate to keep up with his brothers. Before he was tall enough to sit on the seat of a bike and pedal at the same time, he rode the bike standing up. More than once his foot slipped off the pedal, and he crashed. Applied to Lennie, the proverb about getting back on the horse meant putting bandages on his knees and pretending the fall on his bike didn't hurt.

Whether the warp in Lennie's good sense came from the pressures of constant competition, or whether it came from something deeper in his character, no one really knows. Beyond having little fear of skinned knees and broken bones, Lennie also had little fear of adult authority. The possible exception was his father. Lennie was scared to death of him.

His mother was another matter. She was one of the few people with whom Lennie cooperated. She had devised a clever way to get him to do as she asked, by coaxing him with Black Jack chewing gum. Neither Lennie nor any of the other kids liked gum that tasted like licorice, but that didn't interfere with the deal she had with Lennie. Training Lennie with gum was like training a dog with kibble.

If his mother held out gum and told Lennie to put on his shoes, he kept an eye on the gum and did as she asked. Lennie would walk the dog around the block for gum. He'd spend Saturday morning raking leaves in the yard for the same paltry reward. It wasn't clear whether, apart from the bribe, Lennie would have listened to his mother any better than he listened to anyone else.

Beneath his bed Lennie kept a cigar box for his Black Jack assets. Because Lennie neither chewed the gum nor shared it, the quantity grew, and when the cigar box got full, Lennie would transfer some of his inventory to a trunk in the attic. It was secured with a padlock, the key for which Lennie carried on a cord around his neck. In the summer when he would sweat, the cord left a red ring around his neck when he was clean and a grimy ring when he wasn't. The cigar box under the bed he guarded closely, lining it up exactly along the planks of the hardwood floor so he could tell if it had been moved, and sometimes he placed a strand of hair across the edge of the lid so he could tell if anyone had lifted it.

Lennie's mother never gave Black Jack chewing gum to any of the other kids. Wrigley's sometimes or Beechnut maybe. She often had Chiclets in her purse that she would chew very briefly as a breath-freshener. "Chewing gum is not chic," she'd say, "but coffee on the breath is worse." Black Jack chewing gum was in a category apart. His mother knew that were Lennie to see anyone else with his special gum, he would conclude immediately that it was stolen, and once Lennie headed toward a fight, it was hard to back him off.

Unlike his mother, Lennie's father didn't make deals with children. Willard Barone wasn't a persuader. He was an enforcer. Ross avoided the force of his father's discipline by being a model child. Charlie avoided it by being sneaky. But poor Lennie. He blundered into trouble and got punished. Sometimes it was a pinch on his upper arm that made Lennie yelp. Sometimes it was a hard swat on his backside that nearly knocked Lennie off his feet. More than once, Lennie had a red ear after his father steered him around by it. The worst punishment was what happened after Lennie lifted ten dollars from his dad's wallet.

His father might not have noticed the bill was missing because his wallet was usually flush with bills, but Lennie made a mistake. He took the bill out of his pocket to brag about it to Ross and Charlie out on the porch. Ten dollars was a lot of money for a kid, and Lennie knew it would get attention. Unfortunately, at the very moment Lennie was showing off the money, his father came through the screen door.

"Where did you get that?" he asked.

"Somebody gave it to me," said Lennie.

"People don't give ten bucks to kids for nothing. Who gave it to you and for what?"

"Can't remember," said Lennie. He couldn't come up with a credible alibi on the spot.

Willard Barone took out his wallet and looked at the money in it as if he knew every bill personally. He went through them slowly, flipping them with his thumb while Lennie watched. "There's one missing," he said.

Lennie stood there twisting his thumbs together and biting his lip. He was too scared to realize he was being baited by a master interrogator. The truth broke through when Lennie began to cry and say he was sorry.

"I won't have a thief in my house," said his father as he picked Lennie up with one hand on his collar and the other on his belt. As he walked Lennie into the house, the boy's feet were going a mile a minute, like a frantic squirrel trying to escape a predator that had him in its jaws. The screen door slapped shut, and the stunned kids out on the porch stood frozen in silence.

"You rotten good-for-nothing," they heard Willard yell. "If I'd known what a pain in the neck you'd be, I'd have put you in the trash when you were born. You may think I'm stuck with you now. You're wrong. So help me, I'll pound some sense into you if it's the last thing I do. Don't even think of touching my wallet again, because I'll snap your scrawny little neck in two with my bare hands." Grandpa Willard's way with words was always ruthlessly inventive when he was in a rage, but this time he outdid himself.

The kids on the porch could hear Lennie pleading, "Not your belt. No, Dad, please, don't. I'm sorry. I didn't mean to do it. I just wanted to show the kids. I was going to put it back."

"I'll show you what you didn't mean to do," the loud voice said. "Let go!"

They heard the slapping of leather against Lennie's flesh. There were muffled cries with each blow. Finally there was the sound of Willard's voice again. "Pull up your pants. Ugh, you've wet yourself, you baby. Go to your room! Clean yourself!"

All the while Aunt Lillian was recounting the ugly scene, Jenna was chewing something loose on the side of her thumb. The thought of someone whipping a boy with a belt made her sick, and the leather snapping against a little boy's pale flesh made her furious. She got a shivery feeling. "Did my dad just stand there and watch this happen? And where was Gramma Jeanne? Why didn't she do something?"

"She was at the hairdresser," said Aunt Lillian. "I want to believe if she'd been there, she wouldn't have allowed it, but once it was done . . . well, it was done. What could she do about it?"

"She could report him," Jenna said. "Call the police."

"Oh, Jenna," said Aunt Lillian, "when we were young it wasn't illegal to beat kids. All sorts of fathers did that. And some of the men who beat their kids also beat their wives."

"That's disgusting," Jenna said. "That's absolutely disgusting."

"I agree," said Aunt Lillian, "but I'm also telling you the truth."

"What happened to Lennie after he went to his room?"

Lillian heard her mother going in and out of Lennie's room during the night. She heard Lennie whining and sniffling. From the kitchen she heard the freezer door open and close and the familiar clink of ice cubes. His mother's voice was soft as she spoke to Lennie. It wasn't until a day later that Lennie appeared again. He had long pants on and his mother told him he should wear shorts, because it was going to be a very hot day. "I'm cold," said Lennie, and then fearing what would happen if his father heard him lie, Lennie corrected what he said. "I don't want shorts today. I'd rather have long pants."

Lillian couldn't remember how many days Lennie wore his loose corduroy winter pants in the heat of an Illinois summer. She vaguely remembered that Lennie, the avid swimmer, didn't go to the pool when Ross and Charlie did. And she remembered that when Lennie's legs appeared again, they had dapples of green and yellow across the backs. The bruises were slowly being absorbed, but not the hurt.

When summer was over and the kids were back in school, Lennie had trouble controlling his temper. His teacher told him to put his work away in his desk, but he hadn't finished his last math question, so he ignored her. She repeated her request. "You're a stupid bitch," Lennie said as he took his pencil in two hands and broke it in half. The sharp edges of the pencil's wood dug into his hands, but he didn't care. And he didn't care that for the rest of the day he sat outside of the principal's office on the bench known as the "The Penitent's Perch," where kids walking by would ask each other in a whisper "What did Lennie do this time?" By the end of the day everyone knew what Lennie had done. The news of Lennie Barone's bad day at school was repeated that evening around supper tables in Evanston, but in the Barone household not a word of it was spoken. At least in this way the children were loyal to each other.

Lennie had temper tantrums when he was playing with children and no adults were around. The boys would say, "Watch out, Lennie's going ape-shit again!" The girls were more likely to say, "Let's get outta here, Lennie's going bananas!" Only Lennie's mother seemed to have genuine sympathy for him. She would tell the children to be kind to him. "He's hurt and scared," she'd say. "Don't make it worse. Don't set him off."

After high school and a few tries at jobs he didn't like, Lennie joined the Marines. Ross and Charlie had both been in the reserves, and Lennie looked up to them when they came back from basic training fit and proud. He enlisted. Mastering basic training, being issued a rifle, all those things were thrilling for Lennie. Finally, he could prove he was as good as or better than his brothers, but there was one difference. His brothers had served in the reserves during peacetime; Lennie enlisted during the Vietnam War.

When Lennie's tour of duty was done, he came home and moved in with his parents in the big house in Evanston. From the day of his arrival, Lennie planned to re-up, but he wanted a break "to take care of some matters." Top on the list was marrying Joyce. During one of his furloughs Lennie had dated Joyce a few times, and from the first time they met, he was convinced she was the girl for him. During his deployment he carried her picture and told his buddies he was going to get married once he was permanently assigned stateside.

Lennie's devotion to Joyce was out of kilter. Their relationship was dreamed up by Lennie while he was away, and it was a hook on which to hang his memories of home, but it didn't have much to do with Joyce. He wrote to her about his life in the jungles and mud of Vietnam, the terrible heat, treatment for bug bites, hiding out in a rice paddy during a lightning storm, and a detailed report of his method for drying out his socks, which were always wet either from sweat or from slogging through flooded fields. Joyce's letters back commended Lennie for his bravery in dealing with these challenges, which she cited in her letter to him one by one, and then she signed off with love and her best wishes that he'd make it home safe. She was a faithful pen pal because she thought it was her patriotic duty.

In the beginning Joyce did miss Lennie a little. He'd made a good first impression. A Marine, physically fit and well groomed. A strong man carrying out a brave mission. But as time wore on, Joyce realized the letters were all about Lennie, and he didn't seem that interested in learning about her. He barely seemed to notice when she wrote to him that she'd moved back home to Missouri to be nearer to her family. She didn't tell Lennie that there were other men paying attention to her. Joyce was cute, and men noticed her. She had no difficulty filling her dance card.

When Lennie came home, ready to call in the commitment he'd made to Joyce, there was tension. He wanted her to move back to Chicago. She wasn't eager to do that, and Lennie took her hesitation as abandonment of him. She took his persistence as proof that being in a relationship with Lennie Barone meant the end of her freedom.

The military had taught Lennie to fight for what was his. When it became clear that letters and phone calls weren't convincing Joyce to move back to Chicago, Lennie shifted his center of operations to Missouri, where he found a room in a boarding house. He demanded to know Joyce's schedule for the week so he could give her rides to work. She refused to give it. Lennie stepped up his surveillance and discovered that Joyce was dating. And then it wasn't long and Lennie realized that she was seeing one guy in particular. The notes Lennie left at Joyce's apartment and the things he said to her when he intercepted her on the street after work turned unfriendly.

Disaster struck the night Lennie parked himself outside Joyce's apartment and saw her leave with Bud. He followed them to a restaurant and waited down the street in his car. He followed them back to Joyce's apartment and watched them go inside together. When he could bear it no longer, Lennie went to the door and rang the bell. Joyce didn't answer immediately, but when she did, Bud was standing behind her, and she told Lennie to go away and never come back.

Lennie left, but he wasn't gone long. He came back and went to the door a second time with a knife tucked into his sock and a baseball bat held behind his back. This time it was Bud who opened the door. In a rapid move, through the narrow opening, Lennie the warrior snapped into action. He pushed the door open and struck Bud with the bat. Before Bud could raise a hand to defend himself, he lay crumpled on the floor.

Lennie stepped over Bud's limp body and pulled him away from the door so he could close and lock it. Joyce was cowering in the corner. "Don't do this," she cried, "don't make trouble. Bud, say something. What have you done, Lennie? Just go away!" But Lennie wasn't done. He twisted Joyce's arm behind her back and led her to the kitchen where he ordered her to sit down on a chair. With the duct tape he had in the pocket of his jacket, Lennie bound

Joyce to the chair. Then Lennie dragged Bud by his feet into the kitchen, putting him directly in front of Joyce, where he took the hunting knife out of his sock and in several firm swipes slit Bud's throat.

Standing over Bud like a hunter over big game, Lennie watched his victim bleed out. Once the blood had drained from Bud and pooled across the kitchen floor, Lennie made his last move. In Vietnam he'd learned to take trophies after a kill. He sliced off Bud's ears and tucked them into the pocket of his jacket. Then, Lennie left.

There is no knowing how long Joyce might have stayed there, frozen in fear, terrorized by the body on the floor and the thought that Lennie would return to kill her. When the blood reached the hallway, it leaked through the cracks in the hardwood floor, and as liquid is prone to, it followed the course of least resistance, until it began to drip from the ceiling register into the apartment below. The landlord, who lived on the first floor, thought it was water. A dishpan or a bathtub or even a toilet overflowing. When he wiped up the first drips, it was obvious what it was, and he called the police.

Jenna listened in fascinated shock to the story of her uncle. On the one hand she couldn't believe something like this could happen in her family. On the other hand, she couldn't believe she had never been told about it.

"What happened to Joyce?" Jenna asked. "What happened to Bud's family?"

"Joyce had a breakdown and was hospitalized. When she left the hospital, she went to live with her parents. I can't imagine what hell it was for her to face Lennie in a courtroom," Aunt Lillian closed her eyes tight and shook her head in disbelief.

"Did anybody try to contact her?" Jenna asked.

"No. Why would she want to have anything to do with Lennie's family?"

"I get that," said Jenna, "but didn't you want Joyce to know how sorry the family was about what happened to her? And what about Bud's family? You can't just walk away from things like that, can you? It sounds like a lot of unfinished business."

"There was no way to finish it." Aunt Lillian said in a quiet voice.

"What happened to Lennie?" Jenna asked, intentionally not calling him "Uncle Lennie."

"He went to prison. Life without parole."

"Did you visit him? Did anybody visit him?"

"Your dad did. He was responsible for dealing with Lennie's lawyers and putting money on Lennie's prison account," Aunt Lillian explained. "Mama visited him too, whenever she could. She went through the pat-downs and didn't object when she was told to remove the gold chain and crucifix she always wore around her neck. She didn't make a fuss when visitation was cancelled for no apparent reason, after she'd travelled five hours to get there and was already waiting in the visitor's room. Once she returned home with black finger tips because they'd insisted on finger-printing all the approved visitors. Mom submitted to whatever indignities were foisted on her in order to visit her boy. Long ago she'd learned to do the best she could within limits over which she had no control."

Chapter 11

WHY THE SECRECY? Why had the grandchildren in the Barone family never been told about things that happened in the past? Jenna didn't understand. Her mom and her Gramma Jeanne were strong women. Why did they give in to this?

"Were my mom and your mom enablers? Codependents or something?" Jenna asked Aunt Lillian.

"Oh, here we go again," Aunt Lillian said with a contemptuous chuckle. "That codependence stuff is just a bundle of sharp-edged words that help families dump blame on the ones who are tender-hearted. Codependence is bunk. It's a word people use when they make a virtue out of being indifferent. Of course, they don't admit the coldness. They call it strength. When someone's hurt and struggling there are two kinds of people. The one kind moves in to help, and the other kind walks away. Listen to the way people talk and you'd think the Good Samaritan was a codependent. The ones who walk away think they're superior because they don't get involved.

"I'm sorry I brought it up." Jenna avoided her aunt's glance and scrambled to think of a way to change the subject. She didn't like seeing Aunt Lillian this way. It reminded her of Grandpa Willard, a person who could be smiling one minute and steaming the next. Aunt Lillian sometimes had his tone of voice and that little slip and slide in her speech that set them apart. Jenna felt like the little girl in Evanston. Not the happy one; the scared one.

"It's good you brought it up," Aunt Lillian said. "I've had my own season in the doghouse when I was blamed for being an enabler. I flatly reject the idea. It's a cruel way to blame someone who doesn't give up. Does that make sense? Really, Darling, does it?" Aunt Lillian's voice was pushy. If Jenna had known the word, she might have described Aunt Lillian's comments as imperious.

"Now I've made you angry. I'm really sorry," Jenna said. "That's not what I was getting at when I asked about my mom and Gramma Jeanne. I loved them both. I still love them, really. I'm not critical of them."

"Oh, honey, I'm angry, but not with you. You didn't intend to offend *me*. I know that," said Aunt Lillian. "And by the way I love them both too. They are two of the best people I've ever known. But seriously, this codependence thing. You didn't come up with that term on your own. Tell me the truth, someone accused you of being codependent, and it stung like an angry hornet."

"I had a fight with my sister Laura when I was married to Jak. She accused me of being Jak's enabler," Jenna admitted. "I wanted Jak to stop spending money we didn't have. I wanted him to stop carrying on with other women. He wouldn't, but I stayed with him anyway. We had kids, and I wasn't working. What was I supposed to do, call a taxi and tell them all I was leaving because I didn't want to be an enabler? Later it all came up again with Steven. After he broke ties with other members of the family, he still came around to see me. Sometimes he stayed with us, or I lent him money. Laura warned me that my help would kill him. 'You're giving him the rope with which he's going to hang himself,' she said. 'You're our family's worst codependent, and when disaster strikes, you'll have to answer for it.' It's hard to get her words out of my head."

"Shame on her for putting those words in there!" Aunt Lillian's neck was red, and she spit a tiny bit as she spoke.

"After Steven was dead, Mom told me she wished she'd helped him more, not less." Jenna didn't want Aunt Lillian to think badly of her mother. "I can't count the number of times I've cried about Steven and wished I could have rescued him. I still feel guilty because I couldn't. I mean," Jenna swallowed and paused to catch her breath, "what's love worth anyway? So maybe we're all codependent. Maybe we're all enablers. It's going to be hard either way. Anyway, thanks for defending me, Aunt Lillian."

"You'll always be my Darling Jenna," she said. "I wish there were more people like you."

"Thanks. I appreciate that. I don't feel so good about myself." Jenna was beginning to feel a little spark of anger catch her own kindling. "I finally took everybody's advice and left Jak. When he needed me most, I didn't take care of him. He's not doing well, and when I see how kind my kids are to him, I feel guilty. He loves them as much as ever, and they love him back. That's why I'm defensive. When someone mentions Jak and tells me how smart I was to leave him, I don't think they know what they're talking about. What right does anyone else have to make that call . . . I mean it . . . either judging me or judging Jak?" Tears welled up in Jenna's eyes, and she flushed.

"When people sided with you, they stopped seeing the good in Jak, but you don't have to do that. You're entitled to see it both ways. You loved him enough to marry him. What about that? And you got confused enough that you had to leave. Those both are true. You don't have to vote for one side or the other. Ignore what the others say." Aunt Lillian's voice still was raised slightly. Jenna wondered if she was talking about Jak or about Raymond, and she wondered how much Aunt Lillian knew about Jak.

"I know about your marriage to Jak," said Aunt Lillian, as if she were reading Jenna's mind, "because your Gramma Jeanne sent me pictures of your wedding. You were such a beautiful bride. I framed the family picture taken at your wedding and kept it on a table in my living room. Your mother told me about wonderful times she spent with your family and at your home. Maggie adored your children and the creative family life you and Jak gave them. She admired Jak. His free spirit fascinated her. There was a good dose of that in Maggie, too, you know. I think she envied Jak sometimes, but she also understood that it was hard for you to be married to him. I know about your divorce too. Maggie never questioned your choices. She understood that it's never simple, Jenna."

"I had no idea," said Jenna.

"You didn't think I knew about what was going on in my family back home? As long as your Grandpa Willard was alive, I didn't feel welcomed, and I didn't want to be there, but Maggie and your Gramma Jeanne kept me informed. You know what your mother used to say to me? 'You can hide, Lillian, but you're still part of this family.' She wouldn't let me drift away completely. When I lived in France, Mama came to visit her parents, and I made sure I was there during her visits. She'd tell stories and gush about her grandchildren. I think women do this, Jenna. We maintain a whole tangle of connections because sorting them out all in one place and all at one time is impossible."

Jenna tucked a stray lock behind her ear and took a deep breath before she spoke. "It feels strange that there are people who know about me, but I have no idea that they know. I'm not sure how I feel about that. I thought that only happened to people in Hollywood or in politics. Paparazzi victims, you know, that stuff. It scares me that people have opinions about me, and I don't know what they think because it never gets back to me. Something about that isn't fair. Did Raymond know about me?"

"Of course, he did." Lillian leaned over and patted Jenna's arm. "Remember, your wedding picture with your family was on my table, and he lived there too. Sometimes he said you were my other daughter. He knew Margot, but that was more complicated. I had to be careful claiming her as a daughter because she had a mother who raised her. Lines of connection aren't as tidy as we might like them to be. Our heart connections and our public connections . . . Oh, my goodness . . . don't even try to figure out whether or not they match. But don't stop listening to your heart, Jenna. Don't worry about what people know. There are stories about us floating around, and those stories are beyond our control. Best not to rent them space in your head."

"You make it sound easy," said Jenna. "I'm not sure I feel that way."

"You know one of the reasons I continued to be so fond of you?" Aunt Lillian asked. It's because of what your mother told me. She watched with admiration that you didn't turn around and hurt Jak back when he hurt you. People who loved you were watching from the sidelines, seeing what a good person you are. Maybe Laura thought you should be harsh, but that's not what your mother and grandmother thought. They thought you were magnificent. Forget about the person who called you an enabler and said you were codependent. Instead of fighting with the wounded, we should fight back against those people who want to put mean labels on us."

When Jenna got the call from her sister Laura that the work on genealogy was turning up new information about their family, she leveled with Aunt Lillian. "Sometimes it's hard to talk to Laura," Jenna told her aunt. "She jumps to conclusions about people."

"And Will?"

"He's more tolerant than Laura. Cocky and abrupt sometimes, but not judgmental. He lives in a glass house, so he doesn't throw stones."

"What about Rowland?" Aunt Lillian asked.

"He's easy to talk to, but I'm careful because I don't know how much he keeps to himself. When he repeats a story, he dresses it up or drops out details that don't fit with his opinion. I'm not sure he remembers they're stories about real people. He's a little unpredictable, but he has a good heart."

"Oh, so he's like me? A little unpredictable, and he doesn't keep secrets? Good for Rowland," said Aunt Lillian. "He's breaking the Barone family mold." Jenna was stunned that Aunt Lillian could say this so confidently; she barely knew Rowland.

"As far as I'm concerned," said Aunt Lillian, "you may tell your brothers or your sister anything I've told you. You may tell your children too. The stories belong to you now. Just remember, none of us owes it to anyone to answer every question asked. We get to decide what to do with what we know. We get to decide who to trust."

"I always thought I could trust Gramma Jeanne," Jenna said. She closed her eyes. She could see Gramma Jeanne's white hair and the wrinkles around her blue-gray eyes. Jenna could remember her voice. There was a little slip and slide in the way she spoke that made it sound soft and round. When they visited her, Gramma Jeanne kissed Jenna on both cheeks and had special surprises for her. She taught Jenna to knit, and let her use her sewing machine; the summer before Jenna started high school, Gramma Jeanne helped her sew a wrap-around skirt.

Jenna opened her eyes and realized Aunt Lillian was watching her. "It's really true," Jenna said. "I always felt I could trust Gramma Jeanne and Mom. Sometimes it feels to me like the women are the center of our family, even though the men act as if they are."

"Let's have tea," said Aunt Lillian.

"We can have tea, but I'm not finished with this," Jenna insisted. "I want to know about my dad, and not just because Laura wants information about him. First, I need to tell you that my dad was the best dad I could ever have wished for. He was sweet to me. He helped me out of some really tough situations when I was married to Jak. And when my dad was dying, I saw him nearly every day. The time we spent together was so special. What am I trying to say? Um . . . this, I guess . . . no dumping on my dad. Still, I want to know how Ross Barone fit into your complicated family."

Jenna was determined to make Aunt Lillian practice what she preached, if she didn't want to be like all those other members of the Barone family who kept secrets. "You need to tell me. Why did his name get changed? Why didn't he tell us about his childhood? Who is Leo, anyway? Did my Dad know him?" She looked squarely at Aunt Lillian, and with a voice just short of bossy said, "Tell me about Grandpa Willard too! Please don't hold back, Aunt Lillian; tell me what you know! Tell me about all the weirdness."

Part Three

Ross's Story

Chapter 12

"Ross was born near Beauvais, a town in Northern France that has occupied the junction of two rivers since the time of the Romans. At birth he was christened Philippe Guillaume. He was named after his mother's father." Aunt Lillian spoke in a formal voice as she began her introduction.

"Where did the Guillaume part come from, and who was my dad's father?" Jenna asked.

"Guillaume is the French form of William, and Willard is that name after it was altered to fit your grandfather's tastes." Lillian chortled derisively. "Your Grandpa Willard was Ross's father. No doubt about it." Aunt Lillian shook her head, as if she were disapproving of something and also sure she was right about it.

"My dad had a different last name at first. Why was that if Grandpa Willard was his father?" This was the riddle Laura had been trying to solve for months, and Jenna was impatient to move on with the full story. "C'mon, Aunt Lillian, explain it!"

"Jeanne de Roose had been married to a man who died in the war. When she met Willard, she was a war widow. At the time of Ross's birth Jeanne and Willard weren't married, nor were they living together, so her baby was given her last name. It was her married name from her first marriage, and she kept that name when she became a widow, out of respect for her lost husband."

"It's hard to think of Gramma Jeanne as a widow," said Jenna.

"It was a chaotic time during the war. Willard was planning to go to America and start a new life as soon as he could arrange it. When Jeanne got pregnant, he chose not to marry her because he didn't want to change his plan." Aunt Lillian paused and looked away. She did this odd thing with her mouth. A nervous gesture. Her tongue pressed into her cheek like she was checking for a bit of meat stuck between her teeth, or alternatively as if she were trying not to cry. "Jeanne and little Ross didn't join Willard in America until later. You want to know why she followed him to America? Why she didn't stay with her family? I'd like to know that too. Her family embraced her through her widowhood. They were steady for her when she became a mother. Why did she leave them?" Aunt Lillian looked genuinely puzzled.

"You don't know the answer to that?" Jenna asked.

"I don't. It's a mystery. Her decision doesn't make sense to me at all. And think of all the things that would be different if she hadn't made that choice."

"My dad and you wouldn't have been born, for starters. And my brothers and sister and me, we wouldn't be here either. But, Aunt Lillian, that's sort of beside the point, isn't it? Why did Gramma Jeanne follow him? Maybe she loved him," Jenna guessed. "Or maybe she wanted her baby to have a father. There's no way to know unless she told you."

"By the time I was part of the picture, their marriage didn't seem like a great love," Lillian said. "Ross managed his first years just fine without a father. It doesn't seem likely she made her choice for him. Maybe she was like someone in the middle of a river who knows there's no use turning back. Better to give in to the current and try for the other shore. Some odd drive to complete what's started."

"And the names?" asked Jenna.

"Your Grandpa Willard didn't want your dad to have a French name that would mark him as a foreigner for the rest of his life. Once Grandpa Willard and Gramma Jeanne were married, he wanted everyone in the family to have the same last name. He liked things to be tidy. Uniform. Not unusual. He was the one who decided to change your dad's name. I don't think he even asked your Gramma Jeanne. He just went ahead and did it. Ross was a nod to de Roose, and Barone was your Grandpa Willard's surname. That's how your dad became Ross Barone."

"That's all?" Jenna asked. "Big secret!"

"There's another layer," said Aunt Lillian. "This one is uglier, and your sister Laura is not going to find it in the documents she's tracking down on the internet."

"No use stopping now," Jenna said. She didn't want Aunt Lillian to get distracted.

"Willard told people he was born in the United States, in Maine. He wanted to start his life over in America and leave the past behind him. By not admitting there was a past, he thought he could side-step questions. Claiming he was born in America was a source of pride for him, but of course, it wasn't true. A child born in France, who didn't come to live with his father until he was nearly four years old, was an embarrassing wrinkle in Willard's carefully fabricated story."

"He lied?"

"He did. He lied so often about being born in Maine that finally he believed his lie himself. He was more comfortable with the story he made up than with the story he lived."

"What about Gramma Jeanne? She played along?"

"Oh, what tangled webs we weave when first we practice to deceive," said Lillian. "That's what Mama used to say about your Grandpa Willard's lies."

Once when Willard was discussing an employee who took credit for work someone else had done, he said, "A shoe made for another man's foot is not going to be easy for walking." Jeanne thought about Willard's lies and wondered when he would discover that his own shoe didn't fit. She confronted him. He became furious and slapped her. It was hard enough to leave a bruise along the side of her face, and it was enough to show her that she was defenseless. She decided to bide her time, because she knew the truth would find its way out eventually.

What Jeanne could not have guessed was that Ross would ask the awkward question that cracked open the secret. He was doing his homework when he asked his mother where he was born. They were studying the states at school.

"I was born in Illinois, right?" Ross asked.

"No, my dear, you were born in France. That is another country across the ocean. But you came here when you were very little, and you are a citizen, so that's as good as being born in Illinois. You are an American, like all the people who were born here."

"Where were you born, Mama?" Ross asked.

Jeanne could imagine the gears turning in his little head. He was trying to adjust the family map to accommodate this new information. "I was born in France too," she said.

"Did me and you come here together?" Ross asked.

"We did. On a ship. You were little. Do you remember it?"

"Maybe. I think I remember a big river and a bridge," he said. "Are you American?"

"Yes," said Jeanne, and that seemed to satisfy his curiosity.

At dinner in the evening Ross asked his father, "Papa, where were you born?"

"Why do you ask?" It was so like Willard to parry a question with another question, as if a little boy as smart as Ross wouldn't notice he was being evasive.

"We're studying the states in school. What state are you from?"

"New England," said Willard.

"That's not a state, Papa. I'm learning the capitals, and if I learn them all I'll get a flag. Which state is yours, Papa?" There was a brief silence as Willard calculated his odds.

"Maine," said Willard. It was the state where he first touched down when arriving in America. For all anyone could tell, Willard believed that the part of his life that mattered began in Maine and the part before that was of no consequence. By giving the location where he began, just not at birth, he wasn't lying to his son. "Do you know the capital?" Willard asked Ross, quizzing him about geography to change the trajectory of the boy's questions.

"Augusta," said Ross.

"Good work, son. I think you'll earn that flag."

What began as a fib to distract a boy from an awkward fact got layered into more fabrications. At a reception he attended with Jeanne, Willard told acquaintances that his family had been in Maine since the first trading posts were established there. He later elaborated on the story, when retelling it on another occasion.

The odd little lisps in Willard's speech were remnants of his past that he had never been able to iron out completely. He noticed, though, that others easily accepted his accent as one of those backcountry Maine hangers-on, so he built that into his story too. He explained that he grew up speaking French as well as English because Maine borders on Quebec. Although he studiously avoided looking at his wife when he was weaving his lies, Willard knew she was too loyal to contradict him in front of others. He was oddly satisfied when she didn't contradict him later in private either.

Jeanne was troubled by Willard's fictions, and she went to the priest to ask advice. The priest understood the stresses of war, and he also knew that families don't have perfect, unscarred family trees. He listened patiently to her story as she confessed the circumstances of Ross's birth. Taking the charitable approach, the priest advised Jeanne to follow the course that would do least harm to the most innocent victim. He advised Jeanne to say nothing to Ross that would tarnish his image of his father.

Later Ross asked his mother again, and this time in the presence of his father, where she was born. Apparently, he was fact-checking.

"Remember, I told you that I was born in France, and that's a different country," she explained to Ross.

"I don't get it," Ross said. "If Papa was in Maine and you were in France, how did you have me together?" The question was a schoolboy's innocent query about the map.

Jeanne glanced at Willard. It was his question to answer, and she hoped he would set the record straight. "Well," said Willard, "your Mama had you when she was in France before she came to be with me in America."

"Did I have a Papa in France?" Ross asked.

"Yes," said Willard, "but he died, and I'm your Papa now. You're a good boy and I'm glad to take care of you."

Jeanne listened in disbelief as Willard disowned his son and gave him up to a phantom father. Was he ashamed to admit the circumstances of Ross's birth? Although he was willing to go to extreme lengths to protect his own honor, he was unconcerned about Jeanne's or Ross's.

Jeanne didn't know what to do. Should she get into a battle with her husband in front of their son? Should she take Ross aside later and tell him the truth? Again, she asked the priest, who repeated his earlier advice that she should act out of kindness to the most innocent victim. And that is how the false story gained its status. Willard let Ross believe he was an orphan taken in by a kind man in America. The mold was cast, and little Ross had to prove that he deserved the generosity of the man who rescued him when he was fatherless. That cruel secret drove their relationship.

"What father would do that?" Jenna asked. "Grandpa Willard denied his own son? Was he crazy or something?"

"No," said Aunt Lillian. "He wasn't crazy. He was vain. He didn't want to admit that he'd had a child out of wedlock and abandoned the child and its mother so he could go off and seek his fortune in America. Once the lie started, he didn't want to admit that he was a fraud. Your Grandpa Willard was too proud to admit mistakes, so he revised the story and turned himself into a hero."

"And Gramma Jeanne played along," Jenna said, as if she were finally drawing the obvious conclusion.

"She couldn't stand up to a powerful man. She had no resources," said Aunt Lillian. "All the power was on his side. Remember, he'd slapped her when she challenged him before and left bruises on her face. This was a far bigger confrontation. She had no idea what he would do if she exposed him, and she decided to keep the peace for the sake of her children."

Jenna felt a surge of anger toward Grandpa Willard. Toward Gramma Jeanne too, and even toward her dad for not standing up for himself. "Peace at Dad's expense?" she asked.

"That's exactly right," said Aunt Lillian. "Peace at your dad's expense."

"Dad must have found out sooner or later. He did, didn't he? Why didn't my dad get mad and make them own up to it?" Jenna asked.

"By the time he was a teenager Ross had figured it out, but as with so many things your Grandpa Willard did, the crisis that would have been created by correcting the story wasn't worth it." Aunt Lillian shrugged. "Maybe Ross thought that as time went on it would be water under the bridge and it wouldn't matter anymore. I don't know if he forgave his father, but he certainly forgave his mother. He loved her dearly to the last day of her life."

"Did Mom know?" Jenna asked. "Do you think my dad ever told my mom?"

"She knew, but as easily as Ross seemed to move beyond the lies, Maggie couldn't. There was no love lost between Maggie and Willard Barone. She was loving toward everyone else in the family, but around her father-in-law there was a deep freeze." Lillian paused for a moment. "Your mother avoided using Willard's name when addressing him. In speaking of him to others she referred to him as 'that man.' I guess that tells you what she thought of him."

"Meanwhile my dad kept working for his dad?" asked Jenna. "That must have been hard."

"Ross and Charlie both worked in the family business, but Charlie couldn't handle the constant criticism from his dad. They squabbled, and Charlie drank. After a few serious mistakes by Charlie, your Grandpa Willard decided Charlie needed to earn a living some other way; he fired him. Both Ross and Charlie had been given shares in the company, and it was a mess when Charlie was fired. In the end they sold the company. By then your Grandpa Willard had made enough to live comfortably on savings and investments, and he retired."

"And my dad? What happened to him?"

"Closing the family business was Ross's lucky break. I wasn't around when that all happened," said Aunt Lillian, "but I know that was when he got the job with the bank. Your dad was successful in his own right. Smart and reliable. Good at handling business accounts. The painful part was that his father always took the credit for Ross's accomplishments. It infuriated your mother when 'that man' bragged about giving Ross a start in business and claimed that he was the one who taught Ross everything he knew about money. Even after Ross left the family business, he still did heavy lifting for his parents. He bought and sold property for them, managed their assets, and was responsible for Grandpa Willard and

Gramma Jeanne's comfortable retirement income. Ross never got over trying to be the worthy son of a phantom father."

Chapter 13

IN ALL LIKELIHOOD Ross Barone had only the barest memory of his arrival in America. He was a little boy obediently staying in step with his mother as she made a journey alone into an unknown world. The years before Ross's arrival in his new home were without the influence of his father, Willard. How much Ross knew about Willard or what he called him is a detail of the story that has been lost to time. The recollections about little Ross that Jeanne later shared with Lillian begin with the trip she made from one side of the Atlantic to the other.

As Jeanne stood at the rail with Ross by her side, the beginning outlines of land on the horizon grew larger before her eyes. At last, they entered a bay with land on both sides and sailed under a bridge. The little boy standing beside her asked, "Is that big bridge America, Mama?"

"It's all America," she told him. "Everything you see."

Jeanne noticed a steeple, and then another. The farewell blessing of her parish priest had included advice to attend Mass faithfully. "The church always will be your port in a storm," he'd said. She wondered if that could really be true. Her priest had never been to New York. He didn't know much more about America than she did.

A few minutes later Ross pointed back at the bridge. "You didn't tell me there would be a bridge, Mama. You told me there would be mountains and a big river. Are you sure this is America?"

"Yes," she said, "that bridge is New York, and all the rest that you see is America too, but America is very large and not all of it looks like this. In some parts of America there are mountains." She spoke as if she knew what the rest of it looked like, while in actuality she had seen no more of it than her little boy had. Ross looked at her and smiled, not doubting at all that his mother was right. "It's big," the boy said in a wispy voice. There was a strong wind, and he was shivering.

Standing near Jeanne was the woman whose stateroom was next to hers. She'd been a friendly neighbor during the crossing, and Jeanne had shared that she was going to meet the man she planned to marry. She also told her neighbor that her fiancé had changed his name from Guillaume to Willard. Her neighbor corrected Jeanne's pronunciation. "You'll have to practice saying it over and over if you want it to sound the way Americans say it. You'll need to get your teeth out of the way and purse your lips."

There at the rail a wave of panic had come over Jeanne. There was no turning back, and soon she'd have to leave the ship. What would she do if no one was at the dock to meet her? She had never seen a city so vast and buildings so tall. How would she find her way? *No matter what happens this will not be the worst day of my life. I have already lived through that one,* she told herself. She remembered the farewell advice of a neighbor. "No matter what you face, there's always a way out. Look and listen, and you'll find it."

Jeanne watched as the river's edge passed by in a slow panorama. Men were fishing on the bank. Smoke came up from tall chimneys. Small boats loaded with people crossed the water. Seagulls were diving. Everything her little boy saw turned into an excited question. "What is that, Mama? Are we going to go over there? Will that man talk to us? Will we fish too? Is that house ours?"

Jeanne leaned over and told Ross that no matter what, when they left the ship, he must hold her hand and not step ahead of her or fall behind. She didn't tell him she'd heard horror stories of families getting separated from each other when they disembarked. A mother who knew no English got swept into the crowd away from her family as they left the ship, and she was never seen again. Little children were grabbed and sold off to strangers.

Like all the other passengers standing at the rail as the longshoremen secured the huge dock lines of the ship, Jeanne was scanning the faces below. Then she saw him. He was wearing a suit, a white shirt, and a tie. In his hand was a fedora that he'd removed from his head, just as all the other men had, so they wouldn't lose their hats to the wind. She waved. The slow turn of his head stopped when his eyes reached her. He put his hat back on for a moment, tipped it to her, and quickly took it off again. Then he waved.

At the bottom of the gangway Willard kissed Jeanne lightly on the cheek and reached for his son, picking him up and holding him away enough to get a look at him. He reached into his pocket for a small wooden truck that he handed to the boy as a welcome gift. Then he turned again to Jeanne. "Was the passage good?" he asked. "Was the ship comfortable?" It was a courteous reception. No grand embrace. There was no sign that the test of their love was over, and they had crossed over into the land of happily ever after. It was nothing like the movies.

Willard led Jeanne and the little boy to a line that had formed in front of a wicket. To the papers Jeanne had brought with her, Willard added some that he took out of the breast pocket of his coat. When it was their turn, he observed carefully as the official put stamps on the documents. The official didn't question Jeanne. When the papers were handed back to Willard, he carefully folded them and put them back into his breast pocket. Then he gestured to Jeanne and the boy to follow him, as he walked off toward the large double doors, beyond which she could see cars passing in the street outside. The little family of three stepped out onto the streets of New York, and Jeanne entered America without saying a word.

The car to which Willard led them was black and had big seats. He placed the boy in the back and opened the passenger door for Jeanne in the front. They said little. They were accustomed to long stretches of silence between the letters they sent back and forth over the Atlantic, but more striking than the silence was his speech because she had not heard his voice for several years. "We will cross the river to New Jersey," he said. "I have a motel there for tonight. Tomorrow we will start driving to Chicago, Illinois. That's where we live."

Jeanne noticed how strangely Willard said "Chicago" and "Illinois," and she repeated it back to him as a question. "Chee, ka, go'... is that it?" she asked, putting the accent at the end.

"No, that's not the way we say it." He repeated it for her several times. "Say it back," he instructed her. When he was satisfied that she had mastered the pronunciation of Chicago, he started on Illinois. That was harder for her. "You're going to have to learn English," he instructed her.

Willard's way of speaking to Jeanne was matter-of-fact. Business-like. Not playful like her neighbor on the ship. In the years when Jeanne had not heard his voice, she had imagined it. What she heard now was different. In place of the youthful lover who used to come to the back door of the house to visit her, she now saw a grown man maneuvering the gear stick and turning the wheel of a large black automobile, inside of which she floated through a sea of cars over a road along which she recognized nothing familiar.

"There will be changes," he said. "We may as well begin with them right away. I am not Guillaume in America. Please do not use that name. I am Willard. That is my name now." He said it very clearly, making it obvious that he wanted Jeanne to notice his pronunciation. "Try to say it now the way I say it," he instructed her. He was pleased by how well she pronounced it, and she didn't tell him about all the times she had practiced his new name with her neighbor on the ship.

"There are some other things we should begin with right away. You will be Joan. Philippe will be Ross. I thought it best to let him keep his surname as a given name. De Roose will become Ross, and that is his first name. He will take my last name. Beginning today he will be Ross Philip Barone. You must explain to him that he has a new name, from now on you and I will both call him 'Ross.' I've already made the change on his entry documents. The more immediately we make these changes ourselves, the easier it will be. I'll speak English with the boy, and I'll speak English with you too, whenever I can. Delay will only make it harder."

By the time they arrived at their lodging in New Jersey, Jeanne wondered what she had done to herself and to the little boy, who was sitting in the back of the car gazing out of the windows. Even small things seemed strange. In the back pocket of his suit pants Willard carried a small square of leather in which he kept little documents and paper money. Coins and the keys of his car he carried in the front pocket of his trouser, where he also kept a white handkerchief.

In the restaurant, Jeanne and the boy were silent while Willard ordered food for them. The woman who served them had very red lipstick, and she wore a strange hat shaped like the crown princesses wear, but this one was made of faded cotton and held in place with a black bobby pin on each side. In the center of the table was a basket with breads. Jeanne took one for herself after she saw Willard put one on Ross's plate and then take one for himself. She tore hers in two and took a bite. It was soft and sponge-like with no taste except a bit of sweetness. She thought it odd to eat cake before the meal. Following Willard's lead, she put butter on it, but it wasn't butter. It was pale and greasy. "Margarine," Willard said. "In America we use margarine."

They stayed in a strange hotel that was a long row of rooms, each with an outside door, and a car parked in front. There was no staff. There was no hallway. Willard asked which suitcase she and Ross would need for the night. She pointed to the small one, and Willard carried it in himself, along with a small soft bag that she assumed contained the things he needed. The rest Willard left in the large compartment at the back of the car.

In the bathroom there was a tub where Jeanne gave Ross a bath before putting him into familiar pajamas and tucking him into a small cot that had been prepared for him. She then changed into her own nightgown. Willard went into the bathroom and returned in a cotton suit with pale stripes, which Jeanne guessed was his sleeping costume. They each went to a side of the bed. He sat down and over his shoulder said, "I am happy to see you, but we'll deal with these matters later. For now, with the child in the room, I think it wouldn't be fitting."

"I agree," she said. "He's just a little boy, and there's a great deal he'll need to get used to. Thank you for being considerate of him tonight."

Willard, like Ross, slept soon. Jeanne couldn't sleep. Her thoughts went back across the ocean to her parents asleep in their beds. Up the steep stairs to the loft in their little house in Beauvais, like a ghost, her imagination wandered. Her sisters were sleeping in the large room on the left. In the smaller room under the eaves her three brothers were sleeping, and tucked into a small bed along the wall was a little boy. She paused to say a prayer at the foot of his bed, and then kissing the tip of her own index finger, she imagined lightly placing it on his cheek.

Like a wandering spirit, Jeanne drifted to the small village in the countryside where she had lived happy years before the war. Those were days in which she couldn't have even imagined where she was now or the events that brought her here. She recollected the sound of the front door of her own house closing, and she floated along the main street past the other houses and toward the shops. Curtains parted slightly as neighbors peeked out to see who was walking by. She knew the neighbors behind each curtain. On she walked until she heard in her imagination the familiar bell on the door of the bakery. The smell of morning bread came to her, and she felt the warmth of the fresh baguette under her arm as she walked back through the village toward home.

As Jeanne floated past the church in the village square, she recalled the creaking sound of pews and the smell of candle wax, the swish of vestments, and the padding footsteps when the priest crossed the altar, paused to genuflect, and then moved on across and through the vestry door. In her thoughts, Jeanne paused in the church to say a prayer for her sleeping family in their familiar home, and for herself and the little boy who was asleep near her on a cot in the corner of a room an ocean away from them. The memories through which she floated were a brief comfort, but the ache of homesickness kept her awake.

Jeanne had been so eager to leave, but now she wondered what she had done. Had she made this choice for them, or had she allowed herself to be swept along with choices others made for her? She had lived in limbo until the day a letter arrived telling her when her ship would sail and where she could pick up the tickets that had been purchased for her. How did all this happen?

In her wakefulness Jeanne tried to recall the scene she had imagined during weeks of preparing for her reunion with Guillaume. That dream was already beginning to fade because the day had been so different than what she had envisioned. Jeanne lay facing her side of the bed, away from Willard, this stranger whom she would now begin to call by his new name. Tears rolled into the crease at the side of her eye, from where they spilled onto the pillow. Quietly she touched the crucifix around her neck and said her evening prayer. Sometime later she slept. Her first night in America.

The distance, the coolness of Jeanne's exchanges with Willard, did not go away immediately. They had practiced distance for a long time. Already when they were lovers in her small village, they had kept their distance. When he visited her, he came after dark and to the back door of her house. When unexpectedly they met on the street, they behaved as if they barely knew each other. A polite greeting and that was all. "Hello Madame de Roose," he would say. "Hello Mister Barone," she would reply. They did not stop for conversation, which some might have considered rude, but others thought only proper for a widow greeting a foreigner during wartime.

After Willard left for the United States, he sent his letters to her by way of the village priest. When Jeanne replied she brought her letter to the priest, who sent it off for her. Words scribbled onto the thin paper of aerogrammes have a different feel than the words lovers whisper to each other when both their heads are on one pillow and there is no one to overhear them.

No one ever asked Jeanne how Willard was doing. A few did ask the priest if he knew what happened to the wool salesman, Guillaume Barone, because he didn't pass through their village anymore. There was a shortage of products in the shops, and what was on the shelves was of inferior quality. The priest explained that, as far he knew, the wool salesman had gone to seek his fortune in America.

One might wonder why Jeanne and Willard followed through with their plan to reunite. They each had their own reasons. He was a man of his word who promised to come back to fulfill an act of penance left over from his role in the war and to do right by the woman with whom he'd fathered a child. Jeanne was a woman who'd learned through the harsh experiences of war that, when an opportunity presents itself, it mustn't be wasted. Her options were few. There was a shortage of eligible men in the village after the war, and she was a widow with a child. On the occasions when her resolve to reunite wavered, then the little boy, who after his arrival in America became Ross, was enough to tip the balance. She wanted him to have a father.

Despite their best intentions, when Jeanne and Willard were together again, they were still an ocean apart. Jeanne took over the kitchen in the house Willard had bought for them. Day after day she tended to the cleaning, the laundry, and the family shopping. But lying side by side in the same bed at night, theirs was still a trans-Atlantic marriage. On those nights, when in what became a familiar sequence of gestures, he would reach for her, and she would accept his reach with her own longing to be desired as a woman, they were still oceans apart. Flesh against flesh, longing pressed to longing, they remained strangers.

Willard focused on the future. He resisted looking back, and Jeanne did her best to follow his advice. She trained herself not to greet the shopkeepers and other customers when she entered a shop. "Americans don't do that," Willard informed her. "It's an odd French habit that marks you as a foreigner. Why greet strangers anyway? You have to learn to fit in."

There were hard patches. The first winter, Jeanne asked Willard where she could purchase a goose and oysters for Christmas dinner, and he told her to forget it because they were Americans now. "*Père Noël* is Santa Claus and we'll eat ham," he said. "Ask the butcher for a good one." What hurt even more was the holiday dinner at which Jeanne brought out the *Bûche de Noël* that she'd prepared using her mother's recipe. She thought at last the time had come when she could tell her children how she had celebrated Christmas when she was a child. Willard was in an unpleasant mood to begin with that evening, because he resented holidays. When Jeanne came from the kitchen and put the holiday treat out on the table, he asked her to remove it. She picked it up to carry it back to the kitchen, and he followed her. "You need to stop doing this," he said. "Clinging to the past like this is bad for you and bad for our children. If secretly you wish to torture yourself with the past, I can't stop you, but I will not have these displays of it in my house. Buy ladies magazines and find Christmas recipes. Spend what you need. Decorate as you wish. But stop clinging to France. It's past. It's gone."

The day came when Jeanne and Ross joined others, dressed in their best, to stand before an official who swore them in as citizens. Ross looked up to smile at his mother, and he saw a tear trickle down her cheek. She told him that many people are moved by that proud moment. She didn't mention that she was thinking of the place where she was born, the place where she would always be a citizen. She didn't try to explain to him that, when you divide your loyalties between two countries, you never feel completely at home in either one of them again, because wherever you are, something somewhere else is calling you home.

Chapter 14

MUCH OF WHAT Willard set in place in the first days after Jeanne arrived in America became the new habits of their household. There was one change, however, that never took hold even though Willard made numerous attempts. Jeanne refused to change her name. She would not be "Joan." She was willing to call her husband "Willard," and she learned to call her little boy "Ross," but her mouth refused to make the shapes into which it had to be twisted in order to utter the strange name her husband was trying to force on her. When others called her Mrs. Barone or Ross's Mommy, she could accept it. When she heard someone saying, "Hey there Lady," or when behind her back she heard someone speaking of "that strange French woman," she knew whom they meant. But when someone said "Joan," she refused to accept that it was referring to her.

"My name is my name," she told Willard. "That you change your name is your choice, but I've given up enough, and I will not give up my name." She didn't want to give up the name her parents had given to her, and she didn't want to forget how her name was spoken by the first man who loved her, the one she lost in the war and left buried in a French graveyard.

Keeping her name was not Jeanne's resistance to being joined to Willard. She made a good home and took good care of herself in order to be a wife of whom Willard could be proud. She never went to the market or the bakery in the clothes in which she did housework. She tidied her hair, changed her dress, put on polished shoes, and walked on the street like a woman with dignity. As she became more accustomed to American ways, she plucked her eyebrows, shaved her legs, and, when the first strands of gray appeared in her hair, she had the hairdresser at the salon take care of that too. But that is jumping ahead of the story.

Within a year of Jeanne's arrival in America their family began to grow. The first addition was Charles, who very soon was known as Charlie. A baby was a comfort to Jeanne. Ross was ready to begin kindergarten, and always happy to remind his mother that he wasn't a baby anymore. To prove to Willard that he was a big boy, Ross would carry his father's briefcase from the car, run to answer the telephone when it rang, and water the geraniums in the pots on either side of their front porch. For his diligent service, Willard gave Ross an allowance each Saturday morning. It was one shiny quarter that Ross proudly put into the little bank he kept on his dresser.

Ross's claims about being a big boy did not stop Jeanne from squeezing his cheeks and telling him that he was handsome. She kissed Ross on both cheeks when she tucked him into his bed at night, but when he left for school in the morning, she only waved from the doorway as she had observed her neighbors did when sending their children off down the driveway. As a courtesy to Willard, Jeanne did not kiss both cheeks of anyone in public; in fact, she didn't kiss anyone on one cheek either, because Willard insisted that people in America "don't do all that kissing. Especially boys and men would find it strange to be kissed as a greeting. Kissing is for something else entirely. They don't expect to shake your hand either; that's what men do with each other," Willard explained.

"How do they greet each other then?" Jeanne asked Willard. "I find it cold that they treat each other like strangers when they enter a shop or pass by each other on the street."

"Things are done differently here. Try to adjust," Willard replied.

"I'll do my best not to embarrass you," Jeanne conceded.

With the arrival of babies, Willard tried to be a present father instead of an absent one. First and foremost, he was a food, clothing, and shelter father. He bought a house that was ample enough for all of them, in a neighborhood with good schools and proper children with whom his could play. His yard was tended, his car was washed in the driveway each Saturday, and the household allowance he left for Jeanne to use for clothes and food was generous. Business was good, and there was nothing for which the profits were as willingly spent as for his family.

The ocean of distance that Willard and Jeanne had practiced before Jeanne joined him remained an ocean of distance even when they lived in the same house and slept in the same bed. They were not cold to each other, but they stayed out of each other's way. They kept to their roles, and they were in firm agreement most of the time about what those roles should be. When their roles did overlap, they were somewhat formal. Willard was courteous. He always opened doors for her. She was impeccable in making sure that, whenever he needed a starched and ironed white shirt, there was one ready for him. She served dinner on time, and he paid the bills in a timely fashion.

In their bed they also upheld their roles. He was courteous there too. Always cleanly about himself, and careful when he reached for her. And she was pleasantly available as one might expect of a good wife. She was grateful for his courtesy when she heard stories of other women whose husbands were inconsiderate or vulgar. She was not the kind of woman likely to make comments to others about her husband's bedroom skills, although one time she did say to a friend, "Willard is like men who dance well. He takes pride in his skill."

Willard and Jeanne learned how to stretch their marriage without breaking it. One stretch for their marriage was becoming Presbyterian. They both had been raised Catholic, but once in America, attending Mass and reciting Latin felt too much like the old way for Willard. He decided being Presbyterian was a good compromise. That is why one Sunday Charlie was baptized at a font that stood near the communion table in a handsome gothic-revival sanctuary. Morning light cast a scatter of blue and red blessings from the stained-glass windows, where four apostles looked down with grace on the couple and the clergy assigning the mark of a covenant to Charlie's little head.

When the minister, in his black robe, asked the couple, "By what name shall your child be called?" Willard responded "Charles," but he tried so hard to sound thoroughly American in his pronunciation that he sounded instead as if he had something stuck in his throat. And Jeanne, already nervous, had to stifle a giggle, but when she saw Ross sitting in the front pew watching the scene with wide eyes, her chuckle quickly passed because for the life of her she didn't want to tarnish a rare sacred moment in the eyes of this precious son.

No doubt witnessing the baptism of his little brother was reason for Ross to wonder about his own. "Did I get baptized?" he asked his mother.

"You did. You were baptized right after you were born. Babies can't remember things like that, but other people remember it for them," she explained. "I promise; you definitely were baptized."

"Did you have to say what my name was?"

"Yes. I told the priest what you were to be called before he baptized you."

"Did I have my different name then?"

"Yes. You were still called Philippe Guillaume when you were baptized."

"Does it still count now that I have a different name?"

"It does," said his mother. "The blessing goes with you forever."

"Did Papa's blessing go with him too when his name got changed?"

"Yes."

"Is that why you didn't want to change your name?" Ross squinted and his smooth boyish brow drew down from the effort of thinking it through. "Did you want to keep your first blessing?"

"Not exactly. It's complicated, my dear Ross, but don't worry, my blessing goes on forever too. It follows us wherever we go."

"Even to different countries?"

"Of course."

Jeanne didn't see any harm in an extra blessing or two for a little fellow who'd probably need all the blessings he could get to face the life ahead of him. Furthermore, she worried there was something missing in this baptism, and that is why on Monday Jeanne took little Charlie to visit the priest at the parish church in their neighborhood. She was relieved when the priest told her that a Protestant baptism was as valid as a Catholic one. He blessed Charlie in Latin and told Jeanne he would be happy to enter Charlie's name into the parish registry. He entered Ross's name too and made a note that at his actual christening he had been called Philippe Guillaume.

Rightly or wrongly, Jeanne understood the priest was giving permission for Ross and Charlie to be Presbyterian. Partly out of gratitude for this reassurance, and partly because she found comfort in the familiar language, sounds, and smells of her local Catholic church, Jeanne began to drop in a few times each week for Mass. She did not tell Willard, nor did she deny it. She simply said nothing. This was one of those things that fit in the zone of flexible distance in their marriage.

Later, when Leonard was born, and then after him Lillian, the ritual of a Protestant baptism and a second blessing that put the child's name in the registers of the local Catholic parish was repeated. Somewhere in that succession of events Willard became aware of the double baptism. It seems that one of the boys at school told Ross that his mother had seen Ross's mother at Mass. In complete boyish innocence Ross asked Jeanne about this at dinner when Willard was present. Jeanne didn't lie. Willard waited until he and Jeanne were alone to ask her in a calm voice if this was true, and Jeanne answered honestly again. He accepted it graciously. "Don't make a problem of it," he said. "It's okay, as long as you keep it to yourself."

"I've kept it to myself for several years already," Jeanne said. "It was never a problem before, and it won't be a problem now."

"You and I, we have to be able to count on each other to cooperate in these things," said Willard. "There's a lot at stake."

"I understand," she said. As had been the case with the priest not rejecting Charlie's Presbyterian baptism, so with Willard's gracious response to the revelation that Jeanne went to Mass, she took his reaction to mean that he did not object to her being Catholic.

There was one other time that Jeanne reached out to her parish priest for advice. It was to deal with the worst crisis in their marriage. Willard was a hands-on employer, and his expanding business required that he travel to its various locations. In the beginning, he tried to drive back and forth in a day to visit the other stores, but after a while, as he became more prosperous, he stayed over in hotels and returned the next day. Jeanne was used to giving Willard whatever latitude he needed to conduct business. This was his arena, and just as he did not instruct her what brand of laundry soap she should use or how often she should wash the curtains, so she did not presume to tell him what hours he should work or when he should travel.

The arrangement went smoothly, until after a trip Jeanne noticed the tell-tale scent of perfume as she was hanging up his wool sport coat. She said nothing, but her suspicions were confirmed when later in the side pocket of his suitcase she found the receipt for a hotel stay that included two dinners delivered to Willard's room in the evening, and two breakfasts delivered to his room the next morning. She didn't accuse him; she simply told him what she'd observed. He apologized and told her that it wouldn't happen again.

In her distress, Jeanne went to the priest. He knew her to be a faithful parishioner and a devoted mother, and when she put her problem before him, his response was cautious. "This is a difficult situation," he said, "but remember whatever you decide to do with it, you also will be making a decision for your children."

Jeanne was a woman who'd lived through enough struggles in her life to know the costs of fighting back, and she was determined not to create chaos for her children. That was her approach until the day the phone rang, and a girl introducing herself as Sandra said, "You deserve to know that, even if he says it's over, that's not what he tells me. He tells me he will stay with you until the children are older, but he really wants to be with me. Why do you keep him trapped in a miserable marriage? Let him go!"

When Jeanne asked Willard if he wanted her to let him go, he protested. He was angry about the phone call, but had no explanation for it, except to say that Sandra, an employee in one of his stores, was emotionally unstable. He asked Jeanne to ignore it, and for a time he was particularly generous with her. He bought her expensive jewelry and took her to fine restaurants. At Christmas he bought her a full-length mink coat.

While Jeanne did not think it her responsibility to regulate Willard's work hours or his business trips, she had no intention of sharing her bed. Like her name, this was her domain. A few times when Willard reached from his side of the bed to place a hand on her shoulder or brush gently through her hair to let her know of his interest in her, she equally gently brushed his hand away in much the same fashion one would brush away a piece of lint or a smudge on the sleeve of a garment. And Willard, being a gentleman, did not insist.

Even a gentleman can become impatient, so that at last, instead of retreating into guilty silence after she brushed his hand away, Willard said to Jeanne, "This coldness can't go on forever."

"You made the problem," she said. "Why must I be the one to fix it?"

"Because it's over," he said. "We have to let the past be past. It's water under the bridge. There is too much at stake. We have a good life. Our children need us. Don't make trouble."

"I would have thought that too," Jeanne said. "But now I wonder." Because she was afraid of what she would say next, she got up, put on a robe, and walked toward the door.

Willard followed her. "Don't be righteous with me," he said. "I knew you when you were nothing more than a sad girl ready to welcome a visitor in through the back door of your little house in a no-account village."

"Yes," she said, "and you were the visitor at the back door. That makes us equally guilty in that matter."

"Oh no," he said, "there's more. We had four years apart. I know your cozy arrangement with the priest. Those letters he mailed for you, and the letters from me that he read. I'm sure you had your way of paying him back for his kindness. I know very well that your pretended innocence wasn't innocent at all. Those lonely, love-hungry priests aren't any different than other men."

"Stop," she screamed. "Don't you dare speak ill of him. It's not right. No, don't you dare. It won't turn out good."

"Oh," said Willard, "now look who knows what's right. The fallen woman."

Jeanne turned around and walked up close to Willard. She looked into his eye with a rage that covered fear. She wasn't concerned that he'd feel crowded by her close approach or that he'd strike her. "If you ever speak ill of him again, you will regret it. I will not stand for it. Do not make him your scapegoat."

"And what exactly do you think you can do? How do you think you will stop me?"

"You can't stand it, can you," screamed Jeanne, "that there is a man more righteous than you? A man who never took advantage of a lonely woman. He didn't expose you when the people of the village gossiped that my child was his, because you left and he stayed, as if that proved anything. He never told them that the bastard about whom they whispered their speculations had a father who got on a ship and crossed the ocean to seek his fortune, because his fortune was more important than his child. He could have exposed you, but he didn't. He bore the insults for you, and now you can't bear to admit the debt you owe him." Jeanne did not step back. She did not recoil. She stood staring at Willard without flinching. "Do not ever speak of him again to me. You will be sorry if you do."

""You think you can stop me?" Willard said. He was a man who didn't like to be bested in a contest. More than that, he hated to be told what he could and couldn't do, especially by a woman.

"I do think I can stop you," Jeanne said through clenched teeth. "Test me, and I'll divorce you. I'll expose all the lies with which you've built up your own importance. I'll expose you to your children. I'll tell it all. Don't test me, Willard. In comparison to you, I have little to lose by telling the truth . . . little to lose that I haven't lost already. And I know you. If fairness won't stop you, then I know pride will."

A silence fell on them both. She had nothing more to say. And he had nothing more to say because he'd heard her. Willard pulled some clothes from the closet and headed from the room. When he opened the door to the hallway, Jeanne caught a sight that was like a stab in her heart. There just inside the doorway of his own bedroom, standing in the shadows, was Ross.

Jeanne heard the door of the closet near the front door, and then she heard the front door. A minute or so later, watching from her upstairs room, Jeanne saw Willard's dark figure walking toward the sidewalk. Then there was a second set of footsteps in the hallway. She opened the door to Ross, and he came to her waiting arms. "I'm so sorry my precious boy," she said. "You shouldn't have had to hear Mama and Papa fighting."

"Will he come back?" Ross asked. "Will he hurt us?"

"No. I'll keep you safe. You don't have to worry."

In the middle of the night Jeanne heard the front door open and then the sound of the lock after it closed again. She heard footsteps in the hall, and a toilet flush, but Willard did not come to their bed to reclaim the spot where Ross was sleeping. Very early in the morning Willard tiptoed through the room to the closet to gather fresh clothes for the day. He did not look toward her as he crossed the room, and he didn't wait for breakfast before he went to work. When he came home, he told Jeanne that he had gone to the furniture store and ordered new beds. "Twin beds," he said. "The arrangement we have now is too crowded. I need my rest."

Later at a dinner party when one of his business associates made a crack about middle-aged wives who want twin beds, Willard said, "they're all the fashion. They are the rage in Hollywood." Willard gave a knowing smirk and added, "It's rather old-fashioned to think that having two beds would slow down bedroom activity. Lucy and Ricky have twin beds. Give it time. Twin beds are catching on. There's likely an upside to this market. Maybe we should get in ahead of the market and make an investment in a mattress company." And that's exactly what Willard and his associate did. Willard was good at making lemonade from lemons, and he was good at making money.

Chapter 15

MOST SUMMERS ROSS and Maggie took their children for a two-week stay at Gramma Jeanne and Grandpa Willard's cottage. It was a big old cottage on the east side of Lake Michigan where the dunes are high and the beaches broad. The cottage was built by a lumberman who'd spared no expense on an elegant living room with a large window seat, bookcases with glass doors, and a massive fieldstone fireplace that reached to the high ceiling. Some of the finishes had gone dull and the fireplace was streaked with years of soot, but it was still elegant. Next to the living room through an archway was the dining room with wainscoting and a chandelier that hung over a table large enough to accommodate the whole tribe. Across the entire front of the cottage was a huge screened porch with Adirondack chairs and views of the lake.

By contrast to the elegance of the main floor, the upper floors were simple. On the second floor there was a large dormitory-style room for the girls on one end and numerous small bedrooms with old furniture for adults on the other. At each end of the hallway that ran the length of the second floor were two identical bathrooms with black and white floor tiles and clawfoot tubs. One bathroom was for the adults and the other for the girls. On the third floor, one huge room under the open beams was "the boys' barracks."

Each boy had a narrow bed, four hooks on which to hang his towel and a few clothes, and an open locker at the foot of the bed in which he stored the rest of his belongings. A narrow stairway descended in two steep sections all the way from this attic room to the old-fashioned summer kitchen on the first floor, where just outside the back door was a bathroom that had been added onto the back of the cottage. It had one toilet, two sinks, and a cold-water shower. Long ago when the cottage was built, the steep stairway from kitchen to attic allowed maids to haul laundry up for drying when it was raining or too windy to hang laundry outdoors.

Once Grandpa Willard took over the cottage, the stairway was assigned to the boys. "Up and down those stairs is good exercise," he told them when they complained that, from their beds in the attic, two floors down to the bathroom was a long trek in the middle of the night. Steven found the trek most difficult because he was afraid of the dark. He wet his bed sometimes when he was too afraid to go down alone, and the bed-wetting infuriated Grandpa Willard, who was sure it was laziness, not fear, that accounted for the accident. Grandpa Willard never caught on that Will, Rowland, and the older cousins saved steps by lifting the window and peeing out onto the porch roof. Now and then their grandfather observed that some animal must be foraging around the back porch at night and leaving a scent. "A large animal, I suspect," said Grandpa Willard. "The scent is very strong." The boys didn't say a word.

There was a rhythm to cottage days. The beginning of the day was lazy, and Gramma Jeanne indulged children with special breakfasts while adults helped themselves. Under the watchful eye of adults, kids played in sand and water all morning. In the middle of the day the whole gang gathered briefly on the porch to be refueled with sandwiches and fruit that Grandma Jeanne set out, and then it was back to the beach for the afternoon. At 5:00 the atmosphere shifted. Adults came up from the beach to have cocktails on the porch, and children came up the from the beach too, because there were no adults remaining to supervise them. Exactly at 6:30 dinner was announced. No matter the assortment of guests who came to the cottage, Grandpa Willard held court at a family dinner in the large dining room.

Friday night dinner was an especially big deal because Grandpa Willard hired a woman to come in and cook the meal. She bustled around all afternoon, cooking, setting the table with a linen tablecloth and napkins, and laying out the silverware in the right places. The meal was a full menu including dessert. According to

Grandpa Willard's dress code, men and boys wore shirts with collars at dinner. No t-shirts were allowed. On Friday night, because the women in the family had been excused from kitchen duty, they were expected to wear dresses. Fashionable sundresses were acceptable, but shorts or beachwear definitely were not.

When the children appeared for dinner, the boys had hair slicked back from the showers they had taken. The girls' hair was held back with barrettes or headbands. All the young ones knew that at the table children should be seen but not heard. Once everyone was seated, Grandpa Willard served the plates from dishes and platters brought out from the kitchen and placed next to him on a serving cart.

The serving ritual was tense. Grandpa Willard would take a plate and put a portion of each menu item on it, say whose plate it was, and hand it to his child assistant to put it before the waiting diner. Children were expected to thank him when their plates were set down in front of them. They also knew they were expected to eat what was on their plates and remain at the table until after dessert, when Grandpa Willard would tell them they were excused.

As an adult and long after the cottage was sold off to someone else, Jenna recalled those days at the cottage when she reminisced with Aunt Lillian. "Especially for a vacation, the formality seemed overdone. I loved the beach, but I dreaded dinner. If only Grandpa Willard hadn't been there, it would have been a wonderful place."

"Not easy to get rid of Grandpa Willard," Aunt Lillian reminded Jenna. "He owned the place and was convinced he owned the family too."

"At the beach us kids felt free," said Jenna. "Most days Grandpa Willard didn't bother to come down the long stairs that led from the cottage to the beach. He hung out on the porch, supposedly to read. Row and Will cracked a lot of jokes about Grandpa Willard reading with his eyes closed and his mouth hanging open."

Dinner time was another story. Grandpa Willard insisted his grandchildren know how to behave at a formal dinner. He always looked over at Maggie when he said, "These days parents don't put any effort into bringing their children up with manners and good behavior." Grandpa Willard was sure he was doing parents a favor by filling in where they were neglectful.

Years later, in the memory of each child, there were traumatic episodes in which they starred. The dining room was Jenna's chamber of trials because there was always something on the menu she didn't like, and that was Grandpa Willard's opportunity to go to battle with her. In his unquestioned wisdom, Grandpa Willard knew how hungry each child should be, and he decided how much food to put on their plates. Children were expected to eat what was served, whether they were hungry or not.

Ross and Maggie weren't careless about manners, and their children behaved like average kids at the table, but this was way below Grandpa Willard's standards. Jenna's memorable donnybrook was the night they had asparagus. Ross was absent that evening, although Ross's brother Charlie and his entire family were there to witness it.

When Grandpa Willard started putting asparagus on each plate, Jenna, who was sitting next to her mother, whispered "I don't like that green stuff."

"Grandpa Willard, please leave the asparagus off Jenna's plate," Maggie said.

"I'm serving, Maggie, and I don't need your instructions," Grandpa Willard replied without looking up.

When the plate was put down in front of Jenna, she whispered again to Maggie that she didn't like the green things, and her mother said, "Let's use the three-little-bites rule. I'll cut the little flowers off the top of the green things, they're the best part, and you can dip them in the sauce that makes them taste good." All the kids in the family knew the three-little-bites rule that Maggie brought into play when they were suspicious of something she was serving. She expected them to try three small nibbles before deciding they didn't like a food they had never tasted before.

"There's no reason Jenna can't eat what's on her plate," Grandpa Willard said. "When she's an adult no one is going to be impressed if she pulls up her little nose and says she doesn't like green things." He was giving instructions to Maggie, but then turned toward

Jenna. "Start eating right now," he said. "I've heard enough of your complaining."

Jenna didn't want Grandpa Willard to get mad; she stuffed a whole asparagus in her mouth and started chewing. The harder she chewed the more it turned into a big wad of fiber. Grandpa Willard was staring at her, and tears welled up in Jenna's eyes.

"Maggie, your children are spoiled," said Grandpa Willard. "They'll pay the price for your neglect. That little one's got you wrapped around her finger. She's a miniature Sarah Bernhardt, and you fall for it." When Grandpa Willard started a tirade at the table, he just kept going. The words didn't matter as much as the fact that they kept tumbling out of his mouth. Maggie figured he would carry on until someone broke the spell.

"Take your sister upstairs," Maggie said quietly to Laura. "Help her spit that out."

The girls got up and left the room, and Grandpa Willard paused for a moment to catch his breath and get ready for the next round. In the brief silence, everyone at the table could hear the girls' footsteps going up the creaky cottage stairs. They could hear Laura encouraging Jenna to hurry, and then in a bossy big sister voice they heard, "Oh no, Jenna, don't…" followed by a confident, in-charge, sing-song voice saying, "Mom, you'd better come and help; Jenna's just sitting on the steps. She wants you to take her up." And then the voice wasn't sing-song anymore. Now it had an edge of panic. "Mom, are you coming? Oh, no. Stop Jenna . . . Mom, hurry, Jenna puked."

Jenna was shaking her head as she told the story, but then she broke into a smile. "Gramma Jeanne came upstairs to help me get cleaned up. She stayed with me while Laura went back down to have dinner. I was shivering, and Gramma Jeanne put me in a bath to calm me down and warm me up. There was a rocking chair in the room where Mom and Dad stayed. After my bath, Gramma Jeanne wrapped me in a blanket and rocked me to sleep. That part of a horrible night is a sweet memory."

Some Friday nights Ross was traveling for business and arrived back in Chicago late. He'd wait until Saturday morning to drive to the cottage. When Ross was present, Grandpa Willard still ran the show; he'd order his son around as if Ross were a trusted lieutenant and his father the five-star general. Ross's presence reassured Grandpa Willard that his imperial authority was being given proper deference. When Ross was absent for the big production of Friday night dinner, the dynamic changed. Grandpa Willard was uncertain of his ability to control everyone, and consequently he also was less able to control himself. Cottage disasters happened on those nights when Ross was gone.

On one particular Friday night, Will and Row were hoping to finish dinner on time so they could leave the table and go watch a baseball game on TV. There was an old TV set at the cottage, and even though reception wasn't great out there, it was good enough to catch most of the game. Grandpa Willard liked to watch baseball too, but he wouldn't let baseball interrupt Friday dinner.

Will and Row were sitting near the head of the table close to Grandpa Willard, and Will was his serving assistant that evening. Their mom was at the other end of the table with Jenna and Laura on either side of her. Dessert had been served, and Will and Row were eating theirs as fast as they could. "Stop stuffing your mouths and eating like apes," Grandpa Willard said. When Row was done, he leaned forward and caught his mom's eye down at the other end of the table to ask if they could be excused to go watch the baseball game.

"You can go," Maggie said. "We're pretty much finished up here."

"I haven't excused them," said Grandpa Willard. "This is still my house.

"Well, I 've excused them," said Maggie, "and they're still my boys."

"You wouldn't dare to behave that way if Ross were here," said Grandpa Willard.

"I won't allow you to bully my children regardless of whether Ross is here or not." Maggie's face was pale with anger.

Next to Maggie, Jenna started whining, "I want Daddy. I want Daddy. I want Daddy." She said it over and over, like a stuck record. Maggie put a hand on her shoulder and shushed her, but there was no silencing Jenna.

"Take charge, Maggie," said Grandpa Willard. "You can't let kids behave this way at dinner. I won't have it."

Maggie calmly explained to Jenna that her daddy would be back tomorrow. Jenna was silent for a moment as a puzzled look swept across her face. She was trying to process what this meant. They were on their own, at the mercy of Grandpa Willard. The truth sunk in, and Jenna erupted in a terrified wail.

There was another loud noise as Grandpa Willard's fist came down on the table. "That's enough," he shouted. "If you can't keep those kids in line, Maggie, I'll show you how it's done." He pushed his chair back from the table, and as he did, Jenna stopped wailing and froze. Instinctively Rowland popped up out of his chair and went down to the end of the table where Maggie was seated so he could take refuge behind her, putting his hand on her shoulder so she would know he was there. In the next instant Will popped up out of his chair and came to stand next to Rowland. He put his hand on Maggie's other shoulder. Rowland was trembling, but Will wasn't scared. In a loud clear voice he said, "Don't you hurt my sister. And don't yell at Mom."

There they were, two twelve-year-old boys defending their mother and their sisters. Years later as Rowland recalled that moment for Jenna, he choked up as he spoke. "I loved Will so much standing there next to him like that. I could feel warmth radiating from him, and for once we weren't competing. Together we were more powerful than Grandpa Willard. My fear went away, and I felt invincible."

Incensed, Grandpa Willard got up from his chair at the head of the table to come around to the other end and show this unruly little bunch who was in charge. As he stepped forward his foot caught in the edge of the carpet that had been roughed up as he pushed his chair back, and he stumbled forward against the buffet. His hand went out ahead of him to stop the fall, first knocking over a large pitcher of ice water, and then smashing into the mirror on the back of the buffet. He gathered himself up as well as he could, but when he looked at his hand, he saw blood beginning to ooze out. Protectively he held it against the table napkin still tucked in his shirt. As he walked from the room, every set of eyes followed him, and when he disappeared through the swinging door into the kitchen they were left in stunned silence. They heard running water. Then they heard steps, and they heard the screen door on the back entry slap shut. A moment later the sound of the car told them Grandpa Willard was driving away.

The next morning Grandpa Willard's hand was wrapped in gauze, and he began fretting about whether the tendon of his index finger was so badly damaged he would lose the use of it. No one asked him what the doctor had said about it when putting the stitches in his hand, because they didn't want to start the tirade all over again. The kids were ready in a flash when Maggie said she'd go down to the beach with them, and when Ross arrived home in the afternoon, it was a huge relief.

When Jenna was telling Aunt Lillian about the disasters at the cottage, she added in some details she only knew second-hand from Rowland. After Ross had returned and the children were feeling safe again, Rowland asked Will if he was worried about Grandpa Willard's finger. You never could tell if the whole matter would erupt again, but Rowland figured if Will wasn't worried, he needn't worry either. Will's response was sarcastic, "I'm very worried, stupid, if his finger doesn't heal straight, how will he pick his nose?" Together they collapsed in giggles, each imitating their grandfather trying to get a bent finger up his nose. For years after, when the two boys were at Grandpa Willard's house, one or the other of them would lightly tap the end of his nose with a bent finger to see if he could make his brother laugh.

A week or so after the family had packed up and gone home from the cottage, Will and Rowland were in the car with Ross, who was dropping them off at the swimming pool. Rowland, the kid who always talked too much, said, "Dad, at Friday night dinner at the cottage when you were gone, Mom got in a fight with Grandpa Willard. That's how he hurt his hand."

In the back seat, next to Rowland, Will whispered, "Drop it! Don't get into it!"

Their father was silent at first. Then he said, "I know. I'm proud of you for standing by your mother. We men in this family need to protect our women. Your mother and your sisters deserve that. Your gramma too. That's our duty. So, you did the right thing."

"How do you know about it?" Rowland asked his father.

Will gave him a jab with his elbow. "Stop, stupid!" he whispered.

"I have my ways," Ross replied.

"Did you always protect Gramma Jeanne and Aunt Lillian?" Rowland asked.

They drove for nearly a block before Ross said anything. "I should have done better," he said. He didn't turn toward Rowland as he spoke; he didn't even glance back at him in the rearview mirror. But Rowland could see his dad's reflection in the mirror, and he noticed that Ross just kept his eye on the road.

Part Four

*Guillaume Barone
and Jeanne de Roose*

Chapter 16

JEANNE DE ROOSE had a life before she met Guillaume Barone, but after Jeanne and Willard married, they seldom spoke of their past. It had taken place on the other side of an ocean and occurred in a time Willard wanted to forget. He wasn't a man capable of holding a complex story. Even if he had to stoop to outright lies in order to cover his past, Willard was determined to insulate himself from its ugly truth.

For Jeanne it was different. When Lillian went with her to France the first time, she began to share the story. Piece by piece she brought a dark past back to light. Times had changed, but also Jeanne had changed. She was no longer afraid of her own story.

When Jenna asked about those years, Aunt Lillian knew it was time to hand the stories forward to another generation. It wasn't easy to assemble what she'd been told because the events were strewn through time like the debris from a bomb blast. The earliest accounts had come from Jeanne herself, but when Lillian lived in France, she'd gathered many other details from the stories that had lingered in the places where events had taken place. They had become part of local lore.

Long before Guillaume changed his name to Willard, and long before Jeanne first met Guillaume and their destinies were thrown together, Jeanne was married to Gilbert de Roose, the schoolmaster. Even after Gilbert's death, and even after Jeanne married Willard and they had children, Gilbert remained a love Jeanne carried in her heart. When she was an old woman, the memory of Gilbert still put a soft smile on her face. This despite the fact that their life together was hijacked by disaster.

Gilbert and Willard were opposites. As much as Willard disliked reminiscing, Gilbert enjoyed going over events, shaping the story better each time he retold it, and savoring events as much in memory as he had when they first occurred. He was a romantic, and that was one of the delights in Jeanne's marriage to him. Not only were they happy lovers, but they were talkers. They lived through their simple days together, creating hours of warm companionship by going back over their sweet yesterdays. Like children, they never tired of hearing their favorite stories again.

Sitting at their little table, drinking their tea and eating their bread in the evening, Gilbert and Jeanne reviewed how fortunate they had been to meet each other. She would remind him of the first time she had seen him across the row among the vegetable stalls on market day in Lille.

"Immediately I noticed you," she said, "what an intelligent brow you had and what a finely cut face. Your shiny hair and the beautiful shape of your mouth were like an exquisite portrait." She wasn't flattering him. If she closed her eyes and called up her memory of that first glimpse, this was exactly what she saw each time. "You know that funny little wool cap you wore? It was pressed so deep into your curly hair it looked like it was installed permanently."

"That's a comical memory. Too bad about the cap," Gilbert replied. "If I had known that your first glance would be the one you would always remember, I wouldn't have worn that dusty, moth-eaten cap that day. I would've worn something more elegant. Something befitting a Hans Holbein portrait."

"Oh, no, my darling," Jeanne would say. "It wouldn't be the same without that old cap. I always want to remember you exactly as you were. Not the way Holbein, whoever that is, thinks of you, but just the way you were, when I caught my first glimpse of you that day in the market."

They were a sentimental pair. Their syrupy words were little more than an endless variety of ways two young lovers can breathe tenderness over each other. To an outsider looking in on their private moments, the way they lingered on details would be dismissed as purple prose, but to Jeanne and Gilbert each detail was delectable.

Gilbert was slightly older and more educated than Jeanne. If he had given in to self-criticism, he would have realized that their whisperings were juvenile, but he wasn't inclined to question their relationship that way. Instead, he joined his sweet Jeanne exactly where she was. He embraced her simplicity because, as he said to his friends when he met them at the pub for heady conversations, "Jeanne keeps my feet on the ground. She calls me back to earth when I've spent too much time with my head in the clouds where the air is thin and the view restricted."

To Jeanne herself Gilbert would say, "Oh my precious one, you are such a dreamer," and then he'd go on to remember the shine of her smooth mahogany hair, and the fine cut of her straight nose that set apart the rosy glow of her cheeks. "I remember," he would say, "that day at the market, how I smiled at you, and you smiled back. The corners of your mouth rose like the wings of a little butterfly lifting up and floating on a sweet breeze." Sometimes he mixed metaphors, and he knew better, but at the moment it didn't matter. Something else was more important to him. His lines were always more poetic than hers, but like hers they were a recitative of first love that hadn't been bruised yet.

Many years later, when Jeanne told her daughter Lillian of the *pas de deux* of these two young lovers, when she explained how they could make of an ordinary walk in the park a thing of great beauty, she would admit that it sounded like infatuation. "Everyone should experience the flush of infatuation at least once in a lifetime," said Jeanne. "Of course, an observer with a sour temperament could discount our enchantment. The same surge of hormones has been experienced millions of times over, but in the moment when it is being lived, it is truly one of a kind. It takes courage to believe your love outshines all the rest, and courage is a good thing when it comes to love. Who would want to miss out on that? One *should not* miss out on that," Jeanne said to Lillian, "because it would be a terrible waste of opportunity." In the timbre of Jeanne's voice Lillian could feel deep conviction.

Gilbert's parents were city folk, and his father owned boats that transported goods along the river. Outside the town and across the river in an area of farmland that had been fed for centuries with water and silt from the river, his mother's parents owned a farm. In summer, when the city was musty and dirty, Gilbert, along with his mother and his brothers and sisters, went to the countryside to stay with his grandparents.

On that farm across the river the accident occurred that left Gilbert with a limp. Children sometimes went to the fields with the men to harvest hay, and while the men worked, the children played. When they stopped to eat the bread or drink the tea they had brought with them, the children sat on the top of the hay wagon. From that high spot they could see across the fields or they could lie back to watch shapes in the clouds.

That all changed the day the full wagon tipped just slightly as it was pulled from the field onto the road. Gilbert was lying on top. The sway and then jolt of the wagon threw Gilbert off from his high perch and onto the ground where the back wheel of the wagon rolled over his leg.

Gilbert remembered those days, but only through storms of pain. Others remembered his delirium and the packs being placed around him to control the swelling that made his leg look like a huge stuffed sausage. His oldest sister told how the doctor arrived in a black coat and carrying a black bag. He handed them off to her as if she were an assistant waiting to serve him, and he hurried into the room where Gilbert had been put in his parents' bed. Even as he walked toward the bed, the doctor began giving instructions.

Gilbert's mother was already at the bedside with her little boy, and to keep him from thrashing side to side in pain, she held his shoulders down and pressed him into the pillow. The doctor instructed Gilbert's father to place a hand on each of the boy's hips and press into the mattress, while the doctor took the bent and crooked leg and began twisting it to reset the bones. "It was," Gilbert said, "like being struck by lightning and lit on fire at the very same time." Later his older brother reminded Gilbert that when the doctor twisted his leg, Gilbert's eyes fluttered, and he sank into unconsciousness.

Gilbert's mother thought her son had died and began weeping for him. It was not weeping exactly, but long keening, interrupted with "Oh no, no, oh no." It seemed that in her shock she couldn't find words to call out to her dying son as he drifted away from her, but when his eyes opened again, Gilbert's mother began to laugh uncontrollably and called out her thanks to every saint whose name she could bring to mind. This struck Gilbert's brother as the odd behavior of a simple-minded woman, but for Gilbert it was proof that when he reached the gates of heaven, a team of saints, hearing his mother's pleas, had agreed together to send him back into life. "There was something I hadn't finished yet," he said, when he told Jeanne the story, and in her innocence, Jeanne liked to think it had something to do with her.

Gilbert was not inclined to self-pity. When he told Jeanne the story of his injury, he focused more on the faith of his mother than on his own pain. He admired his father's insistence that the children be prepared to "fly from the nest," and the fact that he had a limp made him no exception. That is why after a boyhood in Maastricht, the course of his life swerved, and he ended up training to be a French teacher. He studied in Lille, and that is where he met Jeanne at the market.

Lille was not Jeanne's hometown either. She was there to be trained as a midwife and to learn basic nursing skills. "It was meant to be," Gilbert would say, "because how else could you explain that the right things aligned so that we caught sight of each other that day at the market." Jeanne heard Gilbert repeat this claim to others, and she never questioned the truth of it. Until the end of her life she believed that their love was both accidental and meant to be.

When Jeanne finished training to be a nurse, she went home to live again with her parents in Beauvais. There she waited for Gilbert to finish his studies and earn his certification to teach. He took the first job he could find that would allow him to be near her; it was a small village near Beauvais, and the students weren't brilliant, but it brought Jeanne and Gilbert together. That's what mattered most to both of them.

Gilbert was not a beautiful man, measured by the standards used by young women who walked the town square in the evening, hoping someone would notice them. He did not have the virile handsomeness of the smith, whose muscled arms, steady stance, and honest sweat drew the admiring glances of married women passing by on their way to market, the ones who slowed their pace just slightly to look into his shop and catch a glimpse of him shirtless at work. He was not handsome in the way of the slender clothier, whose well-tailored garments covered the scrawniness of his body and sketched out perfect long lines as he strolled through the village putting his wares on display.

Jeanne heard the whispered remarks of people who watched the schoolteacher walk across the uneven cobblestones of the village lanes. Once Jeanne heard someone say that he looked like a listing sailboat. "It's a shame, isn't it," that voice said, "that the fellow is so disfigured." A few of the crudest were not so careful to keep their voices low when they'd say to each other, "What does she see in a cripple like that? He's lucky to have found a woman at all."

Jeanne did not see these things, or, if she saw them, they didn't matter to her. What she saw was the gloss of Gilbert's curly hair, and she knew the feel of it when she buried her fingers in it. She knew the bright blue of his eyes when he gazed into hers. She heard the silken refinement of his voice. She knew the smell of his neck when she placed her head on his shoulder, a fragrance that had nothing artificial about it. Beyond all that, what mattered to Jeanne most was how deeply loved she felt when she was with Gilbert.

Once they were married, Jeanne reminded herself often, with an inward smile, that these gossiping women had no idea of Gilbert's real beauty. What they thought they saw on the street when they snickered about his heavy built-up shoe had nothing to do with the artist Jeanne knew at night.

All those unkind voices were far from Jeanne's mind on warm summer evenings when the windows were open and the curtains fluttered, while Jeanne and Gilbert were together in their small bedroom at the back of the house. It was there that sometimes he would laugh and tenderly cover her mouth so that the neighbors wouldn't hear her cry out in passion. "Shhh, you'll wake the neighbor's baby," Gilbert would say.

"Oh, no," she would say and laugh at him, "You are the one who is waking the neighbor's baby."

And to this Gilbert would respond, "Oh, my treasure."

These were the words that stayed with Jeanne even when she was an old woman. These are the words she shared with her daughter Lillian in a very intimate moment of recollection. She admitted that the memory of her young husband still brought a smile. It brought back to be savored once again a time of life that should never be lost. Jeanne knew she had been adored by a good man.

Chapter 17

Jeanne and Gilbert struggled to preserve a circle of sunshine in a dark sky, but around them sinister clouds of war were gathering. Their country was being invaded, and young men were leaving the village to join up and be trained. Gilbert, of course, could not go. He was not fit for military service, and it hurt him to be the man left behind because he was loyal to his adopted country and loyal to the children he taught. To Jeanne he said: "I'll find a way to serve. I'll be true to France. I'll show them." This was especially important to Gilbert because in addition to being the "crippled schoolmaster," he was also "that foreign Dutchman."

In a village as small as their village, everyone knew everyone else, if not well enough to visit in each other's homes, then at least well enough to know the difference between a local and a stranger. The atmosphere of war began to change that. People passed through their village along the roads. Strangers stopped in at the café and stayed at the small hotel. This was a migration different from the ordinary trips people made to visit friends and family, or the trips made by merchants to promote their wares to the owners of small shops in the towns and villages that dotted the French countryside outside the big cities. The travelers created by war were different, and locals turned their suspicions on them.

If a stranger traveling through the village had a military bearing but no uniform, the villagers would try to sort out if he was working for France Libre or if he had been sent by the Germans. Inquiries by travelers were not well received. What normally would have been ready answers that indicated courtesy, now were replaced with brief and evasive responses that in some cases were misleading. Neighbors watched each other more closely than they had before. They needed to be cautious about whom they trusted.

The atmosphere in homes changed too. Gilbert continued to be a sweet and loving husband in the day, but in the bedroom a new element of caution took over. "War is not a good time for a baby," he told Jeanne. "We're young. We should wait. This is not a world into which we want to bring a child." From that time on, when he would turn toward her in their bed, he would ask, "Is it safe?"

Jeanne became the keeper of the calendar, the one who parceled the days of the month into safe zones and unsafe zones. Even when she would say, "No . . . no it isn't safe right now," he would kiss her and remind her that he loved her as always, but then he would turn to face the outside of the bed.

It hurt Jeanne. It hurt her so much that one night she asked him, "Do you still desire me as much as you did before, or has war changed that too?" She tried not to be hurt by Gilbert's discipline, but it wounded her that the danger all around had found its way into the tender space between them. He reached for her like a man desperate to tell the truth. He made love to her, but she felt guilty, as if she had seduced him. As Jeanne drifted into sleep, she was aware that Gilbert got up and went into the other room. When she woke again, he was there beside her, but he wasn't sleeping. He was staring at the ceiling and was tense. "I'm sorry," she said. "That wasn't fair to you. I didn't mean to test you that way. It's just that it's so cruel that war can change everything. Sometimes I feel that it's even changing our love."

"I understand, my treasure," he said. "This is a time we must live through, and I don't know what to say, except that I will love you until my dying day and nothing, not even war, will change that." He moved toward her and kissed her cheek tenderly. "Please say you believe me, at least say that if you truly mean it."

"I do," Jeanne said. "If you say it, I know it is true. How could I doubt you?" He knew she was telling the truth.

It wasn't long after that Gilbert came to Jeanne and said, "there is something you and I need to talk about, and I don't like it."

"What have you done?" she asked.

"No. Nothing like that." He paused. "This is about war. I have never kept secrets from you. I don't believe you have kept them from me. Now, because we trust each other, we need to change our agreement. We each need to allow the other to have secrets. If there are things you know that happen here in the village, perhaps things the women tell you, or small things you observe at the market, you must not share them with me. And if there are things that I discover, I won't share them with you. We must keep our risks separate. We must preserve in each other the possibility of saying that we don't know anything, if ever we face hard questions."

"Why would that ever happen? We're in this together," Jeanne protested.

"This is war, and I am a foreigner," he said.

"I trust you," Jeanne said.

"I trust you too," he said. "Can we trust each other's silence?"

Although Jeanne trusted Gilbert, and she knew that he was right about this silence, she began to worry. She tried to talk herself out of wondering. She had bouts of anger. Not toward Gilbert. Toward everything. Toward the fact that their life was taking this terrible turn. She felt anger in the face of the possibility that war was coming for them.

Jeanne had heard about the war through which her mother, Brigitte, had lived when she was young, twenty-five years before. The Great War was a time of testing. There were "curtain peepers," women who lived around the village and watched. By pulling the curtain back an inch or so, standing in the shadow, and peering through the narrow bar of light, they could see who spoke to whom on the street. They noted who left home and returned at what times. They listened in the night and rose from their beds to take note of anything happening under the cover of darkness. They were the village security system.

Jeanne also remembered her mother's story about one of the curtain peepers who couldn't be trusted. She watched as carefully as all the others, but reported to the wrong side. In the night she was taken from her home, gagged and blind-folded, and, as

Jeanne's mother put it tactfully, "she disappeared and does not have a marker in the churchyard."

"Who did it?" Jeanne asked her mother.

"We didn't ask," her mother replied. "There are things you choose not to know during war time, and when the war is over you still choose not to speak about them again. The lessons learned, perhaps they are worth repeating. What has happened between people, that has to be left behind."

"Why? Once it's over, it should be safe to tell it all." Jeanne was only a girl, and she still had an uncorrupted sense of justice. If the losses couldn't be altered, at least the truth about them should be told.

"Life has to go on," her mother said. "We all have to set aside the habits of war and return to living as if we still know what peace is." Brigitte sighed deeply as she spoke. Jeanne knew her mother had doubts about whether peace could be fully realized again. Her mother was a woman who never again dropped her guard completely. She was good and kind, but extremely careful. She taught Jeanne, "Don't blabber information to anyone about anything if it isn't necessary. It can only lead to trouble." And, consistent with her own principles, Jeanne's mother was a woman who never stooped to silly gossip.

Jeanne had just returned home from her work when the postmaster's son came to the door with a message for Gilbert from his family in Maastricht. It was cryptic.

> FATHER TRAVELING = MOTHER ILL
> = COME QUICKLY

Knowing that Gilbert would want to know immediately, Jeanne put on her coat and hurried to the school. He read the message. "I'll finish the day with the children," he said, "and then I'll come home directly so we can decide what I must do."

Jeanne knew what Gilbert would do, because he was a loyal son. His mother had stood by him in the miserable days of his childhood, and he would not leave her unattended now. Jeanne wondered what she should do. Should she go with Gilbert? Should she remain in the village? Should she go to stay with her parents in Beauvais? Jeanne dreaded being at home alone without Gilbert.

By the time Gilbert came home from school, he had decided to cancel the last week of the school term. It was his plan to travel through Belgium and enter the Netherlands along small village roads. The borders and conflict zones were difficult, but he thought he knew a way around them. Jeanne helped him pack his bag. They ate their evening bread in silence.

In their bed Gilbert turned to her and asked the question she had learned to hate. "Is it safe?" he said.

"Yes," she said. "It's safe." In truth she didn't care if it was safe or not. She wanted him before he left. All night long he held her to him. It wasn't real sleep. It was drifting, dozing, stirring to feel the other there, then drifting away again. When light came into their window in the morning, they both knew they had to pull away from each other. Jeanne got up quickly to begin the tea. She wanted to be the first to leave the bed because she couldn't bear the thought of being left there.

Gilbert needed a lunch to carry with him on his trip, and she prepared it carefully as if with every detail she was putting the food in his mouth. She prepared a bottle of tea for him even though she knew that by the time he'd drink it, the tea would no longer be piping hot the way he liked it. "I'm going to walk with you to the train," Jeanne said. "You need an extra set of hands to carry your lunch."

While she stood on the platform, he boarded the train and settled himself into a compartment, and then opened the window and leaned out to look for her. She moved to where he was. There wasn't anything more to say. She stood there with tears streaming down her cheeks, and he, looking pale, kept repeating to her, "You are my love. You are the best thing that ever happened to me."

Jeanne could not respond, but even if she had been able to speak, she would not have wanted to say to him in this fragile moment what she was thinking. *Is this it? Are you going away now never to return? Is the dreadful thing going to happen?"* The train began to move, the way trains do. You think it's stationary, and then a moment later you realize it's moving, but you didn't see it start. Gradually Gilbert shifted out of her view, until she could see only an arm extended from the window. Then the train went around the bend, away from the village, and finally the last of him was gone.

It was several weeks before a message from Gilbert arrived, a very brief note telling her that his travel had been more difficult than he expected. In addition to telling her that his mother was still very ill, he advised her that she needn't write, nor should she be upset if she didn't hear from him. The postal services were in disarray, and he didn't want her to think the worst if she didn't receive a letter.

At night she recited their poem, like a girl reciting a bedtime prayer. At first it brought her near him, just a little. And then, as the nights passed, sometimes the poem was only a reminder of his absence. The time seemed too long. Nearly six weeks. She couldn't understand why he would choose to be away from her all that time. Jeanne thought of keeping a diary so she could tell Gilbert about all the small things that happened in his absence. But she didn't keep a diary. Why should she? What difference would it make? The time was lost. The days without him were gone.

At last, the postmaster's son appeared at the door again. It was another message. Jeanne opened it eagerly, thinking it would tell her that Gilbert was returning.

MOTHER FAILING = FATHER NOT RETURNED
= STAYING LONGER

What did this mean? What could be important enough to keep him away without explanation? If his mother had died, Jeanne would understand that Gilbert had to stay on to attend to family matters. If he had to care for his father's business, why didn't he say that, and why weren't his brothers helping? Apart from the bit of information that he was not coming home, the message gave her nothing. It occurred to her that she should find a way to go to him. It also occurred to her that perhaps he was not coming back and didn't have the heart to tell her. She stopped reciting their poem.

It was nearly time for the school term to begin. She wondered how Gilbert could stay away without giving the village notice that he would not be returning to teach. She wondered how she would support herself without his salary. A week passed, and then another. Finally, she got her answer. It was not a telegram. It was a sound at her door and his voice calling out to her, "My Treasure. Are you here?"

Gilbert said little about his trip. His mother was old and wearing down under the weight of worry. Her days were numbered. The boats on the Maas had been confiscated, and the family business was on the brink of failure. Many men from their neighborhood had been detained, and his father had disappeared. They assumed he'd been arrested, but they had not succeeded in finding out where he'd been taken. His brothers were in hiding. Gilbert was exempt from the round-up because of his limp. Gilbert's voice had grown darker, as if he had aged during the time he was away.

Jeanne wondered if she should tell Gilbert her own worries. That she often felt slightly ill. Tired. Inclined to sleep. Should she wait until she knew more certainly what was happening to her? Gilbert was stressed and weary as it was, and she didn't want to add to it. He had been so careful, and she had not cared. But why wait? "I have something to tell you," she said. "We're going to have a baby."

Gilbert's face lit up. He began to laugh, a confused mixture of surprise and nervousness. "In this time of terrible news, at last one bit of hope," he said. "What a homecoming."

Jeanne put her hand on her stomach. "I really do think it's true," she said. "I wasn't joking." She couldn't tell Gilbert the doubts she was harboring. Gilbert had been right. War is no time for a child. Jeanne wondered what would happen to this small life beginning in her. She worried about what would happen to all three of them.

Chapter 18

Gilbert watched Jeanne grow round in the middle, but pretended not to see that her wrists were thin and her fingers spindly. When they shared food at the table, he pushed some from his plate onto hers. "I'm not very hungry," he'd say, "but I'm sure the little one is. Finish this for me please; I don't want to waste it." Sometimes he took the small jug and asked the farmer down the lane if he could have some extra milk "for the baby." He gave up drinking milk in his own tea so that Jeanne could have it all, and he gave up eating an egg at breakfast so she could have two. "It was a mistake to think that having a baby during war is short-sighted," he said to Jeanne one day. "It's far-sighted. What promises more hope for the future than this little one?"

Jeanne was caught up in worry but also kept busy with work. There were few babies being born in the village now, but Jeanne and the other midwife were caring for the old and sick to fill in for the nurses who had gone to help with those who'd been wounded at the front lines. The midwives were the only ones left to help one elderly doctor.

Gilbert woke and noticed Jeanne was not in their bed. He listened for her and heard her footsteps in the other room. At the same moment he heard the first rooster crowing, and the cow in the barn across the way lowing for its calf. He went to his wife. She was pacing and massaging her tummy. "It's time for the midwife," she said, "and you should send a message for my mother to come. I'll need her."

Gilbert was relieved when Jeanne's mother, Brigitte, arrived because she knew about babies and mothers. She knew what was cause for worry and what was not. Near the front window, Gilbert sat in a chair trying to read. He passed his eyes over the words, but they didn't translate into thoughts, because his attention was elsewhere. He listened for voices from the other room and was comforted that they were calm. A few times he got up to forage for food and make tea. Toward late afternoon he went outdoors and walked back and forth several times along the street, but each time he felt pulled back to their little house. He noticed when the shadows grew long. The night seemed endless. A few times he fell into fitful sleep, but then sounds from the other room would startle him awake. Toward morning he heard the rooster crow again, and he heard the familiar sound of the cow lowing for her calf. After what seemed like an eternity, at last he heard the cries of a baby. Standing by the door he called, "Is everything right?"

Jeanne's mother replied, "It's a little boy, and everything is just as it should be. Give us a few minutes and then come in." When he entered the room, the baby was resting in Jeanne's arms, rooting a little, peering out like someone who squints when bright lights have been turned on. Gilbert told Jeanne how he had heard the rooster and the neighbor's cow calling when she left their bed. "They knew. Nature is wise. They were all cheering you on. Calling out to our little one, and now he's here."

"Oh, Gilbert, you're such a hopeless romantic," said Jeanne in a voice that had an edge with which Gilbert was not familiar. "You'll need to be more practical now. For my part, I'm done being a dreamer. It won't work any longer to be a romantic. It's too hard."

Jeanne's mother turned to Gilbert. "She means well. What she's saying is that you're a father now, and babies aren't practical. Your son won't think when he wakes up in the night that his Papa needs sleep. When you are deep in conversation, he'll interrupt you. First it will be because he doesn't know any better, and then later it will be because he thinks he knows better than you." Brigitte smiled at Gilbert in a motherly way. "It's all good, but it's not romantic."

"I'll take your word for it," said Gilbert to Jeanne's mother. "I've been a father now for ten minutes, and you've been a mother for decades and nine times over. I can't debate with you."

Jeanne noticed that Gilbert unwrapped his son, and looked him over carefully. He checked his feet, each toe, and then ran his hand along the length of each leg. He looked up at Jeanne, and then put his face down toward the baby and kissed each knee. "They're perfect," he said to Jeanne.

"Yes, they are," she replied and noticed Gilbert's pained smile.

"Time heals many things," said Gilbert. "That's true even for a baby born during war."

"I hope so," Jeanne said. "We'll both have to be more practical now, won't we? We have to give him his name." She glanced over toward Gilbert and asked, "Shall we name him as we planned?"

"Yes, of course," he replied, "We agreed on that, didn't we? We'll save the girl's name for the next time."

"Yes, but you should be the one to announce the name," Jeanne said. "Go ahead, you're the father."

Turning to his mother-in-law Gilbert smiled and said, "The little one will be named after my father. We'll call him Leo."

Jeanne's mother went to the baby. "Leo," she said as if she were confirming an announcement. And then making the sign of the cross over the little one and invoking the Trinity, she said, "Leo, child of God, may you be blessed with every good thing." It was unsentimental, but sincere. The voice was solid. No cooing. No baby-talk. This was a grandmother who had witnessed many babies coming into the world. Some came through the portal of life into happiness, and some met struggle at the beginning. Brigitte used the same words each time she blessed a newborn, and then she turned it over to a power beyond her to sort out exactly what the words meant. She was a woman who knew that we continue to wish newborns all the best, while life is still teaching us that the life these infants face is hard, as it is for everyone.

"Should we call the priest and have him baptized?" Jeanne asked. "I feel so anxious. I have a dark feeling. I thought I would feel relieved by this birth, but instead I feel as if I am in the middle because the dog first had detected a stranger and then recognized Gilbert.

Other things changed. Gilbert went to the church more often than before. Sometimes he went for Mass, but he also went at times when no Mass was being offered. She wondered if he was going to confession, and finally when she couldn't hold the question back, she asked him directly. He told her he was going to meet with the two priests so that they could read Latin together and discuss the books that they were lending him. It had never occurred to Jeanne before that Gilbert would lie to her, but she knew he was not telling her the whole truth. She could feel in his silence that it caused him pain to deceive her. She let it go.

The birth of Leo turned her worry loose. Jeanne feared that she could not keep her baby safe. What if Gilbert were doing something for which he could be arrested? What if soldiers came to their house looking for Gilbert, and Jeanne could not protect herself and her baby? Sometimes Jeanne felt relieved to see Gilbert leave the house and go to school in the morning, as if by leaving he was also removing the danger that he brought into their house. But he would be away only for an hour, and she would be impatient for his return. Was he safe? Would he come home again? Who would protect Jeanne and little Leo if Gilbert didn't come back?

Jeanne didn't tell Gilbert about her worries, but when her mother came to visit, she suggested that Jeanne and little Leo return with her to Beauvais. There would be more company in the household there, and she would have help caring for Leo. Jeanne was relieved, and Gilbert was relieved too.

Jeanne's departure was not dramatic. There were no tears. No lingering embrace and repeated kisses for the baby. It was a sober goodbye. In the weeks that followed, Gilbert came to visit when he could. Once he rode along with the mail truck, and once he rode with the mortician. The visits in Beauvais were short, and often they were spent with the rest of the family around the table.

On Easter when Gilbert came to visit, he told Jeanne that he would have to travel to Maastricht again to tend to his mother. She was still very ill. Jeanne looked him in the eye. "Really," she said, "and again no letters or calls?"

"Better not," he replied and glanced away. "I'll be out a great deal arranging what she needs. There won't be much use trying to call. And letters?" He only shook his head. "I'll come back as soon as I can." Jeanne remembered the trip before. It made her angry that Gilbert's mother, who was continually failing, always seemed to defy death. She wondered if he had some other errand to fulfill, but she knew this was part of that other life about which she shouldn't ask.

When Gilbert returned, he came to visit Jeanne and Leo as soon as he could. His appearance had changed. He was thin and weary. His attention to Leo was dutiful, and there was something forced in his affection. "We are getting accustomed to living without each other," Jeanne said to Gilbert. "We don't know how to be together anymore. It's not good."

"It isn't good," Gilbert said. "We both know that. I'm so sorry. I want you to know that I will always love you. Distance doesn't alter that. I think of you and the little one each day and all through the day. I live for you. And then when I am with you, my mind is cluttered with all sorts of other things. I don't know what to do. You may find that hard to believe, but it's true. This war has changed how we can live our love together, and neither of us can hide that." There was agony in the slope of Gilbert's shoulders, and he was short of breath as he spoke. Jeanne looked away to give him privacy.

Chapter 19

In May of 1940, tensions ratcheted up in the village. Men went off to fight against the invading forces, and, as one of the men remaining in the village, Gilbert had to work hard to hold his head high. It was not an honor to be left behind when all the able-bodied men were defending their country. To demonstrate that he too was committed to his village and to France, Gilbert diligently limped his way to school each day, meeting with the students, and teaching them exactly as he would have if there had not been a war that had taken over the life of the village.

Carrying on as usual was Gilbert's way of serving. That is what he told his students when they talked to him about the war. They talked about their fathers and brothers who were fighting. They talked about towns nearby whose food supplies were depleted. Some of the older and braver students promised that as soon as they could, they would join the resistance. Gilbert listened and continued to teach.

Two priests who served the church at the far end of the village square had not gone off to war either. Amongst themselves, the villagers referred to them, behind their backs, as the old priest and the young priest. When addressing them to their faces, they still called the priests "Father." Many locals were taking on the new habit of not using names when addressing each other. When they met in a shop or on the street, they nodded in recognition or said "Good morning." What in other times would have been bad manners was now understood as necessary for anonymity. This shift in habits kept the village alert to the difference between insiders and outsiders. Some of the outsiders were those who wore uniforms and drove jeeps, and other outsiders were visitors who wore plain clothes and wandered through the towns observing.

On one particular afternoon a car roared into the village along the main road and stopped in the middle of the street, not in front of the church, but next to it in front of the square stone house where the priests lived. The woman who later told the story recounted that it happened on a Saturday. She watched and listened from an apartment on an upper floor where the window was slightly ajar. It was a warm day, and she was sitting behind the curtain in a place from which she could watch the street below.

The old priest and the young priest were at home, and the teacher was not at school with his students. Earlier he had played chess outdoors with some of his students, but now he was reading Latin with the priests. Gilbert went to read Latin more often now that his wife had gone to live with her parents in Beauvais.

Two men in uniforms got out of the vehicle and walked to the door of the building. One of them pounded loudly with the knocker on the wooden door, then paced a bit until the woman who cooked for the priests came to answer. They spoke to her briefly and then pushed their way in. A few minutes later they came out. The old priest was being pushed forward by a young soldier who had a gun in one hand and the other hand against the old priest's back. The young priest was cuffed and being prodded forward by the butt of a gun nudging his back. Limping along behind was Gilbert.

The three men were led across the street and told to line up against the wall. The sun was shining in their eyes, and they squinted. It was hot where they stood. The old priest had sweat streaming off his head. He brushed it out of his eyes with his sleeve. The young priest was sweating too, but he could do nothing about the sweat dripping into his eyes, because his hands were manacled behind him. Gilbert stood motionless with his hands folded in front of him, like a boy waiting at the communion rail. The German officer in charge told a young soldier to stay with the detainees, while the officer himself found a comfortable place to stand in the shade of a tree so he could smoke a cigarette.

Another officer arrived shortly with a young man whom the woman in the window recognized. He was a fellow who from time to time passed through the village selling woolen goods to the local shops. He was not in uniform. In German the officer instructed the young man to inform the schoolmaster and the two priests that information was needed from them. The young man repeated what the officer said, and his French was good. He didn't sound like a German speaking French. The woman, listening through her window, guessed he was Alsatian. Perhaps he'd been picked up and forced into service by the Germans who needed an interpreter.

A man in uniform began with the old priest, asking him questions about people and places. He seemed especially concerned with radios and weapons. To each question the priest answered, "I have nothing to tell you."

The officer repeated his questions several times, adding harsher threats each time. In the exchanges, as he answered, the priest was putting in little bits of advice to the young interpreter. "I forgive you for your questions, tell him I have nothing to say." Or "fear not my son, may God be with you; you are not guilty for the questions you are asking, but tell him that I have no names of people and places for him." Or "may God almighty give us all the courage we need; I have already told him I have no names or places."

It was obvious that the old priest was coaching the interpreter. Fearing how the German officers would react, the interpreter left out much of the priestly advice as he relayed the answers to the officers. Meanwhile the German officer was getting impatient. He ordered the priest to his knees. The old priest stumbled a bit as he put a foot forward. "Help him," the officer ordered the interpreter, and he did.

"Thank you, my son, and may God have mercy on us all," the priest said to the young interpreter.

"What did he say?" the German officer asked when the interpreter delayed.

"He thanked me for helping him," the interpreter said.

"Translate it all," said the captain. "I don't need you to choose what I do or do not need to know."

"I'm sorry, sir," said the interpreter.

On his knees the old priest began reciting the *Pater Noster*. The interpreter did not translate. He turned toward the German officer and said, with a nod to what was obvious, "*das Vaterunser.*"

The officer made a gesture of brushing the comment aside to indicate that he did not need the interpreter to recite the Lord's Prayer to him. It made the officer angry that the priest had the nerve to ignore him and carry on a conversation with someone he judged to be more important.

"We'll see if God helps you," said the German officer. Abruptly with one step forward he drew his pistol and shot the old priest in the top of his head. The sound echoed in the village square. The words stopped, the body slumped forward, twitched a few times, and the old priest was gone. It was so abrupt and unexpected that everyone gasped, including the interpreter and a young German soldier standing nearby. They watched as blood pooled and soaked into the dirt.

The young priest had been watching, and, when the old priest began to pray, the young priest had whispered along with him. Maybe it was a habit formed by the many times they had celebrated Mass together, or maybe it was an effort at solidarity and comfort. Who really knows what gestures that look like courage truly mean in these circumstances? In any case, when the old priest fell silent, the young priest continued.

"Shut up," the German officer said.

The interpreter translated it. "The officer says he wants you to stop praying," he said, as if by assigning the uncouth words to the man in the uniform and softening the message he delivered to the priest, the interpreter could detach himself from the words that came to his ear and a moment later came out of his mouth.

"You see what happens to those who don't cooperate?" said the officer. "Just some information. Just some names. It's not much to ask. Why do you resist? It's stupid of you, because you know what will happen. Look around you. You're not in charge. I am. Are you going to cooperate?" The officer asked it as a question, and the interpreter translated it that way. And then the officer began all over again, asking the same questions. Names. Locations of safe houses. Drop-off points for weapons. Questions about radios.

The officer paused and walked a few paces in each direction, to the left and to the right. Then he came back and stood directly in front of the young priest. "It's hot standing in the sun. You'd be more comfortable in the shade." He smiled an oily smile at the young priest. "Move him!" he said to the soldier standing by him. "Let him stand in the shade of the tree, and give him water!" The officer's tone of voice was almost civil.

The soldier who'd been ordered to offer water looked puzzled. "Yes, of course, from your own canteen. Give it to him," the officer instructed the soldier. "He's thirsty. He needs water." The soldier opened his canteen and held it to the lips of the young priest.

"Thank you," the young priest said. "May God reward you for your mercy."

"What did he say," the officer asked.

"He thanked the soldier for giving him water," the interpreter said.

"Yes, that should help," said the officer, "but you should be thanking me." He looked directly at the young priest and waited until the priest made eye contact with him. "I'm giving the orders here. I don't want to harm you, but don't test me. You won't win. Just give me the answers. Okay. Let's try again."

The young priest stood in silence for a moment, and then without waiting for the officer to begin the questioning, the young priest began again to pray the *Pater Noster*.

"Oh, no . . . no . . . no! Not this again," the officer shouted. "I've had enough of this foolishness. Don't be stupid. You know this won't help us get this work done. Old ladies mumble prayers when all hope is lost. It's a last-ditch effort of fools. You should know better. You're young. You could still have a long life, but of course only if you cooperate." He turned then to his assistant and said something quickly. The only word that was clear was "*Seil*."

Perhaps the young priest thought the officer was showing some concern for him. Maybe he was remembering a bit of German he'd learned at school. "*Seele?*" he said softly as if whispering to himself.

"No, I'm not asking about your soul. I'm asking about your compatriots. Leave the translating to the interpreter." He nodded to the soldier who had gone to the jeep and come back with a rope. "Over the tree," he said to the soldier. "Let the French kid hold the other end," the officer said tipping his head in the direction of the interpreter. When the rope fell down from the other side of the large branch, the officer said to the soldier, "Yes, that's good. Now put the other end around the priest's neck."

The soldier was clumsy and struggled to tie the knot. The young priest was sweating and trembling. The soldier was trying to look efficient, but the harder he tried, the less successful he was. When at last the noose was around the priest's neck, it rested above his collar like a second collar. His neck was thin, and the rope moved slightly when he swallowed. The interpreter stood with one end of the rope in his hand and looked at the other end that was looped around the priest's neck. He looked nearly as frightened as the young priest. There was nothing to translate in the silence, but the meaning of what was happening was obvious.

When the noose was in place, the officer said to the soldier, "Take the other end now and tighten it, just a little. Show him we mean business, but not so tight that he can't talk. We're done with this silly schoolboy misunderstanding. I'm going to ask you one more time. This is your last chance. Either you cooperate or soon you will be swinging by your neck. It's an ugly way to die, especially for no good reason. You will twitch like a little bunny caught in a snare. You will shit yourself, and your eyes will bug out. You may think you are being a hero now, but once the noose tightens, all your dignity will be gone." The officer stepped directly in front of the young priest. "Are you ready?"

"I'm ready to meet my maker," said the young priest, and the interpreter repeated it.

"That's not what I asked. You have some other work to finish first." It seems the confidence of the young priest angered the officer. "Maybe this would help," the officer said. He drew his pistol from his side and put it in the priest's ear. Then in an afterthought he stepped back and looked around very deliberately as if he were searching for something. He picked up a small twig that had fallen from the tree. Slowly he turned it in his hand as if he were measuring its size. He looked back and forth first at the priest and then at the twig. There was arrogance in his slow-motion movements.

"Ah, yes," the officer said. "Of course, you don't hear me clearly. You must have something in your ear. We can clean it out." He walked over to the young priest. Walked around him and looked him over carefully. Then stopped beside him and stared at him. He reached up, put the small stick in the priest's ear, drove it in deep, and twisted it.

The young priest winced. His whole body reacted. He exhaled in a deep throaty cry of pain. "Oh, God have mercy," he said. The twig remained in place sticking from his ear. He shook his head, but the twig didn't fall out.

"A little tighter," the officer said to the soldier holding the rope. "Help him get the point. Not too tight, though. We're nearly done, but not quite." The officer lit a cigarette. He approached his victim and held out the cigarette. "This will hurt," he said, "almost anywhere I touch you with it there will be pain. But some spots more than others. We can find them." The officer let his eyes drop down and then up again in a vertical line along the priest's body. He moved up close and looked carefully at the priest's face. "The eyes are the worst," he said.

The young priest closed his eyes. His lips were moving, but there was no sound.

"Open your eyes," the officer snarled.

The young priest didn't open his eyes, but his lips continued to move. He didn't see it when the officer's rage broke loose, when he reached for his pistol and fired it into the young priest's temple. His body slumped, but he did not fall because the soldier was holding the other end of the rope, holding it with all his might against the dead weight on the other end.

"Drop it," the officer sneered at the young soldier. "We're done with him. What do you think you're doing? Holding the rope until he's raised from the dead?"

"Now you," the officer said with a sour look as he turned toward Gilbert. "What's wrong with your leg?"

"I injured it when I was a boy," he said.

"Lucky you," said the officer. "Good excuse. You don't have to fight. You can stay at home with these village cowards. You know what they say behind your backs, don't you?"

The interpreter translated without expression, and the young teacher said nothing.

"I asked you a question," said the officer. "You know what they say, don't you?"

"No," said the teacher.

"They call you cowards. That's what they have to say about you. Do you have a wife?" asked the officer.

"Yes."

"Have you made children?"

"Yes."

"Would it clear your mind so you can remember names and places if I brought your wife and children here? It's not much I'm asking. Why be stubborn? Why would you sacrifice your wife and children for something so trivial? A name or two. A place or two. If I don't get them from you, I'll get them from someone else. Spare your family. Take a minute. Think about it." The officer took a deep breath and let it out. He stared at the ground as if he were taking a little rest from unnecessary exertion.

Gilbert's eyes dropped. His breath was heavy. He looked to the right where the two priests were lying. He shuddered. His eyes moved across the buildings that lined the village square, as if he were searching for something. Searching desperately. Waiting for help to appear, or searching for something that wasn't there. And then it burst forth, as if he couldn't hold his breath anymore. "It's no use," he said. "I'm just a teacher. What would I know? You're right what they say about us. We don't amount to much."

That's when they took him away. The next morning the teacher's body was in the cemetery of the churchyard. Both his legs had been broken, and there were cigarette burns on his body. It had been a hard night. Maybe he didn't have much to tell. Maybe he was only reading Latin with the priests, and the only secrets he had to tell were the same ones that were barely secrets and known by everyone in the village. Maybe he told them that the pharmacist still had some medicines despite the fact that he'd been ordered to turn them all in. Perhaps he told them that the priests still had a telephone line with which they made contact with brother priests in the south. These were the same secrets they could have gouged out of anyone who'd been walking the streets, going to market, attending Mass all those weeks when the people of the village were doing what they could to survive.

"It's possible," said the woman who had watched from the second-floor apartment at the north end of the town square, "it's possible that he told them nothing at all. Gilbert was a good man. Everyone trusted him. Who knows why they were so brutal to him?"

The old priest, the young priest, and Gilbert were buried next to the church as soon as it could be arranged to send a priest to celebrate the funeral Mass. Dressed in black and hidden behind a widow's veil, Jeanne stood between her mother and her father, each with a hand on her arm. Later she remarked that it was as if she had not been there.

Some neighbors attended because they were devout and others attended because it was their civic duty. The church was full, and it was somber. No one arrived early to gather village news, and they did not linger on the steps after the Mass so they could catch up with their neighbors. They came quietly and left quietly. The priest who came for the burials stayed at the square stone house next to the church, and after the funeral he remained. The village was his new assignment, and he did his best to pick up where his brother priests, the old priest and the young priest, had left off. Soon in the village he was known as "the new priest."

Father Jerome was transferred from the south, from as far away as one could get from this new assignment. His dialect was not a good match to the dialect of the citizens he had been sent to comfort. He didn't sound at all like they sounded when they met each other in the street, or at the market, or when they gathered around for a celebration of the few things left to celebrate. On those occasions the new priest would attend, because he knew he should, but he wouldn't stay long, because he knew he shouldn't. He was an outsider. He knew they wouldn't trust him until he'd proved himself. He could not step into the shoes of the old priest and the young priest, who there in the center of the village under the tree across from the church had shown they could stand up to the test of loyalty.

The people of the village got used to having neighbors come and go. Some left to go to other places that seemed safer; others left to be with their families in the anxious circumstances of war. The milling of people from village to village and through the countryside continued. Farmers planted again. Messages were delivered to spread the news about where old neighbors had resettled, but by no stretch of the imagination could it be said that life was normal.

The villagers were surprised when Jeanne appeared again at the market. "I'm coming back," she told her neighbors. "I'm not going to let the enemy have the last word. I'm not going to forget that Gilbert considered this village his home to the very end."

Living in the little house that she'd shared with Gilbert, the place where Leo was born, forced Jeanne to accept Gilbert's absence. He wasn't away caring for his mother, or away at school teaching his students. He wouldn't be coming home for dinner. He was gone. To bring life into the emptiness Jeanne worked long hours. Most weeks Leo remained with her family in Beauvais where she visited him on the weekend if she could. Only rarely could he be brought to visit her, and when he was, she took him to the cemetery and together they stood beside the grave. "This is where we brought your father when his work was done. He was a good man. Now he is keeping other good men company in heaven," she told the little boy. She didn't know herself what these words meant. They were the kind of words people often used to honor the dead. It was the best Jeanne could weave together to remind her son that, though an orphan, he was the orphan of a hero.

Chapter 20

ONE EVENING AS JEANNE sat by the table in the front room of her house to have tea with bread and cheese, her view out the window revealed a man coming along the street. She didn't recognize him and was surprised when he turned in at her house and knocked on her door.

The visitor introduced himself as Guillaume Barone. His speech was hurried, and he rattled out a cluster of apologies: for the late hour, for coming unannounced, because he was a stranger, and because it was the supper hour. She noticed immediately from his speech that he was a foreigner.

"Why are you here? What do you want?" Jeanne asked.

After a long pause, he said: "I'm here to make an apology, and I have a message for you." He sounded like a nervous schoolboy reciting lines from memory. What followed was his halting account of a dreadful day when he was peddling woolen goods in the area and was forced by the occupation officers to be their interpreter. He had been there with Gilbert on his last tormented day.

Guillaume tried to explain that it was not his choice to be there during an execution. He was as much a hostage as the other men who were marched into the village square. His crime was that he spoke both French and German, and this made him what the German soldiers needed for their interrogation of the men they'd arrested. He was not recruited; he was coerced.

Guillaume was a traveling salesman who sold wool socks and woolen underwear both on the German side of the occupation border and in France. "Socks and underwear aren't political," he explained. "When winter comes, the cold is no respecter of persons." Guillaume had been stopped by the military at a checkpoint along the road, and when the soldiers identified him as someone from Alsace who spoke both French and German, they brought him to their headquarters. While he was waiting, terrified of what they intended for him, he heard an officer say, "These bastards who can speak out of both sides of their mouths are an asset now. If you find them, pick them up and bring them in. We can use them."

Still standing at the front door, Jeanne listened quietly, neither welcoming Guillaume into her house nor sending him away. She wondered why he had come to tell her all these things, most of which she already knew from the accounts given by villagers who had been present to see the horror of that day. As he spoke, however, Jeanne realized Guillaume was there with good intentions, and those intentions became clear when he told her that he had promised Gilbert to be a witness to his resistance. Guillaume had promised to bring back the truth: Gilbert never broke or betrayed his neighbors.

"I'm here to keep that promise," Guillaume told Jeanne.

"Come in then," Jeanne said and led him to her table, offering him her chair while she took the one in which Gilbert used to sit for their small meals. "Tell me more," she said.

On the day he was detained, Guillaume had no idea why. They took him first to their headquarters and then in a jeep to the square where he saw the old priest, the young priest, and the schoolmaster standing near the big tree across from the priory. Guillaume was given no explanation of his role other than the order to interpret. "That was just the beginning of the terror," he said.

As Guillaume spoke, he buried his face in his hands. Jeanne could hear him, but she couldn't see his expression. He was making a confession in a husky voice just above a whisper. Repeatedly he asserted that he was forced to speak words that were not his. He glanced up briefly now and then to see if Jeanne understood. He wanted her to believe that his words that day were the officer's, the priests', and finally also Gilbert's words, but they were not his own. As Guillaume told the story, he grasped for reassurance. "Am I guilty? Did I do something wrong?"

Guillaume told about the interrogation that lasted all night. As he recounted the worst of it, he stopped and wept into his own hands, and then when he gained enough composure to go on, he filled in more details for Jeanne. He told of the misery on Gilbert's face. "It looked like the crucifix at the altar in your church here. Such agony. The thought of it fills me with guilt. I don't even know for what I should ask to be forgiven," Guillaume said, "but I know I'm guilty of something. I can feel the weight of it. His suffering haunts me at night, and my own guilt is in my thoughts every day. Am I guilty for even being near such a horror? Am I guilty because I never could have done what he did?" Guillaume began sobbing again, and tears were spilling onto his shirt. When he looked up, he realized that tears were streaming down Jeanne's face too, but her tears were silent.

At last Guillaume said "Your husband asked me to bring you a message. Twice in the night the officer and soldiers went outside to smoke. I stayed with Gilbert, and he said to me, 'Tell them you saw it all! Tell my wife I didn't betray her!' I will never forget the look in his eyes as he gazed at me. He saw through me and beyond me. I never in my life have seen eyes like that."

"His eyes were deep blue." Jeanne said. "He could say so much with them. But you wouldn't know that. You didn't know him. You were only his interpreter. Why would he trust you? Why should I trust you?" Jeanne put her head down to the table and let out a cry of agony. It was loud, and it was angry. It frightened Guillaume. He thought for a moment of leaving. He had fulfilled his promise and was not prepared to take on a new terror.

"I had no choice. Can't you see that? They were holding the gun on me too. For all I knew they would begin to interrogate me next. They would think I wasn't cooperating, that I was part of the resistance."

"Did you know the priests?"

"No, I had never met them."

"Did you know Gilbert?"

"No, not him either."

"Why were you there, then?" Jeanne asked.

"I don't know how to answer that question. Bad luck, I guess, although that doesn't seem to be a proper answer." Guillaume sighed a deep, painful sigh. "May I have a glass with water. My mouth is very dry."

Jeanne went to get him water. She got water for herself too. They drank it in silence. "Why are you here?" she asked. She knew he had already told her, but she wasn't satisfied with his answer.

"I promised him," Guillaume replied. "I promised to tell how he suffered and that he never gave in. They broke his bones, and burned him, but he didn't turn on you or his neighbors. As he got weak toward morning he could barely speak. Once more he whispered 'Tell her!' And, I said, 'I will. I promise.' I'm here now with you to keep that promise." Guillaume's hands trembled as he spoke. "I don't know how he bore it. They must have injured his insides when they beat and kicked him because he grew pale. He gasped. No words. Just a terrible sound, and then his head fell back as if he were falling asleep. And he didn't speak anymore. He didn't open his eyes again either."

Guillaume explained that he felt guilty for surviving. "When they turned me loose, they instructed me that I should tell no one what I'd seen or done. But why would I repeat what I'd witnessed? Why would I want anyone to know that I was part of it? I had no desire to tell anyone." His own terror wasn't finished when the officers turned him loose. He'd told them that he had brothers serving with the German forces so they wouldn't be suspicious of him. He had allowed them to think he was on their side. In the days that followed, Guillaume was haunted by the faces of the three good men whose murders he had witnessed. He felt he had betrayed them by what he had said about his brothers. That is in part why he promised himself and God that if he survived, he would go back to the village to tell their neighbors that those men had remained loyal. "Telling you what I witnessed is my act of penance. Can you forgive me?"

"What could you have done?" Jeanne asked.

"If only I'd refused to interpret. If only they'd shot me first."

"I wouldn't have known what to do either," Jeanne said. "If I'd been there, I would have screamed, or thrown myself on the ground, or begged for mercy. I could have thrown myself at them so that they'd kill me too. Would that have made any difference? Besides I wasn't there." Guillaume began to weep again as she spoke. Jeanne leaned forward and said, "We must stop this. You've done your penance. Gilbert would forgive you. I suppose I must forgive you now too. Does that help?"

Jeanne was a nurse, used to calling on her inner strength to comfort the wounded. "Can I serve you some wine," Jeanne asked. "Would you like some bread?"

"I'll accept tea," Guillaume said, "but I have already had my food for the evening."

He sat with her at the table sipping his tea while she ate her bread. She wanted to tell Guillaume who Gilbert was. She wanted him to know that at first their life was good, but then it had changed when the shadows of war came over them. She couldn't bring the words together. She said nothing.

Having done his penance, and having made peace with Jeanne, the salesman of woolen goods came to Jeanne's door again a few more times. Once he brought wool socks and a pullover for little Leo. Another time he brought a package of sugar for Jeanne to thank her for her hospitality, because she'd offered him tea when he'd visited. He was careful to explain that he was in town to do business with merchants to whom he sold woolen goods. He didn't want Jeanne to think he was coming specifically to visit her. And he was careful to speak schoolboy French and not his own foreign-sounding dialect.

Once when Jeanne came home, she found a note from Guillaume under her door. He had stopped to see her, and not finding her home, he suggested that he might stop again the following week, when he would come back through her village on his way home. She didn't admit to herself that she looked forward to seeing him. She allowed herself to think that it would be discourteous to let him come twice to a closed door.

When Guillaume stopped, it was late, and instead of coming to her front door, he came to the back door of her house and tapped lightly. When she opened the door, he greeted her much more warmly than she expected. She served him a glass of wine and shared her evening bread with him. He lingered. Finally, she asked him where he'd be staying for the night, suggesting that he should be on his way if he had any distance to travel. He admitted that he hadn't arranged a place for himself and would find somewhere on one of the country roads. "It won't be the first time I've slept in a hayloft," he said with a laugh.

"Stay here with me then," Jeanne said. "But you will have to leave early in the morning and go from my back door, through the field, and to the back road."

"You're a widow, and I'm a single man. What objection could there be?"

"I know you mean well," she said, "but you speak German and haven't proved yourself. You're from the city. You don't understand the ways of a village."

"I'm French," he said. "How can you accuse me of being German?"

"I'm not accusing you," she said. "It's my neighbors who will accuse you. After you leave to go on your way, I still have to live with them."

Guillaume didn't give up. He stopped occasionally at her door, staying outside while he spoke with her, making it appear that he was dropping off some item from his inventory, although he was actually there to ask if he could visit. If she agreed, he returned later in the night or in the early hours of the morning, coming from the back road through the lane that went along the edge of the field, and then to her back door, which she left unlatched. There were no lights left on for him, but he knew he was welcome, and he moved silently through the dark house and crawled in beside her in a bed that was already warm for him.

A few hours later, Guillaume moved again through the dark house and out the back door, from which he disappeared through the field and to the road that led away from the village. Left alone there in her bed, Jeanne wondered how she could allow a stranger into the bed she had shared with Gilbert. How different those nights with Gilbert were from these brief encounters, ushered in goods. This was Axel Barone's introduction to the family business and also his introduction to Deborah Blum.

Axel was a hard-working teen, but also a young man with curiosity and imagination. Tucked away in the family's attic he had found an old concertina, and by trial and error he had learned to play it. The chords and melodies that came naturally to him were those of local folk music. He had a clear, steady tenor voice and learned to sing the songs he listened to at regional celebrations and festivals. Gradually his own reputation as a folksinger grew.

This ear for song served Axel well the day he went to the Blum workshop to bring a bolt of wool. As he waited along the front wall of the building for a clerk to write a message for him to carry back to his father's shop, Axel heard music. It was the clear voice of a girl singing a lieder, accompanied by a piano. Axel was spell-bound, unable to tear himself away until he had heard the piece to its end. The voice, he was to learn, was that of Deborah Blum, who was not only a singer but also the pianist. She didn't know she had an audience beneath the window, but Axel was determined to meet her. From then on, he was the first to volunteer for messages or deliveries in the afternoon, when he knew Deborah would be practicing in the salon of the family's quarters above the workplace.

Long before Axel ever saw Deborah's face, he knew her voice. In fact, he knew it so well he could hear it in his imagination. As he walked through the streets on his daily errands, he would whistle the tune of the song he had heard her sing. On one occasion, a man carrying a violin case paused to look at the whistler. "Schubert?" he asked. "No," Axel replied "Barone," because he thought the man had mistaken him for someone he knew.

Not knowing the source of Deborah's music or the names of the composers, Axel did his best to recreate the songs for himself by working them out on his concertina. His picture of Deborah began to fill in more completely, however, the day he saw an announcement for a recital by Deborah Blum to be offered in one of the meeting rooms of the Synagogue du Quai Kléber. On the program was music by Schubert.

The day could not come soon enough. Axel took a bath, washed his hair, and borrowed his brother's best suit and boots.

Part Four : Guillaume Barone and Jeanne de Roose

Quietly finding a place for himself in the recital room, he waited, wondering who would appear. Later when he recalled the moment that the curtain at the side of the stage parted and a young woman walked out, he claimed that what he saw was exactly what he had imagined all along. He knew her from her music, and she was for him the incarnation of beauty.

There was an obstacle built into Axel's fascination with Deborah. He was Catholic, and she was Jewish. In Strasbourg, which was a cosmopolitan city with more tolerance than the countryside, there were a few mixed marriages, but Axel knew it would not be approved of in his family. Nevertheless, he persisted. He began with brief conversations at the market where he would greet Deborah and compliment her for her music. She was impressed that he knew by name the works she performed. He'd begun doing his homework.

After that initial step, Axel was bold enough to pass notes to Deborah, and eventually he stepped up his efforts and handed her small gifts. She didn't discourage Axel's efforts, and sometimes, when she heard his voice in the shop below her family's quarters, she wandered down to chat with him while he waited for a package or a message.

Axel told his oldest brother about Deborah. He wasn't amused and warned Axel, "It's fine to dream, but keep your feet on the ground. Don't start believing your own love songs. You must see that the prospects are not bright even though you are convinced that she is perfect and beautiful. Do you really want to get tangled in that briar bush?"

There was another place where Axel revealed his growing infatuation. He admitted it in confession. The priest he chose was considered progressive, and he reminded Axel that Jews can convert. It was not necessary for them to revoke their former faith. Jesus was a Jew; so were Peter, Paul, and the other apostles. All that was necessary for becoming Catholic was to learn the rituals of the church and undergo the sacrament of baptism.

The case made by the priest was fortified by the examples of well-known citizens who had converted. Doing so opened doors for them to civic positions, and they were good citizens. Axel asked if it would be acceptable for him to convert to Judaism. The answer was quite different. "No. That can't be done. You can't go back in time. That conversion would require revoking your own faith, and that is a mortal sin." With this response Axel realized that he had reached the limit of his trusted confessor's open mind.

Neither the warning of his brother nor the advice of the priest stopped Axel. He became bolder in finding ways to meet Deborah. She also became bolder in cooperating with him, making sure he knew when she would be at the market or strolling in the park with her cousin. Axel did not begin by presenting the problems; he began by sharing their delight in music. He brought his concertina and sang a song for her. He also showed her pictures of art and wrote poetry for her.

Only after their attachment became obvious on both sides did the love-struck couple admit the encumbrance of their families' religions. There was very little of the rebel in Deborah. She dreaded being a disappointment to her family, but she also could not bear to turn her back on Axel.

When Axel and Deborah declared their intentions to their families, it was a crisis with many layers. Their families shared important business interests, and neither side wanted to lose a major customer if a rift created bad feelings. Deborah's music had opened doors for her participation in community performances, and her talent gave her family status as assimilated Strasbourgeoisie. They didn't want to do anything to counter that.

Axel's family appeared most open-minded on the surface. They were ready to accept Deborah with only one condition. She had to convert. If after that she wanted to have social contact with her family and observe some of the family's holidays, that was not a matter of concern. If she wished to make dietary adaptations in her own household, there was no objection to that. They went so far as to suggest that it would be permissible for her to have future sons circumcised; the twelve apostles all had been. The one non-negotiable was that she had to be baptized.

Deborah's family was in the position of those who have too much to lose by holding their own ground. The Jewish population in Alsace-Lorraine had been moving to the cities and becoming increasingly assimilated in business, the arts, and education. "Getting along" with their neighbors was important. Business interests and social standing were important to Deborah's family, but nothing was more important to her father than avoiding any risk of creating a deep and permanent separation from his daughter. He loved her dearly. Finally, he was the one who broke the stalemate. "I cannot stand in your way," he said. "You have my permission to make your own choice, but do not leave us. Remember your father and your mother."

One does not know what went on behind the walls of each home: bitter words spoken, tears shed, and rancorous negotiations. One cannot know either the fears that Axel and Deborah carried with them. Certainly, all the risks and disadvantages had been paraded before them while they struggled with their decision. They must have known that they were putting themselves outside the safe boundaries of the usual, but once the decision was made, at least on the surface it was a relief. They were seen together at musical performances, the theater, poetry readings, and other cultural events. They appeared happy.

Axel and Deborah were married in a wedding Mass at a church located on a familiar street near the Blum's home; it was also the parish church in which Deborah was baptized. Her family celebrated the marriage at a ceremony of their own, to which were invited the members of her extended family, a few dozen friends, and the members of Axel's immediate family. It was held under a blue sky and a wedding canopy, and seven blessings were spoken by close friends of the family.

The fifth child of Axel Barone and Deborah Blum was christened Guillaume Jakob, the name he shed when he became an American and chose to become Willard Barone instead. His early childhood was happy enough in the circle of the family. He knew his father's extended family well because he moved in and out of their business quarters almost daily, greeting his uncles and his father's long-term employees. He was familiar too with his mother's family, accompanying her on frequent visits to her sisters and going along with her when she joined her family for holidays, for musical events, and to celebrate family milestones such as a bris, bar mitzvah, wedding or burial. It amused Deborah's family how well young Guillaume spoke Yiddish. He lived comfortably in his two worlds. They were separate but not conflicted.

Nevertheless, Guillaume was growing up in a time of significant social transition. At the end of World War I, Germany lost control of Alsace, and it was returned to France. In Strasbourg, local centers of power shifted, and the population adjusted their loyalties in many areas of life. One of the pillars of social stability that helped the Barone family adapt was the Catholic Church, which was influential enough to garner liberties for itself and its members, despite regime change.

There was economic depression and unemployment in some areas, but the Barone family was less impacted by this than most, because the basics they produced continued to be needed. "Every man needs socks in his shoes and a good suit of underwear to keep him warm," Axel reassured his workers. "Our business is not political." Furthermore, the Barone family's sympathies with France had been nurtured even during a time of German control because the Catholic church operated on both sides of the border with little apparent conflict.

Following World War, I the Barone family had trimmed back their business to adjust to the weak economy; a significant portion of their business had continued to be supplying merchandise to clothing shops in French towns. Young Guillaume dreamed of being a designer of fashionable men's clothing, but the downturn in the economy made it impossible for him to go to Paris or Milan to pursue that dream. Instead, he spent his teen years working in his father's business, waiting for the economy to improve. He was single and friendly, and in addition he was handsome. A natural salesman, he traveled to nearby towns to sell woolen goods to the owners of small shops.

When Germany began to assemble its plan to reclaim what it had lost in the Great War, Alsace-Lorraine was prime territory. As Germany began to make incursions at the beginning of World War II, the sales circuit through which Guillaume travelled was on the path of the military campaign. He was cautious not to arouse suspicion among his customers. It would not improve sales if they thought he was secretly working for the wrong side, although there was no right side, because every village and town had divided loyalties.

Guillaume was young and of fighting age, and the fact that he was not serving in the military raised questions. He was quick to explain that he was excused from service because he was a necessary employee in an essential business. Soldiers needed socks and suits of underwear, and the Barone family business in woolen goods supplied them.

Although their business was compatible with war, Axel's own family was enormously stressed by it. Beginning in 1939, Jews living in Alsace were being ordered to leave, and large numbers of them relocated to the south of France. With the capitulation of France and the control of the northern territories by Germany in 1940, Strasbourg came under the control of the German military. Property of Jews who had remained in Strasbourg was confiscated, and the inhabitants fled south to locations from which they hoped to find a way out of France and into countries safer for them. In a wild rampage, the synagogue in Strasbourg was burned to the ground by Hitler Youth, and almost overnight this monumental building that had stood as a testimony to permanence became instead a glaring reminder of impending threat. The hard-earned security of the Jewish community was shattered.

Many of Deborah Blum's relatives left with the first large migration, but in the second her remaining two sisters also left. They and their families went to Paris where, because they were less well-known, they thought they could be anonymous while waiting for documents for their passage to Geneva. Both families were crowded into a small apartment in a rundown building on the outskirts of the city. Guillaume's mother was terrorized. She was sure it was only a matter of time before the same groups that had destroyed the synagogue and driven out her family would come for her.

Ever the devoted husband, Axel tried to assure Deborah that her marriage and conversion made her safe. She was Catholic. This did not reassure Deborah, however, because word had come as far as Strasbourg about the Jewish converts to Catholicism who had been rounded up by the German occupation forces in the Netherlands. They were sent to a detention camp in Poland and were not heard from again.

Axel could not believe this would happen to his family. They were known by their neighbors as good citizens. He had been living in Strasbourg for generations. Their standing could not be so fragile. Furthermore, Axel didn't want to leave behind all the work he'd done to build a successful business, and he could not relocate it without great loss. While carrying on as normally as possible with their life in Strasbourg, Axel committed himself to helping Deborah's family in hiding.

It took money to live in Paris, and even though the family had resources, those resources were in jeopardy. Funds had to be assembled carefully so as not to draw attention, and it had to be moved carefully because there were restrictions on taking funds out of the country. Axel and Deborah took responsibility for gathering funds; Guillaume's special role was carrying the funds to his relatives in Paris. He had good reasons for travel as he called on customers on his sales circuit, and were he stopped and subjected to inspection he would explain that the funds he carried was payment collected from customers he had visited.

While all this was happening to Deborah's sisters, Axel's own family in Strasbourg was in disarray. One of Guillaume's brothers had done what his father had done; he had married a Jewish woman who converted before their marriage. Under German military rule investigations were being done of Jewish men and women in mixed marriages. It was no longer obvious that being Catholic and having an Alsatian name kept them safe. At last convinced that for the safety of his family it was necessary to find a way to Switzerland, Guillaume's brother left for Paris where he awaited the documents that would allow him to leave France.

Guillaume's sister was afraid for a different reason. She had married a man who suffered intermittently from depression. During one of his most severe episodes, he had been hospitalized in a clinic for several months. Word was spreading that the program to create a pure German race included clearing it of "mental incompetents." Already several people from their community had been detained and sent for evaluation. Following the lead of her older brother, Guillaume's sister and her husband also left for Paris.

Before Germany annexed Alsace, Guillaume's family, like so many other families, thought of itself as French Alsatian. After the annexation of Alsace to Germany, they had to decide if they were willing to be German. Guillaume's two brothers, just older than he and also single, had little choice. They were conscripted into the German army, and along with many other French *Malgré-nous* were forced to serve against their will. The brother sent to serve in the occupied territories of Belgium caused them shame, but not worry. The more difficult predicament was the deployment of Guillaume's other brother to the eastern front. Within months of his departure, he was reported missing.

The family clung to the hope that their son and brother had walked off the job and found a way out of German-controlled territory. Under the conditions of occupation, even among close friends and the immediate family, those hopes were harbored but not spoken. Desertion was a death sentence, and those who defended deserters were traitors. As days and weeks passed, the family's fear shifted; the numbers of soldiers being lost on the eastern front was mounting. What if their son and brother had not escaped, but had died in combat? Day by day they waited in dread for the notice that he had made the ultimate sacrifice for the Reich and the German people.

While all this was going on, Axel plodded along with his business in woolen goods, and Guillaume continued to ply the circuit of small towns in order to market the company's products. The business was adequate to support Axel's own household, but the size of the extended family depending on it had grown, and it was necessary for Guillaume to expand his sales trips to bring in additional income.

It was on one of these trips that Guillaume was picked up by the German occupying forces and made to serve as interpreter at the execution of Gilbert and the two village priests. One would think he would never go anywhere near those towns again, but he had little choice. He had established customers, and he had goods he needed to sell. The family needed money, and his last stop on the circuit was Paris, where he delivered money to his relatives. His mother's sisters lived together in one crowded apartment. His brother and family lived in another, and his sister and her husband lived in a single rented room. Each small enclave waited desperately for Guillaume's delivery of funds, often having little food on hand until he would arrive again. On one such trip Guillaume delivered the money that had been raised by selling off the grand piano Deborah's family had given her as a wedding gift. On another he delivered what had been gotten through the sale of the household silver.

Guillaume's stops to see Jeanne were the only points of relief on his trips. As they became more familiar, she asked him about his travel, his work, and his business. He avoided giving straight answers, and she tolerated his evasiveness because it was wartime. Once she realized that she and Guillaume were permanently connected by a child, however, she became more insistent. She pressured Guillaume to stay overnight and spend a full day with her before traveling on. Fearing an ultimatum, Guillaume agreed. As tentative as he was about making a commitment, he did not want to lose Jeanne completely.

When Guillaume left Jeanne after their brief visit, he continued on to Paris. At his aunts' apartment, he discovered it was vacated. The suitcases were gone and much of their clothing. A woman, noticing him lingering in the doorway, asked what he wanted. He replied that he was trying to deliver a package of woolen goods that had been ordered. She advised him to sell his goods to someone else because his customers had been taken away, and they wouldn't be coming back.

"Where have they gone?" Guillaume asked.

"It depends whether they're Jews or rebels," the woman said matter-of-factly. "Wherever they've gone, they won't be returning. People who are taken away in trucks don't come back."

At the apartment of his brother, Guillaume found the rest of the family in turmoil. Someone had already come to tell them that Deborah's sisters and their families had been rounded up and taken to a central location where Jews were being processed. Knowing the pressure would be on them soon too, his brother's family was packed and ready, waiting for Guillaume to deliver the money they needed for their trip over the Alps. "You should have been here four days ago," his brother complained. "If you'd come on time, your aunts and their families could have left the city. Soon they'll be boarding the trains to . . . who knows where?"

Guillaume could see his brother's anger, and he understood his brother's angst about the plight of his aunts, but he couldn't muster the courage to admit that he'd been delayed because he'd lingered with the woman who was about to give birth to his child. "I'm sorry," he said. "Travel has become hard. There are obstacles and delays."

Instead of going back to Strasbourg, Guillaume returned to Jeanne. Through a long night, he revealed to her who he was, about his family, and his guilt about arriving late in Paris.

"Why didn't you tell me sooner?" she asked. "I would have understood and been kinder to you."

"What good would it have done to tell you. It would have put you in danger. Information comes with a risk. It's better not to know. Besides, I'm doomed. Nothing ever turns out right for me. And nothing ever turns out right for anyone who counts on me."

"What will you do now?"

"Return to Strasbourg. Talk to my father. See if there is a way to pick up the pieces. My father is a clever man, but I don't know if he can find his way out of this predicament. When I was a boy, I thought there was nothing my father couldn't do. Not a problem he couldn't solve. Little did I know. I don't know how much more of this I can bear."

"Can I let you know when the baby comes?" Jeanne asked.

"It's not a good idea."

"Wouldn't it at least be one small thing about which you could be happy?"

"Or another thing about which to worry?"

"That's not fair," said Jeanne. "This child is your child too."

"I suppose I owe it to you to know when you have the child. It's fair that you want that. I don't know that I will be able to do much for you or if I will be able to come. When the child arrives, send an inquiry to our shop to ask if we keep a stock in baby clothing. That will be my sign, and I'll see what's possible." Guillaume's voice had turned cold.

Their parting was painful. Jeanne wondered if she would ever see Guillaume again. He seemed broken, distracted, directionless. She heard nothing from him and sent no messages to him until she sent the inquiry about baby clothes. And then she waited.

When Guillaume returned to Strasbourg and told his father what had happened to the relatives in Paris, his father instructed him not to share the bad news with his mother. She was already in a deep depression. She hadn't been able to make contact with her relatives, and Guillaume's apparent lack of news about them confirmed for her that something dreadful had already taken place. "You must go back and find out what happened," she insisted. "You must find a way to help them. At least find out where they are."

"There's no use, Mother. I asked as much as I dared, but no one knows what happened to them. I couldn't go to the government office without implicating myself, and I had to be careful speaking with their neighbors. You never know who will betray you. Let's hope they've moved to a different apartment, or they've already started their trip south. There's nothing to be done under these circumstances except wait and hope. I'm sure they'll be in touch with us when they are able."

"That's a fool's hope," his mother replied. "Wait for what? It can only be bad. It will only tell us that the worst we can imagine has come true."

The family's days were torn apart with worry. On the one side, Guillaume's mother was frantic for news that her sisters and their families had made it to safety. On the other side, she was frantic to hear that her sons, fighting for the Reich, were still alive.

Guillaume continued to travel, in part because it was the only way he knew to earn the money his family needed, and also because it allowed him to be away from the misery at home. Under the guise of delivering needed clothing, he made visits to Jeanne to see the baby. Their visits were hollow, and she felt relieved when he left again.

In late 1943, while Guillaume was on one of his sales trips, doing what he could to keep at least a fragment of the family business alive, his mother took her own life. Guillaume arrived home to find his disconsolate father locked in the drawing room with the drapes closed. In the hearth, broken to pieces and partially burned was his concertina. His mother's burial, according to tradition, had been attended to immediately. There was no funeral Mass.

The death of his mother brought the last of Guillaume's belief in himself tumbling down. He had failed the woman who bore his child by leaving her and being absent for the birth. He had failed his relatives in Paris by allowing himself a detour and arriving too late with the money they needed for their escape. He had failed his mother by being absent when she was most desperate. He could not bear the thought of ever again meeting his brothers who were serving with the Germans. "I have always been in the wrong place doing the wrong thing," Guillaume said to his father. "I need to go away. Somewhere I'm not known. A place where I can begin a new life."

"Go," his father said. "I have nothing to offer you, and there is no reason to stay. Go far away and begin again, if you think you can. As for me, my life is over."

Guillaume's travels took on a new purpose. He sold whatever he could to gather funds for himself. He used his connections and didn't limit himself to woolens. In farm villages he bought produce and resold it in the city. In the city he bought sugar and coffee and sold it in rural villages. Not all of his business was legal because food supplies were rationed, but he was beyond caring about that. The moment the war was over Guillaume planned to leave. He would go as far away as he could; he would go to America where no one would know him. An ocean would separate him from his guilt and anger. An ocean would separate him from his shame and loss. He stopped less often to see Jeanne. On his last visit, he told her he would not appear at her door again.

Chapter 22

Jeanne told the priest she was expecting a baby, and after the birth she confessed to the priest who the father was. She didn't reveal that Guillaume still came to her door for random visits under the cover of night. The last time Guillaume came to see her, he told her he would be leaving soon. She knew he intended to resettle in the United States, but she was shocked that he wasn't planning to take her with him. He was the one who had been making the choice to come back to see her. It wasn't often, but he did return from time to time.

Guillaume made flimsy excuses about the fact that Jeanne had her work and her children tying her to France. The truth is, he was desperate to leave the ghosts of war behind, and she was one of those ghosts. "I need to do it alone," he said. "I can't take care of others. I've failed at that already. My list of failures is so long; I don't want to add you to it."

Jeanne was a war widow who brought flowers to the cemetery, and she also had lost the best of her life on a wretched day in the village square, but Guillaume seemed not able to comprehend this in a way that created sympathy for her. He was so overwhelmed by his own trauma that he couldn't allow himself to see hers.

The stubborn intention with which Guillaume looked forward and never looked back frightened Jeanne. Would she become one more element of his forgotten past? Did he think that when he brought Gilbert's message and defended the dead man's honor, he had fulfilled his penance and could be done with her?

As Guillaume stood at the door to leave for the last time, Jeanne uttered the words that changed her future. She begged him to take her with him to America. Moving against him and clinging to him, she pleaded with him not to desert her. She gripped him with a desperation that made him wonder if she would leave bruises on his back.

Guillaume was not a man who acted on impulse, nor was he one with a flexible imagination. He had already made up his mind, but when he looked at Jeanne, the expectation on her face as she gazed up at him, and the frantic hopefulness of her body against him, he couldn't deny her. Or perhaps it was himself he couldn't deny, because Guillaume did care what others thought of him. "Let me go first," he said, "and if it works out, I'll write to you. Perhaps you can come then with the child, but it will have to wait until I have a place ready for you."

Jeanne didn't doubt Guillaume's good intentions, but she also didn't share his plan with her neighbors. She heard them mention with regret that the merchant, who peddled the best woolen goods, no longer visited their village, and she heard others explain that he had gone to Canada. "They speak French there, you know," one neighbor was quick to add. She did tell her mother and her father what Guillaume had promised. "These things will work themselves out in time," her mother said. "We'll wait and see."

The baby boy, born to the schoolmaster's widow, was given the name Philippe Guillaume de Roose when he was christened in the small village church near Beauvais. Gilbert de Roose was dead, his body had moldered into the ground, his wounds turned to dust, but the memory of him had not faded. He was still a hero. Jeanne de Roose had not remarried, and she was still thought of as the schoolmaster's widow when her neighbors met her in the street and respectfully greeted her as Madame de Roose. Little Philippe, named after Jeanne's father and known in the village as the son of the schoolmaster's widow, carried the honor of two good men. Only later, when his name was changed to Ross Barone, would he be stripped of those honors.

In the village the mystery of the little boy's birth was inextricably linked to concerns about *who* the father might be. There was a shortage of men in the village, as is often the case after war, and hand in glove with this shortage was an atmosphere of possessiveness on the part of women with regard to their own men.

Many in the village noticed accommodating men who, when delivering milk, or eggs, or vegetables at the back doors of widow's homes, stayed longer than necessary. There was speculation about men who did home repairs, or painting, or helped with gardening, especially if they were seen going into a widow's house without ringing the bell or knocking at the door. These rumors were not unique to the schoolmaster's widow, but the birth of Philippe, a child of unclaimed paternity, turned special attention on her. Village women with husbands and teen-age sons wondered if it was a man from their family who had made this baby.

The speculations were especially troubling to other widows who had no husbands but did have lovers. Theirs was a complicated breed of possessiveness. They knew they had no choice but to share a lover with a wife, but it was quite another thing to share a lover with an attractive younger woman who'd had a baby. These women seldom admitted their churning insecurities, but that didn't stop them from gossiping about the schoolmaster's widow.

The village priest soothed the women one at a time, but not in the way one might think. There were priests in some villages who, under the pressures of the shortage of men after war, rationalized a special generosity toward lonely women. This priest was different. One by one he heard the women's fears, and one by one, he told them they had no cause to suspect their own husbands. His assurances were a balm that soothed the worry spreading through the village, a worry triggered by Philippe's birth. The priest knew who the father was, and his assurances to the women of the village were not counterfeit, but to Jeanne herself he suggested she not disclose the identity of the child's father. "Hold the information close," he said; "that will be kinder to your son."

After receiving reassurances from the priest, the women of the village admitted to their husbands that they had confessed their worries and were happy to report that the priest had exonerated them. Not only were the men relieved to know they were no longer under suspicion, but they were thankful to the priest when they noticed their grateful wives were warmer in bed. The birth of Philippe started a ripple effect that went far beyond the little house on the last street at the edge of the village.

The son of the schoolmaster's widow--they still referred to him that way--began to toddle, then talk, then walk beside his mother when she went to market, and he was always beside her in the pew at Mass. The villagers commented about what a well-behaved child he was, and then checked to see if they could identify whose ears he had, and whose nose, whose bright eyes, and whose gait.

The citizens of the village gradually settled on their own conclusion. Their speculations moved from many possibilities, to a few possibilities, and finally settled squarely on the priest. It became a fact. That is why, they surmised, he had been so gracious in not condemning the schoolmaster's widow, and that is why he'd been so confident in assuring the distressed women who came to him that their own men were not the father.

The priest knew about the gossip, and he knew he was not the father. But he was a wise man who also knew that if he could serve his parishioners by bearing the sins of a father in this way, and if he could bring peace of mind back to a village where war had done so much damage, then he was willing to bear the guilt. He had some sleepless nights about it, but went to confession himself, seeking to be absolved of a sin he hadn't committed with the schoolmaster's widow and also the sins he had committed by mercifully deceiving his parishioners.

Faithfully the priest tended to his role. That is what he felt called to do, and he succeeded except for one minor slip. A drunk wandering home from the cafe sidled up to the priest on the street late one evening and whispered that he was not attending Mass anymore because he had figured out that the schoolmaster's widow had become the priest's whore. The priest, tested to his limit, answered back, "You lazy bastard, you've slept your way through Mass for years, only stirring enough to come forward and take the host of which you are unworthy. Not having you there committing sacrilege is a relief." The priest felt guilty for the flash of anger that had eclipsed his pastoral duty to invite the man to confession and after that to return to Mass. The priest admitted his misstep to his own confessor, who, along with absolving him, also assured him that it's good for a priest to be reminded now and again that he is like everyone else.

By bearing the sins of his parishioners, the priest gave the citizens of the village reason to trust him. They stopped noticing that sometimes he still had a strange twist in his speech and a dialect that was not theirs. They came to trust him the way every village wants to trust its familiar, local priest. For reasons right or wrong, the people of the village knew their priest was human, just like all the rest of them.

Life went on for the schoolmaster's widow, but it wasn't easy. Her neighbors kept their eyes on her. She wasn't as chatty as the other women were with the baker and the vegetable vendor. She knew better. She noticed how the wives of the shop owners came out to serve her, even if their husbands were in the front of the shop and could have served her themselves. The wives working in the back put down their work, dried their hands in their aprons, and came out through the curtain that divided the front of the store from the back. They greeted the schoolmaster's widow as if they were surprised to see her, as if they had not heard the alarm bell of her familiar voice from where they were busy working in the back room.

The people of the village were not morally heavy in their judgments of the schoolmaster's widow. Long ago they had swept enough of their own sins under their own carpets. They'd say, "leave judgment to God," while in their own minds they were remembering that during war there are no clean hands and totally pure hearts. They were ready to move on, to get back into the stream of life, and that meant forgiving the past and protecting what was their own.

Though they left the moral judgment to God, the people of the town didn't forget that the schoolmaster's widow was loose, which was another way of saying that she was young, pretty, and alone.

They could not blame her for being a widow, and they did not reject her child. That did not mean they could trust her.

When women were not present, men would say in a half whisper and behind the shield of a cigarette held close to the mouth, "It's a shame to waste a woman like that. Some man should step up and do the honors." The men of the village were as deft at gossip as the women were. They knew better than to say outright that they imagined the satisfaction of helping this woman. They were discreet, but not so discreet as to hide the insinuations of their manliness. They knew how to leave just a hint of bravado, that they too could have been, even if they weren't, the one to fulfill the mission.

All this confusion swirling around the schoolmaster's wife created both envy and admiration for the priest among the men in his parish. They became more forthcoming at confession, where behind the curtain and across the grid they could admit their secret thoughts. One might call their admissions "guilt," but it was only a particular category of guilt, the sort they thought the priest could certainly understand; after all, he was a man too.

The men still didn't admit to the priest that sometimes they shorted their customers on the scales at the market or filled their own baskets with apples and pears in a gesture to "clean up" under the trees of their neighbor's orchards. They doubted that this would interest the priest. But the other guilt, the one about which they were both slightly burdened and slightly proud, this guilt they confessed. A little dalliance with the young girl who came to help in the household. A small tryst with the cheesemaker's daughter who came to market each week. They noticed how young girls admired silk stockings and colorful scarves, and they were sure girls who worked hard should have a little pleasure in life. They fulfilled their obligation to serve the needs of their neighbors with gifts and pleasure, and if they had any uncertainty about the virtue of what they had done, they confessed it to the priest.

And so it went. After the war things improved in general. Life went back to normal. Whatever that is. But it did not improve for the schoolmaster's widow. Around her there continued to be a chill. She was considered "thin ice."

"I can't do this anymore," Jeanne said one day, as she knelt in the confessional. "It is so unbearably lonely. I see their looks; I feel the chill. There is no way to make my life right. I am caught in a chaos from which I can't escape. I feel condemned forever to the sisterhood of those other 'sisters' who meet men down by the river and give them quick pleasure in exchange for a few coins. But I'm not that. You know that, don't you?" she asked the priest. "I've said this all to you before. I know. But do *you* at least believe me? Do you know I'm not the village whore?"

"I do believe you, and what you observe in them is right," said the priest. "It's not fair. It's unkind. In truth, it's downright foolish. Marriage has not kept all the men at home in their own beds, but that seems easier to overlook. I don't know what to say to you, except it is what it is. You are a good woman, and you deserve better." He paused then. "Do you have anything else to confess?"

"Not today," she said. "I'll leave the rest for another time."

"Yes, of course. That's better," he said.

The schoolmaster's wife rose from her knees preparing to leave the confessional, and then she heard his voice. "One moment," he said as he moved out of the confessional and gestured toward a pew. "Perhaps a new start in a new place would give you a chance at the life you deserve. I never met your husband, but a hero who is admired so long must have been a very good man. You were a good wife. Your children are gifts. You should not waste any more of your life fighting wars that will never end here."

"Thank you," she said.

"May the peace of God go with you," the priest said, as he made the sign of the cross.

When Jeanne first told the priest that she and Guillaume had a plan, he didn't warn her that sometimes men go off to start a new life and don't come back to finish the old one. She was relieved that the priest didn't hint at this, because she didn't want to question Guillaume's loyalty, although now and then there was doubt that crossed her mind. She told herself over and over, *if I'm not bound by wedding vows, then I'm bound by hope.*

PART FOUR : GUILLAUME BARONE AND JEANNE DE ROOSE

It was long after Guillaume departed that the first letter came. It was not a love letter, and it did not come to her. It came to the priest. The return address on the outside of the letter was Mr. Willard Barone and Company, Chicago, Illinois. When the priest opened the letter, he found inside a brief note explaining that this letter was from Guillaume who had changed his name to Willard. He asked the priest to forward a message to Jeanne, and folded inside the first envelope was another letter that the priest handed over to Jeanne the next Sunday after Mass.

Except for the appearance of privacy in a letter whose pages were taped closed, there was nothing private in the letter except Willard's request that they carry on their correspondence through the priest. After that first letter they used aerogramme forms to reduce the cost of postage. Jeanne received her letters unopened from the priest, and she brought her responses back to him without address or her return address. By the time the aerogramme was sent from the village post and by the time it arrived in Willard's mailbox, it was from Father Jerome and a rectory in France to Mr. Willard Barone, Purveyor of Fine Woolens, Chicago, Illinois. Jeanne understood. She understood that Guillaume did not want her to know where he was. He did not want her to come to him.

At last, a different letter arrived. It informed Jeanne of the date of her passage and the address of the booking agent from whom she should retrieve her tickets in La Havre. The letter also contained instructions regarding documents she would need when entering the United States. Jeanne wondered why the passage was booked only for her and for Philippe. There was no mention of Leo. She considered what her options might be and went to Beauvais to ask her parents if they would give her funds to buy Leo's passage. They did not deny her request outright, but they begged her to leave Leo with them. Leo had been living with them since he was an infant; he was a member of their household, and he was happy. Why take the boy across the ocean, to a land where he did not understand the language, and into the household of a man who had shown no interest in him?

Jeanne went again to see the priest. He advised her to do what she knew was best for her children, and Jeanne realized that leaving Leo with her parents was the right thing to do. The priest ended their meeting with a blessing for those who travel, for those who prepare for marriage, for those whose fathers are returning from war, and for orphans. "Remember," he said "the church will always be your port in a storm." She found comfort in his words, and she found comfort in being sent off by someone who had always believed in her.

There was time on the voyage to sit on the deck chairs and stare at the sea. There was time to dream in her stateroom while the motors hummed and the waves tapped out the distance along the side of the ship. Jeanne thought of the life she was leaving behind. She cried for Leo, and tried to find comfort by imagining him at the table with her family in Beauvais. She knew he would be loved there. She also remembered with tenderness the day he was born and Gilbert's love for him.

It occurred to Jeanne that Gilbert's spirit was grafted onto this second son with whom she was venturing out into a new life. Although he wasn't Gilbert's son, little Philippe's character had that same quality of solid goodness. She knew Gilbert would approve of him. She thought too of the gossip, the comments made with a grin, suggesting their village priest was no different than all those other priests who want it both ways. They wanted to be Fathers in the parish and fathers in the village. The worth of her little boy was shored up by the honor of this man who kept his priestly vows and did not bend under that gossip. And she thought about Guillaume, who sent tickets to bring Jeanne and a child he barely knew across this immense ocean. She smiled then, to think of a child with three fathers.

Part Five

Stepping Into the River Twice

Chapter 23

Rowland was thinking about the stories Jenna had gleaned from her visits with Aunt Lillian and the long phone calls during which Jenna recounted for him tales about their family and its tangled past. Wandering through his mind was the idea that his own father had three fathers; that's the way Aunt Lillian said their Gramma Jeanne described Ross. Rowland wondered what his father had known about these phantom fathers?

Through the eyes of his mother, Ross was a little boy who'd gathered in the good from wherever he could find it. He'd survived much that wasn't good and still grew up to be a man his mother admired. That's not what Ross looked like through the eyes of a son. From Rowland's point of view, Ross was solid and predictable, never given to impulse or rudeness, and clear about his rules; but when it came to the affection for which Rowland longed, gestures of approval for an insecure boy, Ross had not delivered.

Rowland knew his mother loved him. It wasn't a perfect love from either side, but it was love beyond a doubt. Did his father love him? This was the question that danced like a phantom in Rowland's self-doubts. His father had always fulfilled his paternal duties; the children never lacked for food, clothing, and shelter. But did his dad like him? Did his heart warm to Rowland the way Rowland's heart did when he thought about his own children?

Was it too much to expect a dad to adore his sons the way a mother does? In moments of self-doubt, Rowland accused himself of sentimentality. Maybe kids don't need mushy dads if fathers provide something entirely different than mothers do in shaping their around, saw Rowland and headed over. "Good spot," he said. "Man, it's noisy over there on the other side."

They ordered their burgers. Same burgers as always. Same beers. When Cohen's burger arrived, he opened the bun and removed the lettuce and onion. Then he glanced over at Rowland's burger and said, "Hey buddy, you've got to cut out the cheese on your burgers. It's bad cheese, and even good cheese is bad. But that stuff? It's cooked up in a factory. Who knows if it's ever been anywhere near a cow?"

"Have we had this conversation before?" Rowland asked.

"Déjà vu all over again?" Cohen laughed.

"Something like that," Rowland said. "But anyway, about the cheese: I don't take the lettuce and onion off the burger. I eat them. They're vegetables. It makes up for the cheese."

"Here we go again." Cohen smirked. "Have we talked about this before too? You think virtue cancels vice?"

"How's your mom?" Rowland asked. "By the way, that's an intentional non sequitur."

"About the same, except steadily getting sleepier," Cohen said. "Her doctors think she's had some small strokes. I've been trying to visit her in the morning just before her lunch. When I get there, she brightens up, but within a few minutes she relaxes and starts to drift off. She catches herself and says, 'I just don't know why I'm so sleepy. Sorry, Sammy, it's not that I don't enjoy your visits. Come back tomorrow. I'll try to do better.' I go back the next day, and it's the same thing all over again."

"They're like babies," Rowland said. "They sleep too whenever they feel like it. They flutter their little lids and start to doze off, and we think it's darling. So why not your mom? Let her sleep if she wants to."

Cohen nodded. "You're right. Soon enough she'll be asleep with my father, with all the fathers, I suppose. For now, it's little catnaps before that big sleep."

"Interesting metaphor," said Rowland. "Have you been reading in your dad's old books again?" He laughed.

"Can you tell?" Cohen laughed with him.

They paused to eat. Rowland wiped his chin just in case he'd left some burger drippings on it. He took a long sip of water and cleared his throat. "Remember once we talked about the burdens fathers leave for their children? You said that the mistakes of the fathers can be carried on for generations. You thought the blunders children lay on their parents stick around for only a generation or so at the most."

"Maybe I did say that, if you say so. The sins of youth . . . something like that. But . . . your point is . . . ?" Cohen was waiting; he was not gearing up to offer an answer. He was quieter than usual.

I'm thinking about my family," Rowland said. "My sister Jenna has been having long conversations with our Aunt Lillian. Once you start pulling the knots apart, it's hard to separate your own threads from everyone else's."

"What are you finding out?"

I'm having regrets. Not about my dad. I haven't gotten to him yet, and I don't know if I'll ever get to my grandfather. If anything, I think the regrets should be on their side. But I do have regrets of my own, and they have something to do with bad habits I picked up in my family."

"Such as?"

Rowland knew he could bail now or go on with this conversation. He exhaled long and slow. "Regrets about my brother Steven."

"Your little brother who died?"

"After my folks put him through rehab a couple of times, I was so angry. He'd get out and go right back to buying from his old buddies on the street. Rehab was costly, and what my parents put into it was a waste. I told them not to throw any more money at Steven's problems. I told them to stop trying to give him a second chance. I was ready to give up on him, but I never thought he'd end up dead. In jail maybe, but not dead. I don't know where I thought he'd end up. That one day he'd decide to give up the drugs and lousy company? Get clean? Come home in a victory parade and pick up the good life where he'd left off at age fourteen?"

"You didn't think he'd die," said Cohen. "You thought it was one of those endless aggravations."

"I also didn't think I was part of his problem."

"Were you?"

"My worst regrets go back to a time I came home from college and was holding forth about the fact that everything is relative. Steven was there with my sisters. We were having breakfast together, and I was debating with Laura. She wasn't buying my views."

"Rowland," said Laura, "you're in the wrong department. You're taking courses with all the smart guys who can't make up their minds. You should take some science. No, better yet, take accounting. If you get it wrong in accounting, the numbers tell the truth."

"Zing," said Cohen.

"Laura was smart; she's still smart. But that day I couldn't let it go. I was hell bent on making my point. I told Laura she was dogmatic. Put down a fact and immediately you'll have dissenters, I told her. But put down a good story, and well, there's not much anyone can say except that it's a story. The cool thing is, if it's a good story, it's about something. But as soon as you start taking it apart, one person's view of it is as good as the next."

"That's what you thought then, or that's what you think now?" Cohen asked.

"Then and now. I waver."

"I'm surprised you feel guilty about thinking that way in college. One day we played the realist, the next day we played the skeptic. We tried views on for size, but whenever possible we beat the drums for relativism so we wouldn't have to defend our own answers. It was the view that made us feel smart, and it was such a shrewd attack on our parents. We could tread on what they held sacred, and we could feel progressive doing it. At least we know better now."

"Steven was there with us when I was arguing with my sister," Rowland said. "He was listening. Not saying anything. Suddenly he stood up. Abruptly. There was a glass of orange juice, still half full, on the table. He swept it off onto the floor, and it broke on the tile."

"True or false?" said Steven. "There is or isn't broken glass on the floor? You pointy-headed idiot, Rowland, you don't know shit from Shinola. Welcome to the real world!"

"Steven left the house. He probably was going to hang out with his buddies who knew the difference between shit and Shinola. I know I'm not responsible for Steven using," Rowland said, "but maybe he needed a fix after hanging out with me."

"We both know that it took more than one conversation at breakfast to make Steven use," said Cohen. "But what's your point?"

"After Steven walked away from the table, Jenna wanted to go to him and say she was sorry, but Laura and I told her there was no use. 'He's such an idiot. Just let him go,' I said. Those are the words that stick in my mind." Sweat broke out on Rowland's upper lip. Cohen could see he was witnessing a man in a spasm of remorse, and he didn't interrupt.

"I can remember Steven when he wore pajamas with feet in them and had hair that stuck up in every direction in the morning. I took him places on my bike. It had a long hotdog seat. I sat forward, and Steven sat behind with his arms wrapped tight around me, holding on for dear life. Steven was quirky, but he admired the hell out of me." Rowland looked pained. Cohen listened. "I never let him know he mattered to me. I just let him think I was barely putting up with him." Rowland ran his fingers through his hair, rubbing his head as if he were searching for a familiar bump on his scalp. "I laughed at him that morning at breakfast. I could have gone after him. He probably would have walked away. Why wouldn't he, if he thought I didn't care about him. He'd figured out that what I cared about more was the heady stuff I could use to show people I was the smartest guy in the room."

"That's a lot of pain packed into one story," said Cohen.

Rowland looked at him intently. "Why was I so heartless? Do all brothers do that?"

"Yes. We all do that. Different stories, maybe, but none of us reaches adulthood without planting our regrets. The harvest comes later." Cohen didn't look away. He didn't distract Rowland by fiddling with the remainder of his French fries, or taking a swallow of beer, or even shifting in his seat. "I gather you think I was mistaken about how long the burden of past sins carries on through the generations?" Cohen said at last. "Maybe it's not about how long the burdens last; it's about how different they are. The sins of the fathers are bad judgment; they should know better. The sins of the children are bad timing. When we're young, we take risks because we assume we have time to set things straight. It doesn't occur to us that we may miss our chance."

"What do you mean?" Rowland asked.

"It's too late for you with Steven. I understand that because I've got regrets of my own. We don't like admitting our regrets when it's too late to do anything about them. We're men. We're fixers. We want to repair what's broken, but if what's broken is beyond repair . . . we can't stand that. Our timing is off."

Rowland was still looking down at the table, listening intently to Cohen's voice. His head bobbed up and down slowly in a thoughtful show of agreement. Their voices were soft in the cloister of a booth off in the corner of a noisy sports bar.

"My regrets are from college days too," said Cohen. "Today is the anniversary of my father's death. What we call *Yahrzeit*. When I visited my mother yesterday, I asked her if she wished me to bring the candle."

"Oh no," she said. "Sammy, it's not a year already, is it? We should wait."

"My mother's memory is fading. Her clock and calendar are all tangled up, but my memory isn't fading. My calendar is full of regret."

"You remember the anniversary of your dad's death?" Rowland asked. "I don't do that for my dad. I don't even remember his birthday most years."

"The anniversary takes me back to the day when I was standing at my dad's graveside. My sister was there with my mom. Rachel was there too. And a good dozen of my father's friends were there. The Kaddish was being recited, and I was trying to pay attention so I'd say the responses in the right spot, but I couldn't keep my mind on it. My thoughts kept wandering away to a beach in the Bahamas, where less than a year before I was standing with bare feet at the edge of the water, in my swim trunks and wearing a stupid T-shirt, on which fake tuxedo lapels and buttons had been printed. It had a flimsy bowtie attached at the neck. It was wedding attire."

"Was this a bad trip? Did you smoke some bad stuff?" Rowland asked.

"If only," said Cohen. "The Passover before my dad died, I was at a wedding in the Bahamas. Dad had called me and asked if he could buy tickets to fly us home for the holiday. I made excuses about Rachel spending the holiday with her own family, and then I dropped the news that I was going to the Bahamas with my buddy who was having a wedding on the beach."

"Standing in the sand? That you call a wedding?" my dad said. "And for a wedding on a beach you would miss Passover?"

"I insisted that my buddy was a good friend, and I couldn't say 'no.' My father knew it was nonsense. 'A friend your family doesn't know is such a good friend?' he said. 'If you come to your senses and change your mind, the offer stands. It would make your mother happy.' With that last comment he showed his hand."

Rowland was puzzled, but this was not a moment for questions.

"I didn't change my mind. I went to the beach, but eight months later my dad was dead, and I was standing at his graveside." Cohen swallowed hard. "At the grave I kept thinking of that wedding at the beach, my choice to go on vacation instead of home for Passover. Every year since I remember that. An anniversary for my regret. My buddy, whose wedding I couldn't miss, has divorced. I wouldn't travel across the street to see him now. He doesn't contact me either; so that's not a problem. But that wedding and not going home keeps showing up, and I update my bad conscience to add a few new details each year. Don't ask me why a bad conscience is so sticky."

"Hold it! Maybe I should ask you that question. Maybe that's the least a friend can do." Rowland put out his hand and bobbed his fingers a little to indicate he was expecting Cohen to put something in it. "C'mon," he said. "Hand it over. Why are you so tough on yourself?"

"There's another wrinkle to the mistakes sons make with their fathers," said Cohen. "When my dad offered to get me a ticket to come home for Passover, I didn't believe it was because he wanted to see me. I didn't think he cared that much about me. I thought he was inviting me because he wanted to make Mom happy. He that someone owes us something and they're going to short-change us. We think life in general has short-changed us. We're angry that we don't get what we deserve, and we're dismissive of those who don't meet our standards. We write them off. I've done it myself. You and I do that because we're anxious, Rowland. We worry about not knowing what's going on, and once we find out what's going on, we get even more anxious because we don't know what to do with it. We get caught in the riptides of our own emotions, and it doesn't bring out the best in us."

"I hear you," Rowland said.

"I shouldn't have spoken for Rowland," said Jenna. "Sorry, Row." Jenna looked at him and smiled her soft smile. The one that could always turn Rowland around.

Aunt Lillian made a sweeping gesture as if she were brushing something off the table. It wasn't clear if she was putting aside Jenna's apology or clearing away Rowland's offense. "There's a solution for both of you" said Aunt Lillian. "Come with me to France. Meet the people on the other side of your family. See the little house where your Gramma Jeanne lived, and stand in the square where her world got turned upside down. Put your hands against the walls and let the stones speak for your Grandpa Willard. When you return, you'll have your own version of the stories. Do it soon, though, because I'm not getting any younger; that is, if you want me to go with you."

After everyone had turned in for the night, and Rowland was alone, he called Polly to confess that he'd committed to an international trip and hadn't cleared it with her first. "Of course," she said. "Don't miss an opportunity like this. Your Aunt Lillian isn't going to live forever. But . . . Rowland . . . remember, you owe me . . . after this summer with all your family drama, you owe me a few. I'm counting on you to pitch in with the kids when it's my turn to go to Greece to do my research. And you definitely owe me when you get back from France, and I go to visit my mother. No sputtering then, okay? Meanwhile, do what you have to do."

Before putting his phone on the charger to leave it for the night, Rowland texted Cohen. "Turns out my destination isn't Chicago after all; it's France. Seems you were right. If something keeps crossing my path, it's better not to ignore it. Didn't you once warn me that three strikes and you're out when it comes to ignoring things that show up by coincidence?"

Just as he reached to turn out the light, Rowland heard the chirp from his phone telling him he had a reply from Cohen. "Go for it, Rowland. BTW I'm not the one who said you'll be out after three strikes. I think that was your dad. I wouldn't limit it to three chances. Talk to you when you get back."

Escorted by their Aunt Lillian, the first stop in Rowland and Jenna's trip to France was Beauvais, the city in which their Gramma Jeanne was born. It was the home of Leo, their Gramma Jeanne's first son, who was also the half-brother of Ross and Aunt Lillian. Since the passing of his wife, Camille, Leo was living in the old family home with his daughter Margot. She'd moved back in with him after her divorce, although she still kept a small apartment in Paris.

During a lively conversation around the table, Rowland was thinking quietly to himself. *It's a lot of family togetherness. Imagine that in my family. Everyone adapting for the sake of everyone else. No way. We'd end up with a boatload of obligations, and we'd have a shitload of resentment about the debts others hadn't repaid.*

Jenna asked Margot what it was like for her to discover that Lillian was her birth mother. "Naturally I was furious," Margot said. "I blamed Lillian for deserting me. I blamed Camille and Leo for deceiving me. As soon as I could I left home and went to Paris."

"Seems you've all gotten over it," Jenna said as she looked around the table at Leo, Margot, and Lillian.

"Camille was a good mother. Now from a distance I can see how lucky I was that she raised me, but in my twenties, I was angry," said Margot. "You know, we all need our twenties, don't we? Something to get mad about. Some reason to leave so we can launch our adventures. Somewhere to go where we think 'real life' is going on."

Margot raised an eyebrow and winked at Jenna. "If we can blame our parents for their mistakes, it gives us an excuse for our own."

"Did you ever meet your grandmother?" Jenna asked.

"You mean our grandmother? Jeanne?" Margot asked. "I met her once. She was a pleasant older woman, but I never made a strong connection. She was a spectacle in some ways. A rich American who spoke French. I didn't think of her as my grandmother. My real grandparents were the old people who lived two doors down from us. We sat together with them in their garden. We brought food from our kitchen to their table most evenings. And we were with them in this very house when they died. That's more my idea of a grandmother."

"My Gramma Jeanne was a sweetheart," said Jenna. "Too bad you didn't get to know her better."

"The person from my American family who made the strongest impression is Aunt Lillian. That's what I still call her, even after I discovered she was my birth mother. I was living in Paris, and Lillian kept showing up. My friends thought she was entertaining, and they liked practicing English with her, so I put up with Lillian. When she was speaking English, Lillian was especially bold, setting aside French manners. She'd ask my friends about their families and their lovers. Over long dinners and much wine we had tell-all marathons that lasted all night. Maybe it's easier to talk private matters to a stranger in a foreign language or with one who's had her own flub-ups," Margot said. "In any case, my friends handed over all their scandals and all the details."

Margot tossed a tentative look at Lillian and shrugged. "My friends liked Lillian more than I did. Sometimes they were nicer to her than I was. My dearest friend said to me, 'You have a good mother at home, and in Paris a fun mother who makes your life interesting. Each family is a very old tea set. Plates with cracks and cups with chips. Mine is like that and so is yours. Accept it, Margot!' Now many years later I can begin to see that she was right."

"What about your father?" Jenna asked.

"My father, Leo, is a good man," Margot responded without hesitation. "He's steady. Was good to my mother and protective of me. That other man, who got together with Aunt Lillian to conceive me, never bothered with me. I don't know much about him, and I don't care to know more than I do. He doesn't exist for me. I refer to him as 'Mr. X' and imagine him as the worst stereotype of a fickle American. This is the picture of him I hold in my mind: he's bald, heavy, and wears a shirt with big flowers. He eats pommes frites out of a paper bag and slurps big ice drinks while he drives down the street in an oversize convertible. That picture is how I punish him for deserting me. Leo is my true father."

"Aunt Lillian, haven't you told Margot about Harold?" Jenna asked. "Her Mr. X doesn't fit the picture you paint of him. You said he was handsome and charming."

"Of course, she has told me about him," said Margot. "Her story is too much like the movies. I like my story better."

Rowland looked over quickly at Aunt Lillian to see if she was offended. She was grinning, and when she saw Rowland's glance, she gave him a friendly nod. "Margot's story is good enough for now. She can revise it later. Rome wasn't rebuilt in one day."

"Aunt Lillian, how many times have you revised your own story?" Rowland asked.

"Can't count how many times. I've had lots of therapy and years to do it," said Aunt Lillian. "I don't have the final version yet."

Margot and Leo drove Jenna and Rowland to the village where Leo was born and to the small house on the edge of town where Jeanne and Gilbert began their marriage. They walked the lane between two fields along which Gilbert had passed on dark nights when he went for his secret meetings. Standing by the back road and looking across the field toward the little cottage, Jenna said, "If I let my eyes go slightly out of focus, I can place a young woman in the window of that little house. I so wish Gramma Jeanne could be here with us."

"She's been here many times," said Leo. "I've walked this lane with her. That's how I know the story. I don't remember living here with my father, because I was too young. My first memories are at home with my grandparents. I had a safe and happy childhood, although later I realized it wasn't as safe as I thought." Leo surveyed the rooflines of the village. "When I visit this house, the narrow streets, the school, the graveyard, I feel the presence of my father. He left his mark here." At the cemetery next to the church Leo led them to a stone on which was chiseled:

<blockquote>
Gilbert de Roose
Requiescat in pace
</blockquote>

They walked from the cemetery around to the front of the priory and then to the spot across the square where the two priests and Gilbert were tried by a kangaroo court. The tree on which the noose had hung was no longer there; only an uneven spot was visible where the stump was gradually wasting away. Leo pointed out a window across the square from which a woman had watched the execution. On this day the window was open and the curtains were tied back; no one was there to observe the American visitors.

It bothered Rowland that the square was neglected. Steps away from where the execution had taken place was a trash can. Sparrows were pecking at a crust of bread in the dust, and they fluttered away when a dog slinked around the side of the building and began sniffing a discarded sandwich wrapper. In the street leading from the square, a food truck playing circus music was selling French fries and satay. Two old men were sitting on a bench outside the Tabac shop across the way. Rowland asked Leo to inquire of them if they remembered the war and knew about Gilbert de Roose. With a doubtful shrug, Leo sauntered over to them. As he chatted with the other old men, he leaned on his cane.

"Wouldn't you think they'd take care of this village square?" said Rowland. "Three brave men died here; there isn't even a plaque honoring them."

"Oh, Rowland, don't be so negative," said Jenna. "Isn't it enough that we can stand here and remember Gilbert? It's been overcast all morning, and the sun just came out. Maybe Gramma Jeanne is here with us."

"Geez, Jenna, come back to earth!" Rowland spoke in a low voice so the others couldn't hear him. "Don't try to make something of this because you're feeling sentimental. Look around! You see anything here worth remembering? A garbage can? A skinny dog? A tobacco shop? Get real, Jenna!"

Leo had finished his chat with the old men sitting by the shop. He walked back toward them slowly. It was obvious he was getting tired. "They don't know anything," Leo said. "They weren't here during the war. They're from somewhere else. Much has changed."

Rowland paced back and forth a few times. He took a picture of the stump where the tree once stood in the square and the window across the way on the other side. He also took a video of a boy who kicked a soccer ball as he walked along the front of the buildings. The boy stopped at the truck and bought French fries. Whiffs of fast food drifted across the square and caught Rowland's attention. It made him think of the Breakpoint Bar, and he wondered what Cohen would make of all this.

On their way back to Beauvais, Leo asked to make one more stop. Margot turned into a long drive leading through two rows of plane trees that were trimmed to form a canopy above. Around a long bend, an old stone building came into view. Inside, they walked along a hall with high-beamed ceilings and images of saints, until at the end they entered a porch. Seated in a wheelchair was an old woman watching a bird feeder outside in the garden. Leo bent down to greet her, but he did not introduce Rowland and Jenna.

From nearby they watched as Leo rested his cane over the back of the chair and sat down. He spoke quietly, holding the hand of the old woman. After a very short visit, Leo pushed himself up from the chair, gathered his cane, and bent down to kiss the old woman on both cheeks. Slowly he walked back to where Jenna and Rowland were waiting, gesturing to them to follow. Except for the shuffle of his feet and the tap of his cane, he moved quietly.

Settled again in the car, Leo explained that this old woman was at the priory the day the priests and Gilbert were executed. She was a teenager who came in to help the housekeeper with kitchen chores. Gilbert had joined the priests for their noon meal that day; they had no idea their meal together would be their last.

was his workplace, and, as far as I know, it's his graveyard. It crosses many borders, but it's still his river, as far as I'm concerned."

Late in the evening after Aunt Lillian and Leo had grown tired, Margot stayed with them at the hotel, but Rowland and Jenna took a stroll through the town and back to the bridge to see it by night. They sat at the bar in a small café to have a glass of wine. The bartender was a young and energetic man who now and then spoke to an elderly man sitting at the end of the bar. They conversed in a language Rowland could not understand. At one point the older man went into the kitchen and came back with food for himself. "More family togetherness," said Rowland. "I'll bet that's his father or his uncle."

"How do you know?"

"Just guessing."

"Filling in the story because you wish you had more details?" Jenna asked.

"Maybe. Or just some harmless curiosity. You're not going to let me forget that I insulted Aunt Lillian for making up stories, are you?"

"Nope," she said with the gentle smile he knew so well. It was one part warning and one part mercy.

Their conversation took a light turn. Jenna began sending text messages to her children. Rowland's eyes drifted over to where there was a postcard taped on the wall. Something about it was familiar. The older man sitting nearby noticed that the postcard had caught Rowland's attention, and he gestured to the bartender as he made a remark. "My father wants you to know that's Heraclitus, a famous Greek. We're Greek you know, and my father is proud of it," the younger man said in a knowing, slightly patronizing way. Of course, thought Rowland. It was Heraclitus wringing his hands over the world. He wished Polly were there next to him to see this postcard and chat with the old man in Greek. She would get a kick out of this. Heraclitus in Maastricht. Go figure. Thinking of Polly made him homesick.

"My wife is Greek," Rowland said to the bartender and waited for him to translate it for the old man.

"You like?" the old man asked Rowland and pointed at the postcard.

"I do like it." Nodding toward the postcard, Rowland said, "He's the one who said 'you can't step into the same river twice.' A wise man." The young bartender translated what Rowland said for the older man, and the older man smiled. To himself Rowland reflected how interesting it was to find this postcard stuck on a wall in a café run by a Greek family located next to a river in Maastricht. He knew there was no use explaining what he was thinking and expecting the bartender to translate it for him. He was in over his head, so Rowland just smiled a warm smile and held the old man's gaze. To the young bartender he said, "We're checking out this area because one of my distant relatives lived here during World War II. We think he died on the bridge."

The bartender nodded. "It was a hard time. We didn't live here then. My father was still in Greece during the war. It was hard there too. Most of the old folks who remember those times have passed on now."

As they were leaving the café the old man approached Rowland and extended his hand for a handshake. "*Fiene ries*," he said. And in response to Rowland's puzzled look, the bartender explained, "He's wishing you a fine journey. It's Limburgish. You know . . . like bon voyage."

"Ah, yes. Bon voyage. Thank you," said Rowland as he noticed the warmth and slight tremor of the old man's leathery hand.

After they returned to their hotel, Jenna went inside, but Rowland lingered on the street. He considered calling Polly to tell her that Heraclitus, or at least his quote, had made it all the way to Maastricht, but then he hesitated because he knew at this time of the day Polly would be busy with the kids. He thought of Cohen and how often they spoke of remembering and forgetting the past. How slippery it is when we try to retrieve it. How sad it is when it's lost.

I didn't think much about losing a brother. He was little and not so interesting to me. I was more concerned about losing my mother."

"That separation must have been painful for a young boy," said Jenna.

"Truthfully, I was living with my grandparents most of the time, and I was happy where I was. My mother would come to see me and her parents on weekends or for holidays. When she left to go to America, it was distressing for me because everyone else seemed unhappy about it. I can't remember wishing that she would take me with her, and I can't remember missing my little brother. I only sensed there was something disturbing in the air."

"When Lillian talks to you about her mother, does it sound like your mother too?" Jenna asked Leo.

"Lillian loved and still loves our mother," Leo began. "I barely remember our mother in my young years. One day she placed a St. Christopher medal around my neck and said 'good-bye,' and many years later she came back, bringing a child for me to raise. At first, I thought it was presumptuous of her to put that responsibility on a son she had abandoned. What did I owe her? Nothing. Little did I realize what a gift that child would be. Camille and I were not able to have children of our own, and little Margot was our treasure. It's a tangled story, but I can live with it because there are elements of it for which I'm grateful. I'm grateful for Margot, and I'm grateful that when my mother finally returned, she was loving and kind. I'm grateful for my grandparents, who surrounded me with family. Over time, you see, the balance pans tipped and the good outweighed the rest."

"My papa's been trying to convince me that you can't cast your story aside because there's something in it that disappoints you," said Margot. "He's sure that if you do that, you'll be missing something."

"The better way," said Leo, "is to seek out what really happened. It must be a full story, not just a few scraps gathered from gossip. Gossip is too simple; the real story is always complex."

"Your Grandpa Willard is my Grandpa Guillaume," Margot said to Jenna. "You knew him much better than I know him. I never knew about him or that he was my grandfather until I was nearly adult. By then I had another grandfather. Elderly, worn out by life, but sweet and present every day. When I found out about Guillaume, I assumed he was of no consequence. Discovering that he was unpleasant convinced me of that even more. I put him in the category of that other American who provided some DNA for me but was never my father."

"Your American fathers don't have high ratings," said Jenna. "Sorry to be bearer of such bad news."

"That's true," said Margot. "The story isn't a good one. I have an idea, though. Come with me to Strasbourg, to the city where Guillaume was born. It's fine if you want to call him Willard; I prefer to call him by his French name. He only feels like a lost idea to me, but I think it would help me to walk the streets he walked. Maybe then he would seem like a real person. I'm not sure I will like him more, but at least he will be more than a . . . how do you say it . . . a ghost?"

When they arrived in Strasbourg, they found a hotel in the old city and ventured out for a walk along the cobbled and bricked streets of the pedestrian area. The ground level of the buildings had charming shops with inviting windows. Above the street level were dwellings. Here and there through a doorway someone emerged onto the street, and through the entryway Rowland could see the stairway to the floors above. He wondered what those apartments were like. He wondered if these were the same streets and small lanes through which Axel Barone had navigated when doing his errands as a young boy. Perhaps Grandpa Willard had passed through one of these doorways. Maybe one of his school friends lived here above a shop.

"Do you notice," Rowland asked Jenna, "that these half-timbered buildings are like the house Grandpa Willard and Grandma Jeanne bought in Evanston. These are far older, and the house they bought was set out on a large yard, but the plaster and wood designs are similar."

"You think Grandpa Willard wanted a house that reminded him of the place where he grew up?" Jenna asked. "It's certainly different from the places Gramma Jeanne lived. Maybe he was trying to recreate the home he lost."

"The style of house Grandpa Willard bought in Evanston was called 'Tudor-Revival.' I picked that up in a book about Frank Lloyd Wright. He thought it was a dishonest style of American architecture that appealed to people who were trying to prove they were of British origin. Wright designed one for somebody when he was desperate for money, but he hated that house. It made sense to me that Grandpa Willard's American-Tudor was fake. It was nothing more than a house constructed like all the other houses, but with some fancy wood decoration pasted onto the outside to make it look like something it wasn't. What was it about that house that attracted Grandpa Willard . . . I mean in Evanston? Ya gotta wonder."

"Rowland, stop!"

"What? Why?"

"Oh, I don't know. Just stop!" When he saw the tears in Jenna's eyes he knew he had gone too far.

"Okay, let's say Grandpa Willard tried to buy something that made him feel important," Rowland observed. "Maybe it reminded him of this city, and it was something that made him feel proud. Look around. This city is old, and solid, and elegant. Maybe it's even Grandpa Willard's taste. He didn't have much choice about losing the original. Let's say he replaced it with the best knock-off he could find. Does that feel better?"

"No," said Jenna as she walked away. "For heaven's sake, Rowland. Just once could you stop analyzing. Give Grandpa Willard a break. You make me tired."

Rowland caught up with her and threaded his hand through her arm. She didn't say anything. It felt old-fashioned to be walking with her, arm in arm, through an old city over cobblestone streets. "Say something," he said at last.

"Listen, then," she said. "Stop talking. Look around. It's beautiful, isn't it?" Jenna looked at Rowland to see if he was listening, and then she scanned the streetscape. "I'm sure Grandpa Willard was proud of this city. I wouldn't apologize for being from here. I can imagine being proud to call a city like this my home. Walking these streets and considering that my grandpa was from here makes me sort of proud of it, like second-hand proud of it."

"If you insist. I can grant you that," Rowland said.

"You have to grant me this too," said Jenna. "It all got ruined. He lost it all. It was taken away from him for no reason, and in the process, he felt like a failure because he couldn't do anything about it. He lost a war. I mean he lost his own personal battle. Why does it surprise you that he was bitter?"

"Okay," said Rowland. "But why did he get stuck there? Why didn't he ever move beyond it?"

"Oh, Rowland. He's not the only one who's stuck. You of all people should understand that." She looked at Rowland, but he didn't like what he saw in her face. It felt a little like pity, and he also felt judged.

"Let's not get too personal," he said. "Enough already."

They walked through the streets that were once the Jewish quarter. Using information Leo and Margot had gathered, they tried to guess where Deborah Blum's family may have lived. Nearby was the church in which Deborah Blum was baptized, and a few blocks away was the place where along the water the grandest synagogue in Europe had once stood. Rowland brought up images of the synagogue on his cell phone. They could hardly believe that something so monumental had been torn down and destroyed by a mob.

"I can feel where Guillaume's anger comes from," Margot said.

"And Deborah's despair. It begins to make sense to me," said Jenna. "I wonder what Grandpa Willard would think of us coming here to figure out his past. Would he be relieved that we finally understand him? Or would he feel we're sticking our noses into something we'll never be able to understand."

"This is hard," said Margot. "We're uncovering secrets he tried to cover up. Maybe he never wanted to look at them again, and wouldn't want us to either. You know that awful feeling when someone says to you that they feel sorry about something that happened to you, and you're thinking to yourself 'you have no idea what you're talking about. You'd only know if you'd gone through what I've gone through. And if you did go through it, you wouldn't be chatting about it.' Maybe that's what happened to Grandpa Willard, and maybe that's why he couldn't get over his anger."

Rowland stopped near a corner and leaned against a wall. Jenna could see the sadness welling up in Rowland. She walked alongside him and threaded her arm through his again. "It's so beautiful and so sad at the same time," she said.

At the end of their walk, they went to Saint Peter's and lit a candle to remember Axel Barone, who was likely christened there. They walked to the Synagogue de la Paix that was built to replace the synagogue that had been destroyed. As they stood there, Jenna put her hands against the stone wall. "It's warm," she said. "It's the sun," said Rowland.

They went to a park by the river and sat quietly for a few minutes to remember Deborah Blum. "I wonder if she walked here on a sunny day like this one and under a blue sky," Margot said. "I wonder if some of these trees were here then. Before today I've never given serious thought to the fact that I had a great grandmother named Deborah. I have no idea what she looked like. Maybe she had straight hair like mine or curly hair like yours, Jenna. Who knows?"

"We should do something for Grandpa Willard too," Jenna said.

"Not right now," said Rowland. "Let's think it over. It has to be the right thing." Rowland didn't like to admit to himself or to the others that he found these "ceremonial gestures" embarrassing. Awkward. A girlish thing to do. He'd been willing to go along with it because he didn't like to come across as uptight, but putting on a show for Grandpa Willard was too much. Even Grandpa Willard would have sneered at that. Anyway, Rowland wasn't ready.

As they were driving away from Strasbourg, Rowland asked Jenna, "When you think of Grandpa Willard, what image comes to mind? Has visiting Strasbourg changed it?"

"The clearest picture I have of Grandpa Willard is at the house in Evanston. He had his own special chair in the living room near the window. Do you remember that?" Jenna asked. "I have a photo of him sitting there. He's wearing a suit and tie. He must have been dressed up and ready to go somewhere."

"I remember that no one else ever took that chair. It definitely was his," Rowland said. "The image I carry with me is him sitting at the head of the dining room table at the cottage, and Dad sitting at the foot of the table trying to keep it all under control."

"Yeah," said Jenna. "At least now we know why."

"That doesn't change the fact that it was miserable for everybody else," Rowland said.

"It was pretty bad sometimes," said Jenna, "but then was then, and now is now. It's time to move on, Rowland."

"That's easy for you to say. You were born with a cheery disposition. That's what Mom always said about you. 'You can count on Jenna to see the bright side.' Mom was right." Rowland gave her that old look she knew so well, the little boy trying to figure out where he stood with his family. In the cluster of siblings Rowland always seemed to be left out, not knowing what his role was.

Jenna said nothing more. They rode on in silence, looking out of the windows, noticing the countryside as it streamed past them. They were relieved when Margot said, "It's time to stop for lunch. We need a break. Let's pick a place with an outdoor patio and a good view."

When they got out of the car, Jenna turned to Rowland and gave him a hug. No clinging, no desperation. Just a hug. He hoped she was telling him that she would stand with him and love him the best she could, even if he was complicated. Rowland stood very still and let Jenna remind him of his mother.

Part Six

Home

Chapter 26

TIME PASSED QUICKLY, and before they knew it, Rowland and Jenna were on their way to the airport with Aunt Lillian. The flight home was quiet; all three of them were worn out. Bringing Aunt Lillian back to her apartment was sad for Jenna, and returning home to his family was a welcome return to normal for Rowland. In response to friendly questions about their trip, they each patched together a convenient elevator speech, although each time they repeated it they could feel it was a little further from their actual experience. They discovered that tourist reports are interesting only in small doses, and hardly anyone is interested in someone else's personal review of family history.

Before Rowland and Jenna left for France, they had agreed with Laura and Will that they all would gather after the trip, so Jenna and Rowland could share what they had learned. Minneapolis was the most practical meeting place, and Polly warmly invited them to stay with her and Rowland. Laura and Jenna accepted the invitation; Will got a rental car and a hotel near the airport. He gave as his excuse the late arrival time of his flight; he didn't like the idea of inconveniencing anyone.

Jenna and Rowland tried to give a clear account of their travels, but their failure to return with photocopies of documents convinced Laura of what she had suspected all along; her siblings weren't committed to her genealogy project. "I can't believe you strolled right past city hall offices and didn't stop in to ask for copies of birth and death documents. I gave you a list. I reminded you by email. What more did I need to do? Do you just ignore me?"

As usual, Will's business traveled with him. At the table with his sisters and brother, Will took his phone out of his pocket to read and reply to text messages. Several times a phone call took him from the room for a long conversation. Rowland and Jenna didn't say anything about these interruptions. They understood Will had a big project in the works, and his projects were always his highest priority. They also noticed he wasn't very interested in their travels.

When Rowland and Jenna got out pictures from their trip, Will's interest rallied briefly. Like any serious photographer, he recommended that they Photoshop some of their pictures. He also advised downloading them to an online album so family members could view them at their convenience. Laura's comments were more critical. "You guys take pictures of buildings, roads, and bridges. You've got a picture of some place where there used to be a tree, and then you tell us the tree isn't there anymore. Go figure. What bothers me most is all the attention to Gilbert. He's not even a member of our family."

Rowland and Jenna tried to explain that they had been guests and their schedules had depended on the generosity of their hosts. It wouldn't have felt right to spend precious hours collecting documents. "Well, that takes care of that then," said Laura. "I get it. You're leaving all the work to me. I should have known it would turn out this way." She began gathering up her things from the table. Her phone. Her papers. Her pen. She picked up her coffee cup and brought it to the kitchen sink and rinsed it out.

Will watched Laura leave the room. "That's one big ego," Will said under his breath. "When she's done with what interests her, the meeting's over."

"Take it easy, guys," said Jenna.

"Yeah," said Will. "Let's not have trouble."

Will looked up and saw that Jenna was tearful. He smiled. "Hey, we don't have to ruin a good visit. Glad you had a good time in France with Aunt Lillian. She's pretty remarkable . . . a little quirky maybe . . . but still remarkable."

"I'm with you on that," said Jenna. "And now that you've brought it up, I have something to share with you. I was going to wait until Thanksgiving, but now is as good a time as any. Too bad Laura's not here. I'll catch her up on it later." Jenna paused and looked at her brothers. Each had that questioning look that told they were unsure whether this breaking news would be good or bad. She answered their question for them. "Don't get worried. This is good news. I want you to know that I've asked Aunt Lillian to live with me."

"You've got to be kidding," said Rowland. "Not just a visit, but to stay?"

"Yes. To stay."

"Do you know what you're in for, taking on this responsibility?" Will asked.

"That's exactly how Aunt Lillian reacted when I invited her." Jenna grinned. 'If you give this a try,' Aunt Lillian said, 'and after a while I tire you out, you'll want to send me back, but my apartment will be gone. Then what will I do? I don't want you to be stuck with me.' It's a risk for her too," Jenna added. "What if she tires of me? What if she doesn't like living in a household in which adult kids move in for unexpected stays?"

"Well?" said Rowland. "She has a point about losing her apartment. And college kids home for the summer aren't easy guests. They keep odd hours and leave messes in the kitchen. What about that? Aunt Lillian has never had to live with kids, either her own or anyone else's. Seriously, though, there's not much risk she'll tire of you. Everybody gets along with you. Aunt Lillian is another matter. Let's just say she has her own ways. You know, good china tea cups and different sugar for tea and for coffee. She's a bit eccentric. Are you ready for that?"

"When I had children, it never occurred to me that if they tired me out, I'd send them back. It never occurred to me that I was stuck with them either. Apparently you've noticed that one by one my kids are leaving home. But we're still family. Home is home; it's not a temporary thing." Jenna looked again at each of her brothers, challenging them to disagree with her. She knew they wouldn't. Even if they didn't step up to support her the way she wished, and even if sometimes their family connections were complicated and edgy, Jenna was sure her brothers knew what she meant. Rowland had referred to the place their mother lived as "home" until the day she died, and by then he was a middle-aged man with a mortgage of his own to pay and kids to support.

"Are you doing this for Aunt Lillian, or are you doing this for yourself?" asked Will. "This isn't penance for divorcing Jak, is it? And it's not some kind of Mother Theresa thing, I hope."

"Geez, Will," said Rowland. "Could you try to be more direct?" It was so like Rowland to be uneasy about questions he would have asked himself if he dared. He preferred to let Will ask the hard questions, so he could reprimand his brother for it, and still get the answers.

"I'm doing it because I can," said Jenna. "I'm doing this because Aunt Lillian lost her home at a young age. Her whole life she has been longing for home, and it's not fair that she's lived that way. I have a chance to make it right." Jenna's face pinked up slightly, and her eyes were shiny. There was no apology or fear in her voice. "Besides," she said, "I really like Aunt Lillian. She reminds me of Mom, and sometimes I miss Mom terribly. My kids are growing up, and I have a house with plenty of room. Why should I live all alone in it?"

"Dad's the one I feel sorry for," said Rowland. "He spent his whole life trying to prove himself to a father who disowned him, and he never demanded that Grandpa Willard make it right. Dad never left home emotionally because Grandpa Willard kept him trapped there. A good shrink could have had a heyday with Dad."

"I don't know who should have done what, and Dad's a completely different matter," said Jenna. "Maybe we should forgive them all because they didn't know what they were doing. It may be too late to make it right for the others, but I can do something about Aunt Lillian's hurt. Besides, I'm not doing this just for Aunt Lillian. Maybe partly for her, but I'm doing it for Gramma Jeanne too. She knew all about homesickness. And Mom. What about her? Just because she had us doesn't mean she didn't miss her own family. She was an orphan. How do you ever get over that? I'm doing this for our family. I'm doing it for all of us."

"And how about Grandpa Willard and Dad?" asked Will. "Are you doing it to make amends for them? Are you paying what they owed?"

"This isn't about debts," said Jenna. "I want to do something *for* them. I'm going to make it right for them; they got hurt too by things they couldn't control. It's gone on long enough. We can change it if we want to. Those things that happened don't have to get carried forward any further by the way our family does business. You guys think that Dad was uptight and old-fashioned. He didn't show emotion. You couldn't tap into his affection. Well, I saw a different side of him. I got to spend more time with him than you did before he died, and I discovered that just beneath that crusty exterior was a lot of sweetness. He loved his family in his own old-fashioned way. Sometimes his way of being practical seemed cold. And sometimes his seriousness didn't seem very affectionate. But under it was love. I know it for sure. Maybe it was hard to see, but it was there. Maybe that was true of Grandpa Willard too. He was a frightened person, wasn't he? Think of what he went through. No wonder he didn't dare to drop his guard again. I don't believe he wanted to leave us with the impression that we have of him. Anyway . . . ." Jenna smiled. That tender, irresistible smile that had always been her signature. It had the power to melt the ice when the people she loved were freezing up. "Now it's our turn," she said. "I want my kids to see that there's a different way. And your kids too, Rowland. And Laura's."

Will and Rowland were silent. Listening to every word. Overwhelmed by how Jenna had cracked open the problem of their family and stepped in without judgment. It was Rowland who spoke first. "Mom would be proud of you, Jenna. You're a lot like her. She always wanted to bring Aunt Lillian back into the circle. You're right about Mom being an orphan; she understood this thing about home."

"It's a good thing you're doing," said Will. He came to where Jenna was sitting, pulled up his chair so he could sit next to her, and put an arm around the back of her chair. "This might surprise you, but I identify with Aunt Lillian. The member of the family who doesn't fit in. The one who has to keep some distance so things

Chapter 27

Rowland decided to text Cohen. "Burger and Brew? Breakpoint Wed or Thurs at 9?" He went to his desk to work on stuff that had piled up there in his absence. Hundreds of emails from the university filled his inbox; most he deleted without opening them because whatever they were about was already past. The busywork of every day was tedious, and in most cases Rowland was glad when it was past and done. His phone chirped. The text was from Cohen. "CU at 9 Thursday," it said.

Waiting at the Breakpoint Bar for Cohen to show up, Rowland considered that only a few weeks before he had been sitting in this very spot with no idea what lay ahead of him. Now he was back on this spot with a whole download of experiences he was trying to merge into his life. He thought about the things with which he occupied himself on ordinary days. *Did I drop the check in the mail that Polly wrote for our house insurance? Am I on schedule with the things I need to do for my next promotion? Am I putting enough into my kid's college fund? What does Polly expect of me beyond good sex, or is that more about what I expect of her? Oh no, did I forget our anniversary?* Although Rowland was thinking these things silently to himself, he caught himself actually shaking his head in response to his own questions. In response to one he only shrugged.

Rowland saw Cohen come through the door and head to the table. "I was hoping you'd show up," he said as Cohen sat down. "Text messages don't leave much room for error."

"True," said Cohen. "Sorry I'm a little late."

They ordered their beer, and Rowland ordered a burger. Cohen didn't order food because he'd already eaten. He cracked a joke about being there to check if Rowland was still eating the lettuce and onion that gets loaded onto burgers at the Breakpoint Bar. "They do that to bulk up the burger," Rowland said. "There's enough lettuce on the burger to feed the whole family."

"If those are your vegetables," Cohen said, "I'm going to make sure you eat every bite to compensate for that cheese you're still putting on your burgers."

Why do we do this, Rowland thought. *Why do we dive into this trivia the moment we're together again? All the way over here I thought about the serious conversation we'd have. Why this prattle?*

The thought had barely flashed through Rowland's mind when Cohen said, "On to more serious stuff. Tell me about your trip." He listened, asked a few questions, and they stayed on track. Rowland could tell that Cohen was interested because he didn't steer Rowland toward other topics. He didn't elaborate on Rowland's points by bringing up similar experiences of his own either. This time Cohen just listened. At one point Rowland asked him, "Is this too much about my family?"

"No," said Cohen. "It's important stuff. You've listened all the times I talked about my family. It's your turn."

Rowland told Cohen about Beauvais, Maastricht, and Strasbourg. He told him about his Grandpa Willard, the poor cuss who was always in the wrong place at the wrong time. He ventured some guesses with Cohen about why his Grandpa Willard had spent so much of his life constructing a fiction about himself and trying to cover up his shame with lies.

"Cut him some slack," said Cohen. "He navigated his way through hard territory. Despite that he's had four kids, eleven grandkids, and who knows how many great grandkids it will end up being. His spark of life isn't likely to get snuffed out anymore . . . unless we have a global pandemic." Rowland looked at Cohen to see if this was just a tasteless joke, but he was dead serious. "Your Grandpa Willard made it. That counts for something. He didn't do it perfectly, but he did it. You think you could have lived his life better than he did?"

"Who knows if I could have done it better? That's not the point," Rowland said. "This is the point I'm trying to make: I would rather be the off-spring of Gilbert than Guillaume. Old Willard doesn't make me proud. Can't you see that?"

"That's our problem, isn't it?" said Cohen. "We think we deserve to be proud sons and daughters. Our parents owe us that, and, if we aren't proud, then we feel they let us down. We put a lot of effort into figuring out what will make our kids proud of us and steering clear of things that will embarrass them. In that respect we aren't so different from your Grandpa Willard, at least not so different from where he ended up. But think back a ways. When life is really hard, I doubt that people are thinking about whether their kids will be proud of them. They're just trying to get through one day at a time and survive. The future is left for later. If you and I are worrying about whether our kids will be proud of us, it probably means life is pretty darn good, and we aren't being burned out by the present."

"That's an easy out for Willard, and I don't want to show disrespect for your relatives who didn't survive. Still, Cohen, I have a problem with what you're saying."

"Why? Because you prefer Gilbert? Because you think Gilbert was a hero, and Willard wasn't up to your standards? Good luck with that," Cohen said. "You got the grandfather you got. You got the dad you got, and in the long run you'll get the kids you get."

Rowland wondered if Cohen was talking about him or about himself. "The least my Grandpa Willard could have done is tell us the truth about himself," said Rowland. "It's not just DNA he left with us. He left us a mess. My Gramma Jeanne lived with constant tension. My dad never got to throw care to the wind and enjoy life. Grandpa Willard ruined my Uncle Lennie. Aunt Lillian too. Her life could have been so much better. Think of how much life Grandpa Willard wasted. He was like a guy who spent his whole life in a bomb shelter and never enjoyed a sunny day, because he never admitted that no one was out to hurt him and there was no bomb."

"It's tragic that he lived that way," said Cohen. "You have to admit he started out in real danger. He was young and scared, and he couldn't erase that experience. My dad had that same problem. The time of terror got planted deep, and they couldn't root it out. They feared the new season in which it would sprout again. They didn't get help dealing with it from the members of their families. Seriously, do you think they could have told us what happened to them without going through all the hurt again? And then there was the risk that the hurt would be multiplied, because we didn't take them seriously."

"My Grandpa Willard could have tried. He had good kids, and he never gave them a chance," said Rowland.

"Okay. But start with you. You blame your Grandpa Willard more than your dad did. Did your dad understand something about Willard that you never figured out? Were *you* ready to hear his story from him?" Cohen leaned forward to catch Rowland's gaze. "Why would Willard risk repeating his painful story to know-it-all kids who would be thinking the whole while about how they would have done better with his circumstances. You kids couldn't even behave at the dinner table. What could he expect from you during a tell-all family session? Smart solutions to past problems? Keen observations of where he made his mistakes? Confident claims that you are entitled to your own opinions on all sorts of matters? He couldn't trust you to honor him, that you would have mercy. Your hearts weren't big enough to feel his pain, because if you did, you'd be left with some of it? That's the real rub. Some of the pain does get left with us, and that's why we're so resentful. Real empathy aches, and the hurt doesn't go away in a day. In some cases, it never goes away. Judgment is so much easier."

Cohen was lecturing Rowland, and Rowland didn't like it. It reminded him of Grandpa Willard or even of his dad at times. Not tentative. Not caring if Rowland agreed. Just so darn sure of himself. What right did Cohen have to make Rowland feel uncomfortable about how he was putting his own family memories together? *I'm entitled to put my family story together in a way that makes sense to me. I'm entitled to my own opinions.* Rowland thought these things silently to himself, but he knew better than to say them out loud, because he wasn't sure he could defend himself.

"Rowland, you think if you got to pick your own grandfather, you'd have the good sense to pick a hero instead of a villain? I mean at the time; not several generations later when there have been decades to hash it over and sort it out?"

"I think I would. Don't you think you would?"

"I don't know," said Cohen. "Heroes are the ones whose faults we've not heard about. The hero just might be the one who did something courageous for which we remember him, but he might also have slapped his wife's face now and then when he was angry with her. And he might have fooled around with his neighbor's wife a few times because he thought he deserved a better woman than the one he got. He might have been the guy who told small lies for a profit when doing business, only to discover later that the lies weren't small and the reasons not as good as he thought. Or he might have been so strict with his kids that he stifled every flicker of creativity in them. The story of the villain is the flip side of that coin. He's the guy whose mistakes we hang onto, but we forget that he brought wool socks and warm sweaters to a poor widow in the cold of winter; we forget that he delivered money to relatives so they could survive a while longer in hiding; and we forget how hard he tried not to burden his family with the failures of his life. What about that?"

"That's too easy," Rowland said. "You're playing my own story back to me with a twist so you can make your point."

"You think you're ready to pick?" said Cohen. "Why not just take the one you got? Honor him the best you can. Then step up and do your duty. Admit that you're the link between him and your children, between the past and the future. Make it the best link you can. Isn't that enough to deal with?"

"Maybe I have underestimated the complicated life my Grandpa Willard got dealt. I can admit that." Rowland looked at Cohen as he said it. "I wouldn't have wanted his life. I can admit that, if I'd had his life, I might have made some mistakes. Had a surprise baby, been late for a meeting, been embarrassed when my daughter got played by an employee who had me fooled. Those are within the range of what I can accept as 'reasonable blunders.' But why lie? Why not tell the truth about yourself?"

"It's hard to know why people lie," said Cohen "Maybe we underestimate the pressure they're under. Maybe it's not our job to estimate it at all . . . underestimate . . . overestimate . . . it doesn't make any difference in the long run. We don't have to be like them. We can't make their wrongs right or change the course of history. They were who they were. Now it's up to us to carry on. It's up to us to do what's right, a venture at which we'll fall short, no doubt. But maybe we'll avoid some mistakes of our own if we know their story. We won't avoid the mistakes because we're better people. We may be able to avoid a few of their mistakes, if we're able to learn from them. To learn from their mistakes, however, we may have to give up thinking we're superior."

"How did we get back here . . . I mean in our conversation?" Rowland asked.

"You mean the offenses of our fathers bearing down on us, or do you mean our own offenses against our fathers that leave us feeling remorseful?" Cohen went on to answer his own question without pausing to hear what Rowland had to say. "I can only speak for myself," he said. "I try to honor my father, but I go at him armed with all my ready-made judgments. I start out with the assumption that I've evolved beyond him. I tell myself it's okay if I look down on him as long as it's not too much. I definitely don't want to put myself in the position of looking up to him. The problem is that if I can't learn from him, it means I may have to reinvent the wheel. How smart is that? Isn't that how we got here?"

"Well, hold it, Cohen! Maybe we have progressed beyond them. I'd like to claim that much for us."

"Okay. We have smartphones and joint replacements. We can track our own DNA. Our life expectancy is longer than it was a few generations ago. That's progress. No use denying it," said Cohen. "But what about the things we've refused to learn even though they're right in front of us?"

"I hear you," Rowland said; "I get the point. You don't have to belabor it, Cohen. But there's something not right about what you're saying. Don't you think I should try to do a little better than my over-controlling, fibbing Grandpa Willard did? I see why my dad was the way he was, and why Grandpa Willard was the way he was too. My great-grandfather Axel didn't have it easy either--that's one heck of a name, by the way. Sometime I should look up what it means." Rowland grinned; Cohen grinned too. He knew Rowland well enough by now to realize that sometimes, in the middle of a deep conversation, Rowland took a little jog to the side so he could catch up with his own racing thoughts. "The truth is I don't know much about Axel. How far back do I have to go, making excuses for everybody? Or should I take your advice and not make excuses at all, just accept that they were who they were, and that was the best they could do?"

"That's a start," said Cohen.

"Okay," said Rowland, "Don't interrupt me this time. Let's suppose I use the Cohen approach."

"And what approach is that exactly?" Cohen asked.

"It's this," said Rowland. "Hey, all you guys in the generations of my fathers all the way back as far as I can track you; thanks a bundle for getting the DNA passed along."

"Yes," said Cohen. "Keep going. Where does that get you?"

"It doesn't seem like enough. There are people I don't want to let off the hook that way. What about the wretch who shot the priests in the village square? If he was your grandpa, would you honor him by knowing his story? No judgment. No excuses. Just the story, sir, only the story? What do I know about Willard's brother on the eastern front? What did he do? Did he grab food from starving families? How many houses did he burn down, and how many families did he leave homeless during a brutally cold winter? Did he haul a man out of his house and shoot him while his terrorized children watched? I don't care if he is my grandpa's brother; if that's what he did, I want to divorce myself from him."

"Sounds like sorting sheep from goats," said Cohen.

"You're darn straight," said Rowland. "Tell me, Cohen, how do *you* sort sheep from goats?"

"I don't know," said Cohen. "If you're related to them, they end up on your side. Sheep or goats. It's all the same. You don't get to turn them back into strangers again. We feel pretty good about claiming our heroes. If they turn out to be villains, they're still in our family. That's the thing about family."

"What does it mean to honor them then?" Rowland asked.

"Maybe it means not getting too caught up with ourselves either way. Just acknowledging our connections and doing the best we can. Like honoring a coupon or a mortgage. Admitting that it's got my name on it when questions get asked. A clear-eyed look at history isn't just about making us feel good about ourselves, is it?"

"What is it about?" Rowland said. "What good does it do for us to carry forward the shame?"

"I doubt that preserving the shame is good. At least you and I agree about that," said Cohen. "Shame weighs us down. It makes us bitter. We end up wanting to turn our backs on what's happened so we can hide our faces. There has to be an alternative."

"Do you really think there's an alternative?" Rowland was already shaking his head in disagreement with the answer he expected.

"I don't know," Cohen admitted. "Do you think there's anyone who lives with the past without making it into shame? I'm serious. Do you know anyone?"

"I think my Grandma Jeanne did. Her life was as hard as Grandpa Willard's, but she wasn't as bitter. And Jenna. She doesn't let past mistakes break her. And my mom. She had that too, that certain quality. What was it? I don't have a word for it, but they seem able to live with limits or disappointments and not give up or get nasty."

"We honor them for it, don't we?" said Cohen, as if he were giving Rowland time to find the right word. "You're the word-guy; you should be able to find something in your mental thesaurus."

"Forget the word," said Rowland. "Gilbert had it. Leo has it."

"Yeah, and they're the ones we hope are there to advise us," said Cohen. "We'll face the same problems they did, and we'll tackle them with the same limitations. The best we can hope for is that our fathers and our fathers' fathers, our mothers and our mothers' mothers will be whispering advice over our shoulders."

"Willard too?" Rowland said. "I still have to think about that one."

"You and me too." Cohen looked somber. "It's those phantom fathers that take a lot of work. The ones we don't like and never got to know."

For a moment Rowland thought of doing what his brother Will would do. Go back to yakking about lettuce on burgers or watching sports at the bar. He could say it was getting late, and he should be going. But Rowland surprised himself. Instead of winding the conversation down, he spilled a thought that had been trickling through his mind for several days. "I've been thinking I should do something to honor my dad and my grandpa. My dad used to take us boys to clean up around the Barone family graves each Memorial Day. He was very serious about it. I've been thinking, I might get some flowers planted next spring, although that seems like a long time to wait to do something to honor them. I'd have to travel to Chicago to do it myself, or hire somebody to do it, I suppose."

"Don't rush it, Rowland. Give it time. The point of doing something in memory of your grandfather isn't to get it done. The point is to begin remembering him from a different place. It's asking an old question and waiting for a new answer."

"You sound like my brother Will. Sit back and let the universe bring you what you need." Rowland barely stifled a chuckle; he often seemed to chuckle when he quoted Will.

Cohen didn't argue. He took a sip from his water glass.

They sat quietly for a few more minutes. "It's getting late. I should go," said Rowland.

"Yeah, I should go too," said Cohen.

They walked out to the parking lot together.

"Will you have time for a beer next week?" Cohen asked as he opened the door of his car and the interior lights came on.

"I'll be around all week. Polly's going to be gone. She's visiting her mother and taking a break from the kids. From me too, and she deserves it. That means I'm in charge of the kids. How about Thursday at 9:00 on my screened porch? I'll have the kids tucked in by then."

"Sounds good. See you then."

As Cohen pulled out of the parking lot, Rowland stood leaning against his car. He watched the streaming red points of Cohen's taillights drifting down the block, and then as Cohen curved up the ramp leading toward the bridge, Rowland saw the lights disappear. He imagined Cohen crossing the river and heading home.

Rowland got into his own car and drove through the quiet streets. The closer he got to home, the more familiar the neighborhoods were. When he turned into the street where he saw his own house at the end of the cul-de-sac, he let his muscle memory take over: turning into the driveway, raising the garage door with the remote, pulling in beside Polly's SUV, turning off the ignition, lowering the garage door. This was his little world. Still and familiar. In two generations would someone walk down this street, stop in front of this house, and remember that this is where Rowland Barone once lived? Would anyone care?

Rowland sat motionless in the driver's seat, not really seeing the soft lights on the dashboard. He didn't take note of the shadowy tools hanging on the pegboard in his garage. His eyes were elsewhere. Seeing once again the little village outside of Beauvais, the bridge in Maastricht, and the beautifully crooked streets of Strasbourg. He remembered his Grandpa Willard sitting at the head of the table in the dining room at the cottage. As familiar as he was, sitting in the front seat of his own car, memory drew him to the backseat of his father's car. He and Will always took the same spots: Will on the left and Rowland on the right. He felt the urge in his neck and shoulders to move over just enough so that he could see his father's eyes reflected back to him in the rearview mirror. From there in the back seat, he'd been able to watch his father drive, and Ross had always kept his eyes on the road.

Rowland broke into a fleeting smile. What a time-traveler he'd become. He could hear Cohen's voice, as if it were coming over his shoulder and advising him: "Go for it, Rowland. Ask the question and wait for the answer. Give yourself time."

Something shifted then. Rowland wasn't in the car anymore. He was walking along a river, so like other rivers. Like the two rivers that meet in Beauvais, the one that flows under a footbridge in Maastricht, and the rivers and canals of Strasbourg. Like the rivers in Chicago and Minneapolis too. He wondered why people always settle near rivers. For water, of course. But was it also that they were attracted to the stream of life that always comes from somewhere and goes on to somewhere else?

Rowland imagined himself strolling along a river bank. He realized he was not alone. Cohen was there with him, but so was Steven. And Will was there too, reminding Rowland to give noisy kisses to his kids. He looked around and realized he was in a long march of figures moving beside the river. Just ahead of him were Ross and Willard. From just behind he could hear the precious voices of his children. It was a grand procession, all headed in the same direction.

Rowland leaned forward and gripped the steering wheel with both hands; he rested his forehead against it and closed his eyes. He could feel his own breath moving in and out. Upstairs his two precious children, breathing evenly in their sleep, were trusting that he would come home to them, and he had. He thought of his grown children off on their adventures somewhere, but always connected to him. In whatever place they were, he hoped that where he was would be the place they'd call "home." For just a moment he had that glimpse again of himself in that moving throng, in the long stream of the generations. A place where he belonged. And Rowland wept.